I0744109

Making the Dean's List

the With Honors series

Book 2

Addison Winters

Cover Design by Greg Simanson
Edited by Carol Farabee

This is a work of fiction. Names, characters, places, brands, media, and incidents are either the product of the author's imagination or are used fictitiously. Any resemblance to similarly named places or to persons living or deceased is unintentional.

PRINT ISBN 978-1-948143-03-5
EPUB ISBN 978-1-948143-07-3

Library of Congress Control Number: 2018956557

Acknowledgments

I would like to thank Heather for listening to me ramble and all the late-night coffee runs, and Joe for keeping my spirits up and not letting reality affect my words. Also, to Carol who guided me through some long nights, rough drafts, and for having the patience of a Saint! And for Dale...I love you more! This last year has been extremely challenging and you all are responsible for getting me through it with dignity and grace. Words cannot truly express the love I have in my heart for you all.

Plus, all the wonderful emails from readers dying to find out what happens next...Thank you all for all your love and support without which none of this would be possible. You mean the world to me!

For Eric, my sexy man and long summer nights in the
desert mountains at sunset…

CHAPTER 1

MICHELLE AND I MET for lunch about a week after Mason left for Chicago. I rolled the windows down and enjoyed the warm breeze from the late May sun. It was shining brightly and there were a few scattered fluffy clouds drifting around the noon sky. The boys were still in school for several more weeks and I, for the first time in years, was enjoying a little bit of free time.

I parked in the lot across from the science building and locked up my car. The humidity was quickly rising letting me know that we were in for a hot miserable summer ahead. I opened the doors to the science building and was greeted with a cold blast of conditioned air. It was a welcomed change causing goosebumps to immediately arise up and down my arms. I weaved through the students who were there for summer classes and made my way to Michelle's office.

"Good morning," I knocked softly on the open doorway.

"Alex, hi. I was just finishing a few things. Have a seat," she nodded towards the empty chair and continued rearranging the papers on her desk.

"Are you teaching classes this summer?" I asked taking a seat.

"Yes, two. At least they are full of students who want to be here," she grinned. "Are you ready? I'm starved."

"Sure," I stood back up and grabbed my bag. "What are you in the mood for?"

"Chinese? Do you like Chinese?" Michelle picked up her bag and locked her office door.

"Sounds good. P. F. Changs?" I suggested.

"My thoughts exactly."

We decided to walk the several blocks to the restaurant downtown at the mall. It sounded like a good idea at the time, but the lunch hour traffic rushing through the city made us rethink our decision about half way there.

P. F. Changs was crowded with lunchtime diners. We were seated in a corner booth by a host who looked a tad bit overwhelmed. He barely left our menus on the side of the table before he scurried away. Moments later our server came by and took our drink orders. Michelle and I both ordered peach flavored iced teas and then quickly put in our lunch order.

"So, what is this big exciting news you wanted to share with me?" Michelle asked after our server disappeared.

"You remember I told you about my encounter with Mason's dad towards the end of the semester?"

"I still can't believe you didn't kick his childish ass for that. I would have been so offended if I were you." She stated flatly.

"I was and I am. Trust me. He paid dearly for his behavior." I raised my eyebrows at her giving her a look that required no further explanation. "However, last week, the same day Mason left. You wouldn't believe who I got a call from."

"Who?"

"Hayden Brooks, Mason's dad."

"From the look on your face I'm going to venture a guess and say he wasn't trying to reach his son." She shook her head slowly.

"Hardly. He emphasized once more how sorry he was about his son's behavior on his last trip down and how he had wished he had met me under different circumstances." I told her.

"Interesting. Is that all he wanted?"

"He also wanted to know what my plans were for the summer. Hayden asked me if I would care to do some traveling with him. He says he has several trips scheduled for business that he must attend to and thought I might enjoy getting out of the states for a while." I almost laughed. "Can you believe that?"

She thought about for a moment before she responded. "What about your boys?"

"They will be spending most of the summer in Arizona with their Dad."

"Well, you did say that if you'd met Hayden first he would be the man you'd be dating, correct?" Michelle reminded me.

"Yes," The server dropped off a plate of spring rolls. "But I didn't meet him first."

"So? I don't understand the problem. He's handsome, he's successful, and charming." She pointed out.

"And he is Mason's father. Doesn't that sound a little twisted to you?"

"Look Alex," she took a bite of a spring roll, pausing while she chewed. "The way I see it is, they are two separate men. You've always said that you've known your relationship with Mason was never going to last past college. And he's only got one year left, you've got two. Plus, Hayden is much closer to your own age and I would guess you have a great deal more in common with him than his son. That alone makes it possible for you to have a relationship with him that just may have some longevity to it."

"That's beside the point."

"No. That is the point. Mason is never going to be with you forever. You already know this. Why pretend that he's something he's not? Mason is a fling. Yes, a long fling, but a fling nonetheless." Michelle argued.

"Mason is Hayden's son. Don't you find that rather ...?" I wasn't even sure of the right word to end that sentence with.

"Sick, twisted, demented." She offered. "No, not at all. How come it is all right for Jack Nicholson to do it and not you? Personally, I don't see the problem."

"Jack Nicholson?" I gave her a quizzical look.

"Haven't you ever seen the movie, *Something's Gotta Give*?"

"Of course."

"I think it's the second line that Diane Keaton's character writes when she's working on her play and crying; '*I fell in love with my daughter's boyfriend*'." Michelle recalled.

"I had forgotten about that..." I thought for a moment.

"If Hollywood and the rest of the world were okay with that, why are you having such a difficult time with it?"

"Jack Nicholson's character never slept with the daughter for over a year before he got involved with the mother. Kind of an important point, wouldn't you agree?" I pointed out.

"No, I don't think it is. They were still involved. That's the point." She dropped it for a moment when the server showed up and dropped off our plates. "You need to think about what is going to make you happy. I've heard you say numerous times how much grief you've gotten over this trisk with Mason. Your family has been difficult, some of his friends, even your friends make jokes about it. Why would you run away from someone who could possibly make you happy? Someone who could be there for you? Someone who could be everything Mason could never be?"

"There are plenty of men in this world, not just Mason's father." I replied before taking a bite.

"Yes, there is, but you must also know that there is a shortage of good men in this world. They are not exactly falling off trees these days, Alex."

"I know," I muttered, hating to admit she was right.

"So, what did you say to Hayden about this summer?"

"I told him I had to think about it. I said I would give him an answer next weekend when he takes me out to dinner." Michelle raised an eyebrow. "And then I called you." I laughed.

"I think you already answered your own question."

CHAPTER 2

I TRIED ON AT LEAST two dozen outfits nervously trying to find the perfect attire for my dinner with Hayden. My best friend and fellow single soccer mom, Lisa was watching the boys for me. She had volunteered to take them for the night even though I wouldn't confess who my date for the evening was. She was excited that I was *'branching out'* from Mason and looking forward to my return to the dating world with men closer to my own age.

I finally settled on a black mid-thigh skirt and a sheer white blouse. I added a black designer belt and black heels with some simple jewelry to complete the ensemble. It was simple, yet fashionable and elegant. I pulled my hair up into a French twist and applied a little bit a make-up. My hands were shaking so badly. I wasn't this nervous when I went to the prom.

This is ridiculous.

Hayden arrived promptly at seven thirty. He looked stunning in his black slacks, casual black shoes, and a maroon dress shirt as he walked up to my front door. He rang the doorbell and I counted to ten before answering in an attempt not to appear anxious.

"Hello," I greeted him and held the door open.

"Good evening, Alex. You look lovely." He walked in and stood nervously in my foyer.

"Thank you, you look very handsome." I said and picked up my small handbag. "Shall we?"

"Of course," he held the door open and I locked it behind us.

We made small talk about his business adventures, a little about my previous jobs and my son's baseball season. Neither of us brought of the huge pink poke-a-dotted elephant sitting between us on the console…Mason.

I had spoken to Mason last evening. We had talked for a couple of hours. He was staying with his mom and step-dad and admitted that he had only seen his Dad twice since starting his internship. He loved his new job, but his younger siblings were driving him a little insane. He wasn't used to being treated like a kid again and having his mother nag him about everything he did from where he was going to the hours he was keeping. He confessed that he missed me dearly and was anxious to return to me.

I kept that conversation to myself.

Hayden pulled into the Meridian Restaurant and Bar just north the city. It was a beautiful old home originally built in the 1880s turned into a restaurant several years before. The evening was warm without a touch of summer humidity in the air. He walked around and opened the car door for me even offering a hand to help me out. It was a nice touch.

He had apparently made reservations for two and we were seated at a small intimate table beside the fireplace. The renovated home was truly beautiful and still maintained a cozy atmosphere. Hayden pulled out my chair for me before taking his seat across the table.

The waiter took our drink orders, two white wines, and then disappeared to let us peruse the menu.

"Have you ever been here before?" Hayden inquired opening his menu.

"A couple of times with my ex-husband for business dinners." I told him looking at my own.

"Anything in particular you recommend?"

"It looks like they've updated the menu since the last time I was here." I noted giving a quick glance.

"Do you like crab cakes?"

"Yes," I replied.

The waiter magically appeared out of nowhere as if on cue with our drinks and Hayden placed an order for crab cakes for our appetizers. I sipped the wine and it went down smoothly. A little too smoothly and felt incredibly refreshing.

I was having a difficult time not looking at Hayden. He was every bit as handsome as I remembered. I kept trying to remember Michelle's words and see the overall bigger picture that included a life beyond college. One that I knew positively, Mason would not be a part of. And even though I knew it, it was still hard for me to imagine. Yet, here I was, sitting across the table at a high-end, elegant, restaurant with his father.

What the hell are you doing?

"Do you know what you'd like?" Hayden broke my train of thought.

"Yes," I looked up apologetically at the waiter. "I would like the Crepe Lasagna."

"And I will have the Filet of Beef with a baked potato load and assorted vegetables, please." Hayden took my menu and handed them both to the waiter.

Once the waiter disappeared from earshot Hayden took a long drink of his wine. "Are we going to get through this uncomfortableness, Alex? I really like you. And I think you like me too."

"Hayden, I do and if…"

"Alex," he interrupted. "I know it's a little weird. I'm not an idiot. I know what's been going on between you and Mason. And I'm sure you really rocked his world." He stated and despite my best efforts, I laughed. "I'm taking that as a yes."

"I suppose," I tried my best to bring myself back in control.

"And I am positive he loved every minute of it. But here's the tough question; where's this relationship going? Do you see it having any longevity past his graduation?" He looked at me with sincerity.

"Honestly?" I took a deep breath and stalled a moment to take a sip of my wine. "Between us, I don't know where this relationship is going. But I do know that it will not survive past his graduation. I am a realist, I know how we look. I know what we are. And I know there is no long-term future between us."

"Then why not let him go now? Why hold on for another year and let him get even more attached to you than he already is?" He asked.

Because I happen to love playing with my little boy toy.

"It's not like I don't have feelings for him. I do love Mason." I couldn't bring myself to say *'your son'*.

"But are you *in* love with him?" He raised one eyebrow slightly in the same fashion as his son had done to me many times before. I almost physically cringed.

"No, I'm not. But that does not mean I don't love him and care for him deeply. I have been with Mason for over a year now…living with him for over a year now." I pointed out.

"Mason is a child. Surely you must know that."

"Yes, I do. I am under no delusions as to who he is and what we are."

The waiter dropped off our entrees and disappeared once again.

"I understand where this is a little strange for you, but I had such a good time with you the evening we shared pizza. I felt this connection to you. This spark, if you will. And I know how silly that sounds, but it's true. And I don't know about you, but that doesn't happen to me very often. Honestly, it's only ever happened to me once before, so I knew I had to see you again. What I need to know is, is this crazy? Is it too crazy for you?"

"Yes," I said looking at him longingly.

"Yes? Yes, to what? Too crazy for you? Or you felt it too?" He reached across the table and placed his hand over mine.

"Yes, I felt it too." I whispered trying not to make eye contact.

"Do you think you can let Mason go to see if there's any possibility for us?" I couldn't help but note how he never referred to Mason as his son.

"Mason's in Chicago. I am here. How far do you expect me to let him go? I will not see him again until August."

"But you spoke to him last evening."

Damn, I didn't know he knew that.

"He called me." I answered honestly.

"He told me." Hayden took another sip of his wine.

"I realize that."

"He misses you." I sighed deeply and tried to remove my hand from his, but he wouldn't let me go. "Please, don't."

"Hayden," I wasn't sure if I could find the right words. "You don't think this entire thing is sick and twisted?"

"I believe it has its challenges." He chuckled.

"Ya think!" I stated without trying to hide my sarcasm and finished off the rest of the wine in my glass.

We barely touched our dinners despite how good they tasted. Instead, we got a couple of travel boxes and Hayden paid the check. We drove to my place laughing back and forth trading silly tales from our high school antics. After my third glass of wine and the little amount of food I put on my stomach, the wine had gone straight to my head. Thankfully, Hayden only drank about half of what I did and ate more of the appetizers and his entree.

He parked in my driveway and opened my car door for me once again. I felt lightheaded from the wine but did my best to walk casually to the keypad and punch in the code to open the garage door. This was the moment I had been both dreading and looking forward to ever since our first slice of pizza.

The end of the evening and what it might bring.

"Would you like to come in for a nightcap?" I couldn't stop myself from offering.

"Yes," he smiled.

God, why does he have to look identical to Mason? It's not fair. None of this is fair. The timing sucks!

We walked into the kitchen and my shepherd-chow-lab mix, Billy greeted us happily. Hayden bent down and rubbed her just behind the ears talking to her in a soothing voice.

Billy took to him immediately, just as she had to his son. I opened the refrigerator and pulled out the new bottle of white wine that I'd brought earlier in the week from Oliver's Winery. I grabbed two wine glasses from the cupboard and set them down on the island. I uncorked the bottle and poured a genuine amount into each glass.

"You have a lovely home." Hayden remarked standing up right once more.

"Thank you," I handed him the glass and tried not to focus on the fact that barely a year ago I'd stood in this same kitchen and had a similar conversation with this man's son.

"Have you lived here long?" He asked before sampling the wine.

I chuckled to myself and downed my glass in one long drink. "Please stop, just stop." I helped myself to a refill. "I was wrong. I can't do this." I finished the entire glass again in one breath.

"Alex…" Hayden took a step towards me and I took a step back.

"No, this is ridiculous." I picked up the bottle and splashed more into my empty glass. "I mean really, this is ridiculous. How in the hell does this shit even happen? You're standing here in my kitchen, looking the way you look." I raised my hand up and down gesturing wildly for emphasis while polishing off another full glass. "And your son looks like a carbon copy of you. This totally sucks!"

I started to pour me another glass, but Hayden took the bottle from my hand. "I think you've had enough for one night." He said with an adorable smile.

"You mean I have not had nearly enough to even begin processing all of this. Have you even thought about this?" I waved my arms widely once more.

"Yes, but mainly I've thought about doing this." Hayden took a step forward and wrapped his arms around me tightly pulling me too him. He leaned down and kissed me so overpoweringly I was positive my legs were going to give out from under me.

I closed my eyes and felt all resistance within me melt away. I wrapped my arms around him and found myself kissing him with the same hunger he was devouring me with. I had spent so much time focusing on how wrong this would be, but instead, it felt so right, so natural. There was such a marked difference just in the way I felt in his arms…safe and secure. His kisses were that of a man, not of a young man. He had the strong sure hands of a man that took charge of a situation and went after what he wanted.

And despite all the progress Mason had made in the area of sexual adventures, he was still just a twenty-two-year-old kid.

I pulled away from him with great reluctance. "Hayden, we can't do this." I whispered.

"I know," he said breathing hotly into the nap of my neck before tracing his lips over it. "It's complicated."

"Very," but I was already leaning into him.

"Come on," he took my hand and led me back to my bedroom.

"Hayden," I stumbled after him.

He pulled the covers back and lifted me up onto the bed. I almost mentioned that this wasn't my side of the bed, but rather his sons. But my mind was too foggy, so I just curled down under the covers and closed my eyes willing the room to stop spinning. I vaguely remembered him kissing my forehead before he disappeared along with the rest of the world.

CHAPTER 3

MY HEAD WAS SPLITTING open before I even opened my eyes. There's nothing worse in the world than a wine hangover. I felt horrible. My mouth was dry, and my tongue felt like sandpaper. I wanted a shower desperately, but not enough to make me crawl out of bed. Then I realized I was still wearing the same outfit that I had worn on my date last night, minus the heels. I took a deep breath and took comfort that at least if I was dressed than I hadn't done anything stupid, such as sleep with Hayden last night.

I draped my arm over my eyes regretting the fact that I hadn't closed my blinds last night before I went to bed.

How did I get to bed?

It was all still too fuzzy. I sort of recalled Hayden and me drinking wine in the kitchen. I think we kissed. I'm certain we did....

Oh, yes. We did.

I rolled over and pulled the pillow over my head in shame.

How could you do something so stupid?

Then I recalled being in his arms, what it felt like, his lips, his strong hands...the way his body felt against mine. I wanted to scream, but my head hurt too bad to even move.

Slowly and with much effort, I rolled out of bed and made my way to my bathroom.

I started up the shower, brushed my teeth and chewed up a couple of aspirin willing my pounding head to stop pulsating with every beat of my heart.

The shower steamed up the bathroom while I felt my muscles finally relax under the hot water. It felt amazing on my tired and guilty soul. I felt so torn. Mason was gone, we were not engaged, nor had we made any promises regarding the future.

I couldn't think about this now. My head was throbbing. I leaned back against the shower wall and closed my eyes. All I wanted to do was crawl back in bed.

But I couldn't. I had to pick up my boys sometime soon. I couldn't leave them at Lisa's. She had enough on her plate without adding my sons to it. Now I had to simply figure out a way to drive with this pounding headache.

I toweled off and threw on an oversized tee-shirt and a pair of lady's boxer briefs. All I could think about was finding the kitchen and drowning myself in a pot of coffee. I lightly ran a brush through my wet hair before I twisted it into a loose bun on the top my head. I didn't even bother with any make-up. I truthfully didn't care.

I opened my bedroom door and slowly made my way down the short hallway. I could feel the pulsating in my head with each step I took. Then a figure covered in the throw blanket I kept on the back of the couch caught my eye. I stopped.

Who in the hell?

I wasn't sure exactly what to do. The figure was snoring softly. I took another step and the floor creaked. Billy jumped up stirring the figure on my couch. She was sleeping right next to whoever it was, but as soon as he lifted his head, I knew.

Hayden.

"Good morning," he yawned and looked over at me trying to stifle it.

"Good morning. I hadn't realized you'd stayed." I was suddenly aware of what I was wearing and tugged my shirt down as far as I could.

"I didn't want to leave without saying goodbye. And I wanted to make sure you were all right. You weren't in the best of shape when I put you in bed last night." He rubbed the sleep out of his eyes before he stood up.

"Yeah, I'm sorry about that. I don't remember much." I admitted shamefully.

"It's okay. Don't worry about it." He started folding the blanket and placed it on the back of the couch.

"Would you like some coffee?" I felt so awkward and wasn't sure what to say to him.

"Yes, please," he walked over and placed his hand gently on my shoulder giving it a soft squeeze. "I'm just going to visit your bathroom for a moment."

"Okay. I'll get it started."

I watched him disappear into the hall bath before I raced into my room and threw on a pair of gym shorts. Then I returned to the kitchen and started brewing the coffee. I couldn't believe he was still here. I wracked my brain trying desperately to remember anything from last night, but it was all a fuzzy blur.

I remembered the restaurant, the awkward conversation, the wine...way too much wine. And then driving back here and consuming a great deal more wine.

I leaned my elbows down on the counter and rubbed my temples trying to relieve some of the pressure in my pounding temples. I felt like hell.

"Are you all right?" Hayden walked up beside me and leaned against the counter.

"My head is killing me." I answered without looking up or opening my eyes.

"I'm not surprised as much as you drank last night." I could hear the smile in his voice. He rubbed my back gently and then moved behind me and began massaging my shoulders. It felt fabulous. I could feel the tension in my shoulders and neck give way. Hayden's hands were amazing, strong, firm, but extremely gentle.

"Why don't you have a seat on the deck and I'll bring you out some coffee? How do you like it?"

"Cream and sugar. The cream is in the fridge." I barely opened my eyes and made my way out to the deck.

I sat down on the swing and took a deep breath of the late morning air. It was an overcast day, thankfully. I don't think I could have handled the bright sunlight. Big grey clouds hovered overhead just waiting to cut loose at any moment. There was a warm breeze that blew around me like a blanket. I leaned my head back against the plush sage green cushions and closed my eyes. My headache began to ease just enough to be bearable.

Moments later I heard the French doors open and Hayden's steps across the deck. He sat down beside me. "Here," I opened my eyes to see him holding out my favorite mug filled with steaming hot coffee. I took it from him and offered a weak smile.

"Thank you."

"Is there anything I can get you? Some aspirin or something?" He leaned back and made himself comfortable.

"No but thank you. I took some already. It's starting to get a little better." I turned a little towards him and took a sip from my mug. The hot liquid tasted like a little piece of heaven. "And thank you for staying last night. I appreciate you putting me in bed and not taking advantage of the situation. I'm so sorry for my behavior. I promise I normally don't act that way or drink that much."

"There's nothing to apologize for. I know this whole situation is strange."

I accidently snorted in my coffee. "That's an understatement."

"Alex," he reached over and placed his hand over mine. "I like you."

"I like you too," my voice was barely a whisper.

Hayden lifted his hand to my face and lightly traced it with the tip of his finger before cupping my jaw tenderly in his hand. He lifted my chin forcing me to meet his emerald green eyes. Our eyes locked and time stopped. It was as if I was staring into his soul.

All I saw was a gentle, kind, compassionate man who was strong and secure. My headache disappeared in his eyes. I could feel my heart rate increasing. Slowly, Hayden moved towards me and smoothly brushed his lips over mine. My stomach flipped, and I held my breath.

He slipped his hand into my hair and guided my mouth to his. Our lips caressed once more as if in slow motion. I could feel his hot breath and I leaned in pressing my lips against his. His hand tightened on the back of my head pushing me gently towards him. Our lips parted, his tongue touched mine. He tasted sweet, of mocha coffee. His morning stubble brushed lightly against my chin.

My arm wrapped around his neck pulling him closer to me. I could feel his heart beating fast in his chest as mine pressed against his. His lips were strong, powerful. I could feel my knees going weak, my stomach tightening in a knot of anticipation. I wanted him.

There was no denying it any longer.

With his lips still hungrily devouring mine, Hayden took my coffee mug out of my hand and placed it on the little wicker table beside the swing. He scoped me up in his strong arms and carried me back into the house and into my bedroom, his firm lips massaging mine. I could hardly catch my breath. He placed me gently down on my bed and climbed up beside me. His masculine body hovered over mine. I wrapped my arms around him pressing him against me. I wanted him so badly. I pulled on his shirt and ran my nails over his back and then up his chest. His body was rippled with muscles, toned and tight.

Hayden reached under my tee-shirt and caressed my breast. It felt like an electric bolt was sent through my entire body. He pulled my shirt up over my head and tossed it aside. His mouth drifted down to my neck, his lips and tongue dancing over my skin, tracing my collarbone, my chest. His hand firmly grasped my breast.

He brought his mouth down to it and teased my nipple with his tongue and nibbled on it with his teeth. I purred softly as every neuron in my body was set on fire.

Hayden leaned up and removed his shirt, dropping it to the floor. I was astonished at the view before me. His chest and abs were completely ripped.

The man must live in a gym.

He barely had any hair on his chest, just enough to accent his pecs. He was beautiful. My breath caught in my chest. I reached up and ran my fingers over his sculpted torso then leaned up and kissed his warm skin. I wrapped my arms around his waist and grabbed his buttocks firmly. Hayden stroked my hair gently. I smiled up at him deviously and smacked his ass playfully. A grin spread across his shapely lips and his eyes sparked with interest.

I placed my index finger in the center of his breast and nudged him gently. Hayden rested back against the mountain of pillows at my headboard with an intrigued look on his face. I climbed over him, straddling with my hands resting firmly on his chest.

I wonder if he's as compliant as his son?

I leaned over and kissed him deeply. My tongue teased him, danced over his neck and down his chest. I slid down his thighs and kissed his abdomen. I ran my fingers over the top of his pant line. Very slowly I undid the button with my teeth. Haydon's eyes widened with interest. I pulled his zipper down in the same fashion. I could see the top of his smoky gray boxer briefs.

Like father, like son…same damn brand even.

Sitting up on my knees, I slowly began pulling his slacks down. I artfully maneuvered myself around and removed them in a seductive manner. I could see his huge cock twitching in his briefs trying to escape. My fingers danced lightly across the inside of his thighs. Hayden shuddered. I took a deep breath and centered myself mentally. He was so incredibly sexy.

I gazed into his eyes longingly while tracing my fingers across the top of his boxer briefs. He smiled in a devilish way and there was a defiant twinkle in his eye. I freed his throbbing cock from its bindings and tossed his boxers to the floor. I wrapped my fingers around his gorgeous dick. It was the most perfect cock I had ever seen…thick, long, and beautiful with just a glisten of pre-cum dripping down the head. I leaned down and lapped it up hungrily.

I took the head fully in my mouth and ran my tongue around it. A small moan escaped from Hayden as he nudged his hips upwards towards me. I slid his hard cock down my throat massaging it as I sucked my way up and down. Hayden gently pulled my hair back away from my face, so he could watch me work. Our eyes locked as I teased his dick with my tongue and mouth. He tasted so sweet.

"Come here," he whispered and gently lifted me up by my shoulders.

I glided up his body and brought my lips firmly to his. Hayden wrapped his strong arms around me pressing our bodies together. His mouth devouring mine with a fire that pulsated through my entire body. His hands explored my body and gracefully removed my shorts and briefs tossing them aside. He caressed my ass firmly yet gently. There was a confidence in every move he made.

Hayden rolled me over. Even lying on top of me, he kept his weight off me. He paused for a moment and looked down at me. He brushed my hair away from my face.

"You're so beautiful," he said softly.

I could feel the blush rushing to my face. I was speechless. Thankfully, a shy smile spread across his lips and he kissed me tenderly.

"Do you have something?" he asked.

"Yes," I leaned over and opened the top drawer of my nightstand. I briefly searched around the right corner for the box of condoms. I pulled one out and handed it to him and closed the drawer.

I couldn't help but wonder if he knew his son had bought those condoms. I quickly dismissed the thought before it fully sunk into my own head. Instead I forced my focus on the deliciously sculpted man on his knees in front of me between my legs.

Hayden slipped on the condom with ease, hovered down over me and kissed me deeply. His legs gently pushed mine a little further apart and his kiss grew firmer, hungrier.

He moved his hips expertly and slowly, as if teasing me, before he slid his thick throbbing cock inside me. I held my breath in anticipation. Then in a smooth thrust, Hayden pushed his way in. I loved the way he felt deep inside me. My head rolled back, and I moaned loudly grabbing a firm hold of his ass.

Hayden's body moved in perfect harmony with mine. I wrapped my legs around his waist and arched my hips in rhythm with his. He brushed his lips over my curve of my neck.

His breath was hot on my shoulder. My hands explored his chest as I closed my eyes and lost myself in him. His body fit my perfectly as if he was made specifically for me. We melted into each other completely losing ourselves in a place where time nor anyone else existed.

***

I pulled out of my driveway and headed towards Lisa's. I could not believe what I had just done. But it felt so right, so good. The sex was incredible. Borderline best ever. I stopped at the light in the middle of Main Street and leaned my head down on the steering wheel closing my eyes for just a moment.

What the hell did you just do? What the hell were you thinking? How could you do this to Mason?

The questions haunted me. I looked up at myself in the rearview mirror and felt so ashamed at the reflection starring back at me.

The image of Hayden lying on my bed looking up at me with that smoldering look in his eyes caused me to blush again as I heard a car horn honk behind me. I look up and realized that the light had turned green.

I parked in front of Lisa's house and climbed out of my car. The muggy evening air smacked me right in the face. The humidity had risen throughout the day causing the air to feel like a steam bath. It was just sticky and nasty. I quickly made my way to the front door, knocked twice, and walked in.

The kids were all running around the house giggling and chasing each other. The girls were chasing the boys and it seemed the boys could not elude the girls for too long. I found Lisa in the kitchen cleaning up some mess the kids had made earlier.

"How ya doing?" I climbed up on one of the barstools.

"Ready to scream," she sighed and tossed the dishrag into the sink. "This has been going on for the last hour. Brie is trying to kiss Max." I couldn't help but giggle. "It's not funny. I've yelled at them four times already."

"It is a little funny."

"Yeah, for the first five minutes maybe. An hour of it is more than I want to deal with." Lisa looked exhausted.

"Don't worry, I'm going to take my two and get out of your hair." I climbed down.

"Oh, no you don't, Missy. You're going to sit your happy ass back down there and give me all the gritty details from your date last night."

"Momma..." Henry cut her off running up and giving me a big hug.

"Hey, Buddy. Did you behave yourself?" I gave him a big squeeze.

"Yes, but Max didn't." I looked over at Lisa.

"He wasn't that bad," she smiled. "He was bored."

"Momma, can we go now?" Max came barrowing in and hid behind me.

Brie and McKenzie busted into the room and came to a halt a few feet from their mother. They were all dolled up. I was guessing that dress up was somehow part of the afternoon.

"You're supposed to kiss the bride." McKenzie little voice sounded about as cocky as a four-year-old could manage.

"I said no!" Max stuck out his tongue as if he was three again.

"We were having a wedding. Max was the groom." Brie looked embarrassed.

"I was the flower girl." McKenzie added.

"And what was your role?" I looked down at Henry.

"Best man," he said proudly.

"Well, then who was officiating this ceremony?" I asked him.

"I was," Logan entered the kitchen. "But the groom ran away before I could say man and wife."

"I said it was stupid and I didn't want to do it." I could tell from Max's tone he'd had enough.

"Okay, guys. That's enough. Get your things, we're going home." Both boys took off running for their things.

"Thanks for watching the boys." I picked up my purse off the bar.

"Anytime," I gave her a quick hug.

"I'll call you after I get the boys down."

"You'd better."

CHAPTER 4

I DOUBLE CHECKED to make sure everything was locked up tight and glanced in on my sleeping sons one last time before Billy and I crawled into bed. I turned on the television and DVD player. *Harry Potter and the Half Blood Prince* sprang to life on the screen. I had forgotten Henry was watching it in here the other day.

I slipped beneath the covers and Billy curled up on the pillow beside me. I rested back against my pillows and grabbed my cell on the nightstand. I hit Lisa's name and waited for the fallout to begin.

"Hey, it's about time. I've been waiting all evening." She answered.

"I had to get the boys asleep first. Besides your kids couldn't have been down for long." I stated.

"No," she sighed. "I just got McKenzie down. She missed her nap today, so she was really cranky."

"Sorry," I muttered feeling guilty.

"It's all right. They all had a good time," she paused a moment. "Except for maybe Max."

"Yes, I heard all about it on our way home. His tune towards Brie is going to shift in a few years. She's growing into a beautiful young lady." I remarked.

"It scares the hell out of me." Lisa confessed. "And she is crazy about Max. I cannot believe how much he looks like Danny."

"That scares the hell out of me," I laughed. "But I'm glad I only have sons." I noted.

"So, who did you go out with?" she inquired once more.

"I'm afraid to tell you." I bit on my bottom lip trying to figure out how to confess who my mystery date really was.

"It can't be that bad. Was it the muscular sweaty guy from the gym that's always hitting on you? Did you finally cave?" She giggled.

"Ew...No!"

"Okay, what about that single dad that just moved out here with his kids? You know, the one who has custody of them because his ex-wife had an affair with the preacher and ran off with him?"

"You mean the fat balding man with glasses? God no!" I laughed. "He's just gross. And that comb over. Seriously? Why can't he just admit he's losing his hair?"

"It's a male thing. They can't admit to any short comings. You know that."

"I know," I sighed.

"So, who was it then?"

"Promise not to lecture me? I already feel bad enough."

"You didn't..." I could hear the disappointment in her voice.

"I'm afraid so."

"Alex, how could you?"

"I don't know. He caught me at a weak moment and I really like him. He's sweet and charming. And oh my God! He is so beautiful. He's..."

"He's Mason's dad, Alex. That's just plain twisted any way you look at it."

"I know, I know. But in my defense, you haven't seen this man. He's irresistible." I tried to explain.

"You need help woman." She said. "So, spill it. Please tell me you didn't sleep with him last night."

"No, I didn't sleep with him last night." I replied with a mimicking voice. "He took me to dinner at The Meridian. The conversation was awkward to say the least. I had a few classes of wine with dinner, he drove me home and I invited him in for a nightcap. Then of course, it was all very déjà vu and I freaked out on him, lost my demeanor, and downed a large quantity of wine. It wasn't pretty."

"Oh, my God! I'm so sorry. I hate to say I told ya so, but I did. I can't believe you even considered getting involved with him." Lisa pointed out.

"Oh, there's more. That's not even the worst of it." I informed her. "I drank way too much, don't remember it, but apparently he carried me to bed and tucked me in." I could hear Lisa giggling on the other end. "When I woke up this morning, I had the worst hangover I'd ever had in my life. I chewed up a couple of aspirin and took a hot shower. When I went to make me some coffee, guess who was sleeping on my couch?"

"You're kidding," she snorted.

"Yep, curled up with Billy. Damn traitor!" Billy perked up when I mentioned her name.

"Did you get the chance to talk to him this morning?"

"A little," I wasn't sure I wanted to admit what I'd done.

"And?" she urged.

"I like him…" I didn't need to say anything else.

"Dear Lord, you slept with him, didn't you?"

"It wasn't my fault," I stated.

"What? Did you trip and happen to fall on his dick?"

"Something like that…"

"Please tell me you're kidding?"

"I wish I could. I feel horrible about it. I know I shouldn't have." I told her. "Mason's called twice today, and I couldn't bring myself to answer the phone. I don't know what in the world I'm going to say to him."

"Well, how was it?"

"One of the best sexual experiences of my life." I admitted.

"Wow," she was taken aback. "Better than his son?"

"Honestly, there's no comparison between the two. Mason is a boy. Hayden is definitely a man. No road map or neon signs required. He knew exactly what he was doing." I giggled like a young girl infatuated with a boy.

"Damn…"

"I know," I couldn't stop smiling at the memory of our afternoon together.

"So, is it true?"

"Is what true?" I asked.

"Like father, like son? Size-wise?"

"Oh, it's true all right. Down to the last delicious inch."

"You lucky bitch," she laughed. "So, what are you going to do now?"

"I don't know. He headed back to Chicago and said he'd call me."

"Ouch! Do you think he'll really call?"

"Well, I don't believe he came all the way down here just to bang his son's girlfriend. I wasn't just some conquest.

He's slightly more mature than that." At least that's what I'd been trying to convince myself of.

"I hope you're right," she sighed, and I knew what she was thinking because I was thinking it too.

"I can't believe I slept with Hayden. Mason would die if he found out."

"Seriously Alex, I know you like the kid and all but it's not like you have a future with him. You two have nothing in common." She reminded me.

"I know, and I don't always act my age when I'm around him and his friends." My mind went directly to last Halloween and Becca's house among numerous other instances. "And that's not exactly a good thing."

"I get it. I do. You need to be with a man, not some guy who runs off to Cancun to drink with his friends on his dad's credit card." *Ouch, that one hurt.*

"But I still feel guilty," I barely whispered.

"Don't. Your relationship with Mason ran its course and yes, it was fun while it lasted. But now you need to consider your future."

"But you know as well as I do that I couldn't possibly have a future with Hayden. Not after my relationship with Mason." I couldn't see how it could be possible.

"You don't know that. Mason could very likely be getting involved with someone closer to his age this summer and realize that this fling with you could never have any longevity to it. Who knows? Maybe he'd even be supportive of a relationship between you and Hayden." She reasoned.

"I seriously doubt that." I laughed aloud. "Even if he is sleeping with someone new this summer, I don't believe he'd give his father his blessing to get involved with me."

"You never know...," Lisa pointed out. "Men can be weird about relationships and there's no logic to their reasoning."

"Somehow I just don't think Mason would be all too supportive. Besides, I'm probably making this more than it is. I don't know what to think anymore."

"Well, get some sleep and call me tomorrow."

"Thanks again for watching the boys. Sweet dreams."

I hung up the phone and turned off the light. I hunkered down under the covers and curled up with the empty pillow beside me. I could still smell the faint sent of Hayden's cologne clinging to it. I closed my eyes and Lisa's words keep running through my mind. I didn't want to believe I was just another conquest for Hayden. He didn't seem like the type. But then again, they rarely do. I could still see the look in his eyes, feel the way his hand caressed my cheek right before he'd kiss me.

I wish it could have lasted longer than just an afternoon.

CHAPTER 5

THURSDAY EVENING, I parked in the lot next to the baseball field. Henry jumped out and took off running to meet his teammates. Max and Aaron walked off to toss the ball around in the vacant lot beside the diamonds while I made my way to the bleachers to have a seat beside Lisa and the other Moms. It was sticky and humid out. We hadn't had any rain in several weeks and the landscape is starting to reflect it. The grass was turning crispy and course, the plants were starting to wilt under the intense heat and if we didn't get some rain soon the damage might be lasting.

"Hello Ladies," I took a seat beside Lisa, behind Kim.

"Could it get any stickier out here?" Kim turned around and asked. "I'm so sick of this humidity."

"Me too," I agreed. I wasn't about to tell them that I'd been wasting my summer vacation lying in my neighbors pool all day while the boys splashed around in the cool water.

"Has he called?" Lisa leaned over and whispered.

"No," I kept looking straight ahead so she wouldn't see the disappointment in my eyes.

"Who?" Kim asked. "Are you dating someone new?" she asked me.

"Sort of. Not Really. We went on one date last Saturday and he said he'd call me and he hasn't." It sounded so much worse saying it aloud.

"What happened to the college guy you were seeing?" Kim looked over at me.

"We're taking a break. He's doing an internship in Chicago for the summer." I tried to be casual.

"Well, I don't know how either of you do it, being single again," she remarked.

"It's not easy," Lisa told her. "And I got lucky with Erik."

"Yes, you did." I agreed.

I sat there quietly for a while watching Henry play baseball. It was a nice reprieve from my own thoughts of last weekend. Unfortunately, those weren't so easy to escape. I couldn't even bring myself to talk to Mason. He'd called me every day and each day I let it go to voicemail. I hadn't listened to the numerous messages he'd left me nor responded to his texts. I didn't want to hear his voice. I knew it would only make me feel worse.

By Friday afternoon, I'd pretty much written off men in general. I floated around on a raft in the deep end of the pool watching the boys play volleyball in the shallow side. Logan and Aaron had joined my sons for the afternoon and the four of them were having a blast. It seemed the best way to keep cool in this heat and to keep them occupied.

I splashed a little water across my legs and soaked up the sun. Perhaps my love life was in the toilet, but my tan was looking fabulous. I took a long drink of my raspberry ice tea out of the little pocket in my raft. I laid back and closed my eyes drifting aimlessly on the water.

I'd thought about calling Hayden a million times but could never bring myself to do it. If he wanted to talk with me, he certainly knew how to reach me.

That evening, I loaded up the trunk of my car with lawn chairs, blankets, and a tote bag full of Red Vines, Skittles, M&M's, Milk Duds, and Sour Patch Kids. The cooler was stuffed full of iced, bottled water, Root Beer, Sunkist, and fruit punch. I stuffed the four boys in the car and picked up two large pepperoni pizzas on our way to the drive-in.

Henry had been driving me crazy about seeing *How to Train Your Dragon 2* at the drive-in ever since I'd mentioned it was playing there. The only way I got Henry and Aaron on board was that *X-Men: Days of Future Past* was playing directly afterwards.

We got there early and found the perfect spot down front. The two older boys helped me set up the lawn chairs while I tried to keep the younger two from getting in the pizza. They laughed and teased and ran around all over the place acting exactly how they were supposed to act. And I was having a great time trying to wrangle them in. Fortunately, the cartoons appeared on the screen and they settled down to pig out on the pizza. The drive-in was quickly filling up and it wasn't long before the stars were out, and the previews began. I reached into my purse and put my phone on silence. I figured, at least that way I could lie to myself that I was missing Hayden's call. At least until I checked it later.

I curled up with a blanket in my lawn chair chewing on my favorite thing in the world, Red Vines and finally let go of the anxious feeling in the pit of my stomach. It was actually a relief to finally make the conscious decision not to let something bother me.

I finally felt the tension drained from my shoulders and was able to relax and enjoy the movies with my boys.

CHAPTER 6

WITH THE FOUR BOYS tucked in and finally asleep, I crawled into bed and set my cell on my nightstand per usual. I stared at it for a long time considering whether I should check it for missed calls. It was almost one o'clock in the morning. For those thirty seconds between hope and disappointment, my stomach was in a huge knot.

I caved and looked. The only missed call I had was from Mason.

Full of heartache I placed my cell back on the nightstand. I turned off the lamp and rolled over snuggling up to Billy and watched *CSI Miami* reruns. I wasn't sure if I was ready to cry, scream, or laugh. I closed my eyes and tried to concentrate on the voices on my television. I was almost asleep when my phone went off. I heard it from somewhere in a daze and it took me a moment to realize it wasn't the television.

"Hello…?" I answered.

"Alex? Did I wake you?" a man's voice inquired.

"Who is this?" I didn't even bother to open my eyes.

"It's Hayden. I didn't mean to wake you?"

"Do you have any idea what time it is?" I mumbled not even sure myself.

"I'm sorry. I couldn't sleep," he barely whispered.

"So, you decided to call and wake me up?" I was confused. "I haven't even heard from you in a week."

"I know and I'm sorry about that. It just got weird."

"Weird? It *got* weird? Honey, it's been weird since the get go." I rubbed my temple trying to fight off the headache I was certain was coming.

"I know, but I really like you...a lot. And I had a great time with you. I enjoy being with you. I feel like we really have a connection." He paused for a moment as if waiting for me to say something. When I didn't, he continued. "When you jumped out of bed to get something to drink, I watched you walk away naked with your hair flowing down your back. You were the most beautiful lady I've ever seen, and I felt so damn lucky to be lying there in your bed. But then your phone went off. I didn't even think about it and looked over at it on the nightstand. It was Mason. I felt so horrible. I didn't know what to do."

"Why didn't you tell me?" I wish he would have said something rather than leaving me hanging for a week without a clue as to why he hadn't called.

"Yeah, and that would've been romantic," he chuckled. "I could've waited until you curled in beside me and whispered in your ear; 'by the way, my son and your lover, just called you'. How do you think that would have played out?"

"Point taken," it was impossible to argue with that. "Is that why you haven't called me?"

"I wasn't sure what to do," he admitted. "I felt guilty all the way home and when I saw Mason on Monday at work, I felt even worse. I couldn't bring myself to call you. I swore I wouldn't see you again.

But I couldn't get you out of my head. I think about you all the time and I know this doesn't happen to me very often."

"I know what you mean. We have so much in common and I feel so comfortable with you." I admitted.

"I really want to see you again," his voice was so soft.

"Really now?" I relaxed a little.

"Maybe," he teased a little with me.

"Well, if you aren't sure…," I was beginning to enjoy myself.

"Oh, I'm sure all right." He laughed.

We spent the next several hours talking. Once the tension was broken and we relaxed, we finally started confiding in each other. We talked about what we each wanted for our futures. We discussed our childhoods, my boys, his daughter, even our past relationships…everything except Mason. I couldn't remember the last time I made such a connection with a man. It was so incredible and worst of all, comfortable and natural.

***

For the next couple weeks Hayden and I spent countless hours talking on the phone. He couldn't get away from work to come down to Indy and I was busy with the boys end of the year activities, baseball, and preparing all their things for their summer with Danny.

I spent my days floating around the pool working on my tan, taking care of the house, and waiting for the boys to get home from school. My days were peaceful, long, and conflicted. I'd never felt so torn in my entire life.

With each passing day I grew closer with Hayden and further from Mason. I was surprised a little with how easy it was to let Mason slip away. He had finally stopped calling or given up trying to reach me. I wanted to imagine him moving on like Lisa had said, with someone closer to his own age and having the time of his life with her.

***

Our daily conversations had started so casually, turned playful, teasing, and ultimately intimate. I looked forward to them every evening after the boys were finally in bed. Hayden and I would talk for hours. We'd laugh, we'd tease one another, we'd speculate on the future. Each of us was dying to spend more time with the other.

That was the tricky part. But with the boys leaving for the summer, it opened a window of opportunity I couldn't dare to pass up. So, when Hayden asked me again about accompanying him on his business trip to Europe, I didn't hesitate to jump at the chance to spend time with him.

Danny arrived on the early morning flight on the first Saturday after the boys completed another school year and for once, the boys and I were there to meet him. I had given up arguing with him and I think I was just too excited about my upcoming trip that even Danny's little annoyances didn't bother me.

Henry was so excited to see his dad, but Max just stood there playing some game on his new phone looking bored. He'd still not forgiven Danny for blowing him off for Thanksgiving and Christmas last year. I couldn't blame him, but I kept those thoughts to myself.

We dropped Danny's luggage off at the hotel near the interstate, the same one Hayden had stayed in when he showed up last spring and even though I had agreed to give Danny a ride, I still flat out refused to let him stay in our home. But that certainly didn't stop

Danny from his all too familiar round of begging, pleading, and bargaining except this time he tried to throw in a splash of guilt for good measure. That didn't go over to well either.

A short time later we found Lisa, Erik, her ex-husband Brian, and children sitting about halfway up the bleachers. I sat down beside Lisa and Erik while Danny joined Lisa's ex in the row behind us. It was Henry's final game of the season due to their leaving for Arizona on Monday with Danny for the summer.

Their teams still had another month of games left along with the Fourth of July parade. Henry didn't mind missing it, but Max was upset about letting his team down, as he saw his departure.

We had discussed it more than once and it was a battle neither of us were happy about losing. But once plane tickets were bought, it was simply too expensive to change travel plans for the three of them.

"I still can't believe you haven't told Danny where you're going?" Lisa leaned over and whispered.

"Thanks to cell phones, I don't have too. Besides, he'd think the whole thing was sick and twisted. I really don't want to hear it from him." I rolled my eyes in his direction.

"Are you sure they will be able to reach you outside the country?"

"I believe so. I don't see why not." I shrugged.

"How excited are you?" Lisa grinned.

"Like a five-year-old on Christmas Eve," I chuckled. "I know it sounds silly, but I can't help it. I really like him."

"Like who?" Danny stuck his head between us and I hadn't realized he'd been eavesdropping.

"No one," I quickly responded.

"Ah, come on," he nudged me playfully. "Is this guy at least old enough to buy alcohol?" Both our exes started laughing and Erik did his best to hide his snickering.

"You're an ass." I looked over at Lisa and could tell she was doing her best not to smile. "And, he's older than I am." I smacked Danny on the arm.

"So, who is this guy?" Danny pushed.

"No one," I glared over at him before spinning towards Lisa and pointing a finger at her. "And you shush!"

"Oh, this has got to be good." Brian stated.

"How did you meet'm?" Danny asked.

"Drop it…I'm serious." I warned all of them.

"Well, tell us, Alex. Did you jump to the other end of the spectrum to geriatrics? Does this one already qualify for the early bird special?" Brian teased.

"Does he need the little blue pills to make you squeal?" Danny was truly enjoying himself.

"Yes, but it's okay. She can be as loud as he wants he just turns his hearing aids down first." Brian added.

"You guys are such assholes." I rolled my eyes at them.

"He's only a couple years older than her. Give it a rest." Lisa playfully scolded the trio.

"All right fine, but who is he?" Danny asked.

"No one you need to concern yourself with." I informed him.

"Seriously. Are you planning a trip while the boys are with me?" he asked.

"So, what if I am? I'll be back before the boys get home." I turned my back to him.

"And what if something happens and I need to get in touch with you?" he leaned in a little closer so that his head was almost on my shoulder.

"Then you'll have to step up to the plate and actually take care of your sons." I pointed out to his horrified face. "Oh, don't look at me like that. I'll have my cell with me at all times." I looked back at Lisa and rolled my eyes again.

Luckily, the game started, and everyone's focus shifted off me and onto the kids.

After both boys had finished their final game, we all gathered over at Debbie's for a cookout. I sipped my punch and floated around the pool soaking up the sun. I didn't want to think about Mason, but he was haunting me.

I don't know if my own guilt was shining through or the fact that I truly missed him. Either way, the last thing I felt like doing was saying goodbye to the only two men in my life who I couldn't live without.

I found myself going through the motions of the day but not exactly living it, let alone enjoying it. I watched from the sidelines as everyone relished the day all around me.

It was good to see my boys playing volleyball at the other end of the pool. Henry was truly happy, and Max was putting on one hell of a show…for Danny's sake or mine, I wasn't sure.

The hours drug on. We did the grill thing, the drinking thing, the goofing around thing and finally, the cleaning up thing. The boys were barely standing by the end of the evening as I put them in the car to drop Danny back off at his hotel. They were sound asleep before I even got out of our neighborhood.

"Are you okay?" Danny asked quietly.

"I'm fine," he chuckled lowly.

"Which means you're not. What's bothering you? Are you missing the paperboy?" He asked.

"Danny," I tightened my grip on the steering wheel. "Don't…" I almost pleaded.

"I'm just playing with you, Alex." I saw him roll his eyes out of the corner of mine.

"Just like you're playing around with Amanda?" I couldn't help myself, I had to say it.

"I see my sons have been talking." Danny let out a sigh. "She's nothing, Alex. I swear."

"Danny, really, I don't care. That's the beauty of divorce. I don't ever have to care what or who you do anymore." I stated flatly.

"Ah, come on, babe." He slipped his hand over on my thigh and squeezed it gently. "Don't be like that. Don't you ever think about me?"

"Not on my worst days." I smirked and removed his hand dropping it off in his own lap. "Squeeze that, my darling ex."

I pulled into the hotel parking lot and stopped under the awning at the front door. Danny shifted towards me in his seat. He smiled slightly and placed his hand over mine on the gearshift.

"Thanks for letting me tag along today. I really had a great time."

"Sure, the boys had a good time with you today." I couldn't think of anything to say to him.

"You didn't seem to. You seemed rather distant. What's bothering you?" he asked and for a split second I almost believed he cared.

"Good night, Danny. Call me in the morning when you get up." I said as politely as I could manage.

"Fine. Have a good night, Alex." He leaned over and kissed me briefly on the cheek. "Sweet dreams," he climbed out of the car and disappeared inside.

I put the car back in gear and pulled out of the parking lot. I turned back onto Main Street when I felt a hand on my shoulder.

"He's still in love with you." Max popped in between the front seats.

"I thought you were asleep," I patted his hand. "Come on up here."

Max climbed over the seats and buckled himself into the passenger seat. "Nah, I was just resting my eyes."

"You were just eavesdropping," I glanced over at him and smiled.

"I was eavesdropping," he smiled back. "At least you two weren't arguing."

"True."

"I think he misses you," Max said casually.

"I think he misses the idea of me, but he really misses you boys." I tried to turn it in a positive direction.

"Maybe the idea of us," he said sarcastically.

"You're rotten, you know that?" I laughed and shook my head at him.

"Yeah, but you love me that way." Max grinned.

"Yes, I do."

CHAPTER 7

THE HOUSE WAS EMPTY. The boys and Danny were gone and the silence they left behind was driving me batty. I left the lights on in rooms I wasn't using as if the boys were still here and just around the corner going about their nightly activities. I curled up on the couch with Billy and a blanket and flipped on the television. I started surfing through the channels looking for something interesting. Of course, there wasn't anything. So, I settled for a rerun of *Ridiculousness*, one of Max's favorite shows and as stupid as I thought it was, it never failed to make me laugh until I cried.

Halfway through the program my cell phone started buzzing.

"Hello?" I grabbed the phone hoping it was the boys.

"Hello sweetass," greeted a now familiar voice. "How was your weekend?"

"It was okay. The boys both won their games. Then we all had a cookout at Debbie's and went swimming." I told him.

"But you don't *sound* like you had a good day. I'm guessing your boys left with your ex."

"Yes, this afternoon." I painfully admitted.

"I'm sorry. I know how hard that can be," Hayden sympathized. "But on a happier note, are you packed?"

"Of course, but you do realize that it would have been much easier to pack if you'd tell me where we're going?" I teasingly complained.

"I told you, I want it to be a surprise."

"That is so nerve-wrecking. I swear you do it just to irritate me." I laughed.

"I do," Hayden chuckled on the other end. "But it adds a mischievous air of mystery to it don't you agree."

"I cannot believe I agreed to this." I let out a sigh of exasperation. "You're such a pain in my ass."

"It's such a cute ass, who can blame me?" He laughed.

"What time do you think you'll be here tomorrow?" I was so anxious to see him again.

"Around noon," he replied.

"What do you think about having dinner with my friend and her boyfriend? She's been bugging me about meeting you."

"Does she know who I am?" I knew he was referring to rather who he was the father of.

"Yes, she knows. And she's trying to be supportive of us. Of course, it took her by surprise, but after she got over the initial shock. I mean, she never openly disapproved or approved of my...," my words dropped off. It just felt too awkward and wrong to speak of my relationship with Mason to him.

"Previous relationship," his voice dropped a bit.

"Are we insane for even considering pursuing this?"

"Perhaps, but no relationship is perfect, Alex. You know that."

"Perfect?" I couldn't help but laugh. "Hayden, seriously…"

"So, dinner with your friends?" Hayden conveniently changed the subject.

"You really are a pain in my ass." I muttered loud enough for him to hear me. "Yes, dinner with my friend, Lisa and her boyfriend, Erik tomorrow evening. Is that all right?"

"And where are we having this dinner?"

"I was thinking about something casual like a cook-out here or something low key, so they could get a chance to know you." I said.

"Sounds good. After all, you want to make sure we're in a safe environment when your friends interrogate me." He laughed again.

"Hayden…," I began.

"I get it, Alex. I do. This situation is difficult for us to explain to ourselves. I imagine it's even more difficult for others to understand."

Hayden and I chatted until I dozed off because the sound of my phone ringing loudly in my ear startled me half to death. I fumbled with it trying to make that awful noise stop. It was a text from Danny asking if I wanted to video chat. I quickly responded sure and jumped to grab my laptop off my desk.

"Hello Momma," Henry greeted me. He was sitting a little too close to the camera, so his face filled up my screen.

"Sit back a bit, little man," I heard Danny's voice from behind him.

"Hi Momma," Max appeared beside his brother. "How are you?"

"I'm good. How are you guys? How was your flight?"

"Long. Boring. But we made it here." Max replied.

"Max slept, but I didn't." Henry added.

"No, he certainly didn't." Danny mumbled from behind the boys. I couldn't help but smile. Henry appeared to be on a sugar high.

"Did you get everything unpacked?" I asked them.

"I did," Max looked bored.

"Not yet," Henry was literally bouncing around in his seat.

"What are you guys going to do tomorrow?"

"I don't know," Henry practically shouted, and Max shrugged.

"Henry, why don't you take a shower and get yourself cleaned up and ready for bed. Isn't it getting late there?" I glanced at the clock on the mantle. It was almost midnight here.

"All right." His expression dropped for a half second. "Can I call you tomorrow, Momma?"

"Of course, sweetheart. I miss you. I love you. You have sweet dreams tonight, okay?" I blew him a kiss.

"I love you too. Night, momma." He blew me a kiss back and took off to get in the shower.

"He's a little hyper," Danny smiled and took Henry's seat. "Are you all right?"

"Yeah, just missing my boys. The house is too quiet." I told him.

"I know. I go through that every time they leave." Danny empathized.

"Well, I'd better get myself off to bed as well. I'm glad you guys made it there in one piece." I looked directly at Danny. "Please take good care of my boys."

"Don't worry, I will. I promise."

"Goodnight Momma, I love you. I'll call you tomorrow." Max said.

"I love you too, Maximillian. Be good and take care of Henry for me."

"I will. Night." Max half-heartedly blew me a kiss.

"Goodnight, sweetheart." I blew him a kiss back.

I closed my lap top and set it on the coffee table feeling very alone. I forced myself up and turned off all the lights. The silence was still deafening, and I hated it. I missed my boys so much. I couldn't help but wonder how they were really doing and if they were just putting on a brave face in front of their dad. The story I got from Max was always so much different than the one he presented in the presence of Danny.

I climbed into bed and hit the button on the remote. The television sprang to life along with *The Bourne Identity* movie I'd watched about half of the night before I drifted off to sleep. Billy bounced up on the bed and curled up beside me. I ran my fingers through her thick black fur and looked into her old wise eyes.

"How ya doin' ol' girl?" she stared at me with a silent understanding. "I know. I miss them too. But they'll be home by the end of summer." I assured her.

I closed my eyes with my arm still draped across my dearest companion. My mind returned once more to its favorite dilemma — Mason and Hayden. What to do? Who is right? Who is wrong? Was it all wrong?

I didn't know anymore.

Mason — my sweet young lover who tried so desperately to be the man I needed in my life. I honestly loved him, but I knew in my heart I wasn't in love with him. He was fun, playful, and all that I remembered of the exuberance of youth. It was true, he had more in common with Max then me, but he was beautiful, sexy, charming and kind. And I absolutely loved those traits about him.

And Hayden — my forbidden passion. Shouldn't it be the other way around? The soccer mom in every sense of the word lusting after the 21-year-old forbidden son? Somehow my situation was ass-backwards. Hayden was the man I knew I could easily fall in love with.

Not just for his obvious enchanting appeal, but for his personality as well. He was smart, funny, charismatic, generous, thoughtful, kind, and considerate. Not to mention sexy as hell. The fact that he held a strong resemblance to Eric Dane certainly didn't hurt either.

With Hayden it was easy. We talked, shared experiences, and giggled into the night. We were playful with each other, and he made me laugh. More importantly, in his arms, I felt safe and secure. And never did I feel like he was another child I had to parent — like Mason often made me feel.

It was simple. Mason was a boy. Hayden was a man. This I knew. Hayden understood what it was like to work hard, to struggle, to sacrifice everything for your family.

Mason had been given everything and was complaining it wasn't enough. So, he took more in an act of pure childish defiance. And for some reason, that behavior truly bothered me. In some ways it gave me the impression of his sense of entitlement because he truly felt he was owed it.

But what would Mason think if he knew I had slept with his father — that I talked to him daily — that we were planning a romantic vacation getaway together? What would he say? What would he do?

Reluctantly, I reached over and picked up my cell off the night table. Before I could change my mind I quickly hit the button that would connect me with Mason.

"Alex?" he answered on the forth ring.

"Hi. How are you?" I hated to admit I missed the sound of his voice.

"Um...I'm fine. How are you?"

"Good. Just lying in bed with Billy watching a movie. What have you been up to? How is the internship going?" I inquired.

"Hang on just a sec." I could vaguely hear him mumble but I distantly heard him say, 'I've got to take this. It's my mom. My grandma's in the hospital. I'll be right back'.

I took a deep breath silently giving Lisa kudos, she obviously knows men, even young men, better than I.

"Alex? Sorry about that. I had to step outside." Mason apologized.

"It's okay. I'm sorry I caught you at a bad time."

"Well, sort of, I...," he mumbled.

"I understand." I didn't want to hear him say it.

"I miss you." He blurted out.

"I miss you, too."

"It's just hard being apart for such a long time and well, there's this girl I met and...," Mason stumbled over the words.

"And she's there and I'm here." I finished for him.

"Well, yeah. I just figured we were taking the summer off from each other since I haven't heard from you." He explained.

"Does that mean you wouldn't be upset if I dated someone else while you're in Chicago?" I asked.

"Why? Have you met someone?" His tone immediately changed.

"Someone asked me out. Yes."

"Who?"

"Why does it matter?"

"Well, how old is he?" Mason inquired.

"What difference does that make?"

"Is he closer to your age?" I could hear the anger and jealousy seeping into his voice.

"He's a couple years older than me. Why? How old is your date?" I couldn't help myself from asking.

"I never said she was a date," he stated hotly.

"But you said...," I tried to remind him, but he cut me off before I could get the words out.

"Never mind what I said. Do you like this guy? Do you want to go out with him?"

"Mason…," I said softly.

"Where's the boys? Do you think it's a good idea to bring someone new around Max and Henry?"

"The boys are in Arizona with their dad for the next five weeks. So, they're not meeting anyone. You know how I am about my boys. I'm surprised you'd even ask me that."

"I'm sorry. I know it's not my place to say anything, but I love those boys."

"I know you do, Mason." I assured him.

"Alex, I know I have no right to say I don't want you to date this man, especially considering where I am, but it kills me to think of you with anyone else."

"How long have you been seeing this girl?" I wondered.

"A few weeks," he admitted. "It just happened. I'm sorry. I should have told you."

Strangely enough, Mason had given me a guilt free out without even realizing it. Well, not entirely guilt free.

"Mason, have a wonderful, safe summer. We'll talk in August." I didn't know what else to say.

"You too, Alex."

And then he was gone.

I put my cell back on the night table and stared at the television without really seeing it. Something in my gut told me that Hayden had been aware of his son's friend for some time now. I was half tempted to call and ask but I couldn't. I'm not sure why but I really didn't need to. I already knew the answer.

A small part of me hated the thought of Mason being with someone else. Perhaps he did think of our relationship as a fling also and knew it would not survive past college.

I suppose he had every right to move on as well. And even as much as it truly hurt my heart to think of him with someone else, I believe he'd never forgive me if he ever found out whom I was getting involved with.

I closed my eyes and wrapped my arm around Billy. I was really going to miss her while I was gone.

CHAPTER 8

I GOT UP JUST BEFORE THE BREAK OF DAWN. I fixed my coffee and went out on the back deck to watch the sunrise with Billy. I took a seat on the swing and sipped my peppermint mocha coffee. I could feel the hot liquid flowing down my throat as if it was fueling life into my veins.

I sat there holding my oversized mug watching the sky burn from purple to orange to pink and fade into a crystal baby blue. The moon in the far distance washed away for another day. A fresh blanket of dew covered the dying lawn. The humidity was thickening. We desperately needed rain. The flowers and shrubs in my carefully attended to gardens were showing signs of wilting regardless of my watering them twice a day. The intensity of this heat was taking a toll on everything.

Still, the sunrise was breathtaking.

After I finished my coffee, Billy and I went back inside for another. I threw on some old gym shorts and a t-shirt, twisted my hair into a messy bun and turned on some music. I spent the next couple hours cleaning up the house, making a potato salad, deviled eggs, fruit salad and baked beans for the evening cook-out. I danced around getting things done in record time. It was amazing how easy it was to accomplish things so quickly when not being constantly interrupted by my boys.

I showered, shaved and climbed into a cute red and white strapless summer dress that looked fabulous accented against my golden tan. After blow drying my hair, I pulled it up into a French twist and applied a little liner and mascara to accent my eyes. With a pair of strappy sandals, I was ready to go.

Billy and I arrived at my parent's house shortly after nine. My dad was sitting at the kitchen table drinking his morning coffee. My mom was standing over the stove frying up some eggs and bacon. I kissed my dad on the cheek and sat down in the chair across from him and picked up a piece of toast.

"You're up bright and early. I didn't expect to see you before noon." My dad remarked adding more sugar to his coffee.

"I got up early to get the house cleaned and finish packing." I said while smearing some apple butter across my toast. "It's been so long since I took a vacation I know I'm going to forget something."

"I think it's great you're getting away for a while. You've been studying so hard and running yourself ragged with the boys." My dad stated.

"Do you want some eggs and bacon?" Mom offered.

"No thanks. Toast is fine." I replied nibbling on my piece.

"Coffee?" she offered.

"Please," she promptly set a hot cup in front of me.

"So, who are you taking this trip with?" She asked returning to the stove.

"A friend."

"A friend? Are you sure you're not taking that Mason kid with you?" She glanced back over at me.

"No, Mother. Mason is in Chicago for the summer doing an internship." I rolled my eyes and my dad grinned over the top of his coffee cup.

"Well, I hope this friend is a little more suitable for you than that kid." She remarked as she put a plate of bacon and eggs in front of my dad.

"Really, Mother? Let it go."

"I'm just saying," she sat down between us with her own breakfast.

"Did you get someone to mow the lawn while you're gone?" Dad, thankfully, changed the subject.

"Yes, Max's friend, Aaron is going to take care of it for me. And the timers are set for the sprinklers and Debbie's going to collect the mail." I assured him.

"Timer's on the lights?" he asked.

"Yes, I set them. Plus, Debbie is right across the street. She'll be keeping an eye on the house and she's got an extra key should she need it." I smiled over at him.

"Good. Sounds like you're all set." Dad patted my hand. "Just be careful and have fun."

"I will. And thank you for watching Billy for me. I hate the thought of her in a kennel."

"She'll be fine. I promise." He got up and put his plate in the sink.

I stuffed the last of my toast in my mouth and washed it down with the rest of my coffee. I got up and put my mug in the sink. "I've got her food, treats, bowls, and bed out in the car if you want to help me bring them in." I asked him.

"Sure," dad followed me outside.

We walked out to my car with Billy tagging along beside us. The sun was out in full force and blazing down upon us. The heat steaming off the asphalt was hot through my sandals. Billy even hopped off the driveway and scampered over to the grass. I popped open the trunk and helped my dad put all of Billy's things in the garage.

"Thanks," I set her bed by the door. "I appreciate you taking care of her for me."

"No problem, she'll be fine." my dad leaned against his classic car and took out a cigarette and lit it. "So, who is this man you're going away with?"

"Dad...," I shook my head at him.

"I promise, not a word to your mother."

"Okay. His name is Hayden. He's around forty, very sweet, and has a great sense of humor. I really like him."

"Does he treat you well? Is he good to you?"

"Yes, he's very good to me, dad. And perhaps one day I'll introduce you to him when mom's not around. After what she did to Mason I'll never bring another man around her." I had to laugh but he knew I was serious.

"What if you decide to get married again? You'll have to eventually introduce him to your mother." He pointed out with a grin.

"Maybe after the wedding. But definitely not before because he'd never marry me then."

"I see your point. Your mother was a little out of line." He took a long drag on his smoke. "Okay, way out of line. But I hope she'll change her tune with this man." He shrugged his shoulders. "I am sorry about Mason. When did you two break-up?"

"We didn't really, I suppose. We're just taking the summer off while he's in Chicago. I guess we're both using this time to explore our options."

"And by your tone I'm gonna make a wild guess that he's already dating someone else in Chicago? Someone, perhaps, closer to his own age?" My dad gave me a sympathetic look.

"Yes, he is."

"I'm sorry. I know you really care for him."

"I love him, but I'm not in love with him. I knew going in that this relationship would never endure past his graduation." I told him.

"But that doesn't make it any easier to lose someone you care about." He remarked.

"No, it does not." I answered him honestly.

My dad walked me back over to my car and embraced me warmly. "Now you be careful and have a wonderful time. Don't forget to send me a text and let me know where you are and that you've arrived safely."

"I will, I promise." Billy came trotting over to me waiting to jump back into the car. "No, Billy. Stay." I rubbed her behind her ears and leaned down and hugged her. "You be a good girl. I'll be back soon. I love you, ol' girl." With one last rub of her head, I climbed into my car. "Bye Dad, and thanks again. I love you."

"I love you, too," he waved as I backed out of the driveway.

***

Hayden arrived just before noon. He was wearing navy blue shorts and a striped polo looking as handsome as ever. I watched him walk up the drive and came out onto the porch to greet him. I stood on the top step and held my arms open for him.

I wrapped them around his neck as he wrapped his around my waist pulling me to him. I was not quite the same height with him even standing on the steps, so I reached up to him.

"Oh, it's so good to finally see you." He held me tightly for a moment before kissing me hungrily.

"I've missed you." I said breathlessly between kisses.

Hayden held me tight against him and lifted my feet off the ground. He stepped up on the porch and with my feet dangling beneath me he carried me across the threshold kicking the front door closed with his foot.

Our passion for each other took a firm grip on us as we made our way back to my bedroom.

Hayden paused beside my bed and slid the zipper down on the back of my dress. Almost magically, it fell to the floor encircling me. I stood there in my white, silk and lace, strapless bra and matching lacey panties. He slipped his hands under my arms and lifted me up on the bed.

He crawled up beside me with this smoldering look in his eyes. He gently brushed the hair away from my eyes and stared down at me. I paused for a moment to catch my breath. His eyes were such a beautiful deep green.

His hair was the same sandy blonde with just a hint of wavy curls and an occasional gray that only enhanced his looks. The carefully manicured stubble on along his jawline accented his rugged good looks perfectly. I could see the dimples deepening the longer he looked at me that way.

Hayden's lips gently brushed over mine. I closed my eyes and felt his lips caress mine with increasing intensity. His hands explored my body as mine did the same to his. I loved the way he tasted.

The firmness of his lips. The way the stubble on his chin felt on my skin. My legs automatically wrapped around him as our hips grinded together with anticipation.

His lips traced over my neck lightly. My entire body felt electrified. He slid his hand around my back and with one smooth stroke, unclipped my bra and tossed it aside.

His hand cupped my breast as he brought his mouth down to it. His tongue lapped over my nipple, his teeth nibbled teasingly sending bolts of lightning down through my body and landing right between my thighs.

I reached for him, one hand catching his hair in my fingers, the other finding my nails over his shoulder.

He continued his downward journey. When he reached my abdomen, I leaned up enough to grab the back of his shirt and pull it up over his head. His muscular chest hovered over me briefly while I ran my fingers longingly over it. Hayden kissed me softly, gently before he slipped back down to his previous location.

Hayden's tongue teasingly played with my belly ring. He traced his lips across my abdomen. It tickled and a small giggled escaped causing me to squirm. He looked up at me and smiled.

His hands firmly grasped my hips holding me in place. A devilish look gleamed in his eyes. He slowly slid down my thighs along with my panties. His feet touched the floor as he tossed my panties aside.

Hayden nudged my legs just enough tell me to bend my knees up. I complied and rested my feet comfortably on his shoulders. He softly kissed the inside of my thighs. I closed my eyes and relaxed, loving the feel of his tongue and fingers as they explored my inner secrets.

He slid his tongue inside me before adding his fingers, pushing them up and forward immediately locating my G-spot and teasing it relentlessly. He brushed his tongue over my clitoris.

I felt like my thighs were going up in flames. Noticing my reaction, Hayden increased my torment by nibbling and sucking on my clitoris until I thought I was losing my mind.

Then he slipped one of his fingers lower and into my ass. I gasped out in surprise and pleasure. I wanted to scream out in delight as his rhythm picked up. I arched my hips up to him and threw my head back as my body spasmed uncontrollably.

"Come here!" I screamed out trying to pull him up to me. My body was in a frenzy as an orgasm rippled through me. I clawed up his back with my nails in desperation. I had to have him inside me. "Now!" I squealed.

But Hayden simply shook his head and held me in place as my body squirmed in ecstasy.

I yelled out in pure anguish and frustration. I had to have him. I tried desperately to escape him. I reached down and tried pulling him to me, but he still refused to budge.

"Hayden, please ..." I begged through a parched throat.

Instead Hayden slid off the side of the bed taking me with him right to the edge. He stood upright, slipped a condom over his throbbing cock and flipped me over so quickly my head literally spun with the motion of it. My feet suddenly hit the floor and he forced them apart grabbing my hips just before he entered me fully.

I hollered out in hunger and pure animalistic delight. My face hidden in the duvet, I gripped a hold of the covers as Hayden thrusted deep into me, filling me up completely.

I loved every inch of his huge cock and the way he felt inside me. I loved the sounds he made fucking me. Listening to him moaning, his quickened breath...only made me want him more. I reached back and held his muscular thigh, hot and rigid in my hand.

His hands tightened on my hips, his pace increasing. He moaned loudly and thrusted hard into me holding my body tightly to his as his exploded in glorious agony. His body shook for several long seconds while he held his breath. Then he slowly leaned down and lightly kissed the nap of my neck.

"I missed you," he whispered.

***

Lisa and Erik arrived just before four. I made the introductions and we all made casual small talk for a few moments before I offered everyone a drink. Lisa followed me to the kitchen and the men made their way out onto the deck.

"Oh, my God…" Lisa leaned over my shoulder as the back door closed. "He's delicious!"

"Told you," I said.

"I can't believe how much they look alike. It's eerie." She propped herself up against the counter.

"I know," I turned on the blender to mix the martinis.

"Are you sure you know what you're doing?"

"No," I admitted. "He's seeing someone else." I turned off the blender.

"Who? Mason?"

"Yes," I hated to admit.

"Did Hayden tell you that?"

"No. He did. I spoke to him last night." I sighed and poured the drinks in to martini glasses. "Actually, I interrupted a date he was on. I felt like the needy teenage girlfriend chasing after the most popular boy in school. It was so embarrassing."

"I'm so sorry, Alex." She put her hand on my arm in a sympathetic way.

"It's okay," I shrugged and handed her a couple glasses. "Come on. They're waiting on us."

The guys were deep in an NFL debate about the upcoming season by the time Lisa and I reached them. Erik was pointing out all the ways the Colts were superior to the Bears and Hayden was doing his best to rebuttal Erik's position. I sat down beside Hayden on the swing and gave him his drink.

"Hey there, you'd better watch your mouth. You are in Colts country here." I gave Hayden a playful shove.

"All right, I give," he leaned over and kissed me sweetly.

"That's better," I teased.

"So, what do you do for a living, Erik?" Hayden inquired.

"I'm an attorney. The really boring kind, corporate law." Erik wrinkled his nose with a grin.

"Normally, my standard response it, 'how interesting', but I'm sorry I don't think I can even fake that one." I shoved Hayden a little harder this time.

"Behave yourself. These are my friends." I told him.

"I said I'm sorry," Hayden laughed.

"I know, it's boring. And not at all like I envisioned back in college, but it's never dull, and the money is good." Erik chuckled and gave Lisa a gentle squeeze.

"Do you two have any kids?" Hayden asked them.

"I have a nine-year-old daughter that is in love with her son Max, a boy the same age as Henry, that's how we actually met," Lisa smiled over at me. "And a four-year-old daughter who is turning thirty next week," she informed him.

"I have a fourteen-year-old son who knows everything and a son that's the same age as Henry and Logan. We also met at the sports field." Erik said.

"So, is this sports field like the rest of society's version of a bar?" Hayden looked strangely at the three of us.

"Pretty much," I said.

"You know how it is, your kids play sports, so you spend all your evenings and weekends at the diamonds or the football field or the gym for basketball. After a while, you meet the other parents. You have kids, so you understand how it works." Erik finished but an uncomfortable silence hung in the air.

"Well, truth be known I missed out on a lot of my kids' activities over the years. I didn't get along with my ex-wife very well and the relationship only got worse once she remarried."

Hayden shifted awkwardly. "I always took care of them financially but if they had stuff going on during the time they were with her, I didn't attend very often. So, I only got to see the things they had going on during their weekends with me." He glanced over my way. "I'm sure you've heard all this before."

I nodded. I had.

"I guess in a strange way it's a blessing that Danny lives so far away. I don't have to mess with him every other weekend." I stated.

"Yeah, but you also don't have the benefit of every other weekend off either." Lisa pointed out.

"True, but I also don't have to see him nearly as often as you see Brian. That's worth giving up every other weekend for." I chuckled.

"Do you have sole custody of the boys?" Erik asked.

"Yes, but Danny maintains his visitation rights."

"Really? How much did that cost you in attorney fees?" Erik inquired.

"It was put in our original divorce agreement. Danny didn't even fight me on it and as long as he still gets to see the boys he's fine with it. Plus, it makes sense with him living so far away." I noted.

"I suppose, but I could never give my ex sole custody of my kids." Hayden stated.

"Me neither," Erik added.

"I'd like to think that Danny would be more involved with the boys if he lived closer, but I can't honestly say that he would be." I shrugged my shoulders.

"Unfortunately, divorce can make being an active parent challenging at times." Erik remarked. "My ex-wife uses our children as a pawn to control me. And she enjoys her petty torments."

"I don't think it's fair the way some people do that in a divorce. Don't they realize that it's the children who ultimately pay the price?" I asked.

"Erik's ex is a special breed of crazy. She's a drug addict and has a revolving door on her bedroom." Lisa told us. "That woman...," she rolled her eyes. "She's the very definition of a horrible mother. The kids are always filthy when we pick them up, always hungry. She makes me sick every time I see her."

"Lisa...," I widened my eyes at her. Even if she didn't like the woman, she still shouldn't say things like that in front of Erik.

"Oh, don't worry about it. She's right. My ex is a drug addicted whore. She wasn't that way when I married her or at least I convinced myself she wasn't. I knew she enjoyed getting high. Hell, we both did in those days," Erik winked with a cute smirk at Lisa. "I was finishing law school when I met her. She was beautiful, carefree and wild...and living with some machinist she was supposedly engaged too, but somehow that didn't stop her from sleeping with me. However, in retrospect that should have sent up red flags everywhere. And I really shouldn't have been surprised when I came home five years later and caught her in bed with my best friend."

The three of us just stared at him for a moment completely speechless.

"And I thought my ex was a bastard." I laughed uncomfortably.

"Seriously? You never told me all that." Lisa looked confused. "Why didn't you tell me all that before?"

"I told you that before." Erik wrinkled his eyebrows.

"I didn't know she was engaged to someone else when you started sleeping with her. Why would you do that?" She asked.

"Because I was young and stupid," Erik admitted.

"So, what made you think she'd treat you any different than the machinist?" I asked.

"She told me she loved me, and I was stupid enough to believe it." Erik confessed.

"I guess we all know which head you were thinking with." I muttered with a grin.

"What can I say? I was young, dumb, and full of cum." Erik gestured a mock bow.

"And now you're old and stupid." Lisa shoved him playfully.

"And on that happy note, I'm going to get a refill. Anyone else need one?" I asked standing up.

Lisa and I took the empty glasses from our men and wandered back off into the house. I couldn't believe how relaxed and easy the evening was going. I began mixing the martinis and Lisa started pulling things out of the refrigerator for dinner.

I brought the guys their drinks and asked Hayden to start the grill for me. Then I returned to the kitchen to help Lisa put the final touches on the rest of the meal.

After we ate, Hayden and Erik got the fire pit roaring while Lisa and I cleaned up things in the kitchen. I was so happy with the way the evening was going.

The two men were getting along splendidly, and Hayden had certainly worked his charms well on Lisa.

Although I knew she still had some serious reservations about the entire situation, she genuinely liked him as a person. At least that was a step in the right direction.

Several pitchers of martinis and a couple of hours later the four of us sat on the deck lit up like Christmas trees. Lisa and I had tried relentlessly to get Hayden to reveal where he was taking me on our trip but neither of us had been successful in getting any information out of him.

"Okay, fine. Be that way." I pretended to pout and give Hayden the cold shoulder.

"Oh, I know what we can do. Let's play 'I never'." Lisa suggested.

"I'm not familiar with that one," Hayden said. "How do you play it?"

"We take turns saying, 'I never....' and then you state something you've never done and if any of us have done it, then we have to take a drink." Erik explained.

"Ok, I'm in." Hayden sat back in his seat.

"I go first since I thought of it," Lisa jumped in. "I never had to replace the swing on my back porch because it broke during a hot sexual encounter."

"I'm never telling you anything ever again." I took a drink and the guys laughed. "And you shut up!" I pointed my index finger at Lisa.

"I never slept with my ex after we separated or thereafter." Erik smirked at Lisa, but it was me who got the odd glance from Hayden when I also took a drink.

"Really?" he asked.

"Shut up," I muttered.

"Okay then. I never smoked a joint with Axl Rose backstage at a *Guns N' Roses* concert." Hayden tipped his glass in my direction.

"Damn people come on!" I laughed and drank again. "All right, I never streaked the Homecoming game in high school."

"Touché," Hayden took a drink as the rest of us laughed at him. "I was seventeen," he winked. "It seemed like a good idea at the time for a senior prank."

"Didn't you play football? How'd you streak the game if you were playing?" Lisa asked.

"It wasn't easy. I stripped down in the locker room while the coach was lecturing the team at half time. I ran out and streaked while the marching band was doing some formation thing wearing nothing but my birthday suit and a Daffy Duck mask. Then I snuck around the outside of the stadium and cut across the field back to the locker room. It was a bitch trying to get my sweaty gear back on before coach noticed me missing." He let out a hearty laugh.

"I wish I could have seen that." I giggled. The martinis were going straight to my head. "Okay, I never got caught by the police having sex in the backseat of a car on New Year's Eve." I smiled mischievously at Lisa.

"You bitch!" She laughed and took a long drink. "Fine, I never slept with two members of the same family!" Lisa slurred.

A deathly silence swept over the four of us. Lisa looked like she was afraid she'd cross that invisible line none of us dared to mention. Erik looked uncomfortable and just sat there nursing his drink. Hayden downed the rest of his.

"So, Lisa, I guess the gloves are off." Hayden flashed her a wicked smile. "And the pink polka-dotted elephant in the room has been exposed. So...let's get the questions out of the way."

"I'm sorry. I was only playing around. I didn't mean anything by it." Lisa looked embarrassed.

"It's okay. I figured sooner or later this would come up. Alex and I are both aware of how challenging our relationship is — and how unorthodox." Hayden said confidently. "This is not something we foresaw or planned. It just happened."

"If we're being honest here, don't you think Mason is going to have a difficult time swallowing this one?" Erik looked directly at me. "You've been living with him for over a year, sleeping with him. Your sons have grown attached to him as well. What are you going to tell them?"

"At this point, nothing. We don't know where this relationship is going yet and until we do there's no need to upset everyone." I answered honestly. "I know how my boys feel about Mason. They love him. So, do I, but I'm not in love with Mason and that's not fair to him either. But I also don't believe that Mason is truly in love with me either because if he was, he wouldn't already be dating someone else right now."

"You know about Megan?" Hayden looked over at me.

"Yes, he told me."

"I'm sorry," he leaned over and kissed me on the cheek.

"It's how it should be." I muttered in response.

"And on a lighter note, can you at least spill the beans on who's better in bed?" Lisa joked to ease the tension.

"Lisa?" I shook my head and laughed not surprised by her bluntness.

"I think I need a refill." Erik stood up and Hayden joined him.

"Me too," And the two of them disappeared into the house.

"I can't believe you'd ask me that in front of him." I said once the French doors were closed.

"Oh, lighten up. I was just teasing." She shifted a little in her chair. "Something had to be said to ease the tension between us. Besides, you already told me who was better."

"And who was that?" Hayden asked as he walked back out with Erik in tow.

"What?" He caught me off guard.

"Who is better?" Hayden sat back down beside me and handed me a fresh martini. "I'm curious."

"I'm not answering that." I stated flatly.

"And why not?" There was a mischievous gleam in his eyes.

"Because if I say you are, that just strokes your ego. And if I say he is then it's insulting you. But if you don't know you'll always wonder and continue to try hard to please me." I reasoned.

"That's just mean," Hayden laughed.

"I have to agree with him on that one." Erik chimed in.

"Since when do you have an opinion on this matter?" Lisa inquired.

"I just think it's mean and funny. Alex's reasoning for not answering." Erik fumbled his way out.

"Ah, you do, do you? Why don't you tell them what you told me before we left my house?" Lisa challenged with a smirk.

"What did you say?" I turned my attention towards Erik.

"Just a smartass remark. I was only joking around." It was fun watching him squirm.

"So, spit it out," I pushed.

"I said that Thanksgiving would be priceless this year. That I'd love to be a fly on the wall and I wondered who you'd be sitting beside. And I might have said something about father and son comparing performance notes." Erik confessed.

"Oh, my God! How could you?" I laughed.

"Well, thankfully this is Mason's year to spend Thanksgiving with his mom, but Christmas should be fun." Hayden simpered.

"Wonderful," I muttered under my breath while struggling not to laugh.

"No, this is good." Lisa spoke up. "This way we can come up with a plan of attack." She took a long sip of her martini before she continued. "You know, just in case you two decide to make a run of this relationship."

"And what is your plan of attack so to speak?" Hayden asked.

"Well, when you're all gathered around the Christmas tree opening gifts, you could hand him a gift-wrapped box of condoms and say something like 'Sorry Mason, your Dad and I finished off the last box you bought so we thought we'd buy you some more'." She laughed and tipped her glass towards Hayden and me.

"Ouch!" my eyes widened at her words, but my mind immediately went to Mason's stash in my nightstand that Hayden has been using.

"Well, I thought it would go over better than you blurting something like, 'We bought you a new bed for Christmas because I've been sleeping with your dad in your old one'."

"Classy, Lisa," Hayden chuckled.

"Sweet," I rolled my eyes with a smirk at her.

Luckily, Hayden took her words with a grain of salt and laughed them off. I didn't know if it was the alcohol, an extension of his feelings for me, or his overall polite nature. But whichever one it was, I was thankful he took it in stride.

I, on the other hand, knew that there was a smidgen of truth behind her words. While she was trying her best to be a good friend to me, I knew she was struggling with my relationship with Hayden.

And I couldn't blame her. I was struggling with it myself. It was impossible for me to expect her to understand something, I myself, was still trying to wrap my brain around.

The evening wrapped up with Hayden agreeing to leave his car in my garage for the duration of our trip as opposed to the alternative of long-parking at the airport. Lisa and Erik had offered to drive us to the airport in the morning.

I was touched by their offer considering that we had to be at the airport at four thirty in the morning and I knew Lisa was not exactly a morning person.

After they left, Hayden followed me back to my room. I was still more than a little buzzed from the numerous martinis. My head felt fuzzy and things were more than a bit hazy.

I felt like I was floating around in a world that was somehow paralleled to the reality I was facing. And I liked it. It felt easier than facing what I was actually doing.

Hayden came up behind me and kissed the curve of my neck. His lips danced lightly across my skin like an electric pulse. His arms wrapped around me and I leaned back and melted into him.

"Your friends were pretty wonderful," he whispered.

"Thanks, I think so."

"I think you're pretty wonderful." His breath was hot against my neck.

"Really?" I turned to face him." Well, I happen to think you're pretty amazing." I leaned up on my tippy-toes and lightly brushed my lips against his.

Hayden picked me up and carried me over to my bed. He laid me down gently and climbed up beside me. His deep green eyes sparkled in the soft glow from the lamp on the night stand. His shapely lips were curved slightly upwards as he looked upon me.

"You are so beautiful," he said in soft voice before he pressed his lips over mine. They parted just enough so that his tongue lightly touched mine for just a brief moment. He brought his hand up and cupped my face.

His kisses became more feverish, desperate with his desire. He pulled off my sun dress and tossed it aside. Then he sat upright for a moment and discarded his own clothes.

Hayden's well-defined chest and arms reflected in the shadows of the soft light. I couldn't stop myself from leaning up and running my fingers over his soft skin. It was deliciously warm to my touch. His hair was tussled out of place in a way that made him look years younger. I wanted nothing more than to devour him.

Unfortunately, the clock on my nightstand informed me that it was close to midnight. We had to get up in a few hours and as much as I desired him, somewhere in the far recesses of my brain, I knew I would oversleep the alarm if I didn't sleep off at least a little bit of the effects from the martinis.

"Hayden," I pulled away from him reluctantly. "Look at the time."

"So?" He glanced at the clock and shrugged.

"We should get some sleep." I elaborated.

"I'll be fine," he tried to pull me back, but I resisted.

"But I won't be," I assured him. "I need to get at least a couple hours of sleep. I'm sorry."

"All right," he pretended to pout for a moment. "I'll behave."

I slid off the bed and disappeared into the bathroom. I started the shower, letting the water warm up and steam fill the room while I removed my make-up and brushed my teeth. Hayden joined me at the sink and began brushing his teeth as well. We climbed into the shower together and for once, simply showered…although rather playfully.

CHAPTER 9

"EXCUSE ME?" I said a little too loudly. "Are you kidding me?" I said to Hayden as I waved goodbye to Lisa and Erik as they drove away from the airport terminal.

"No, I'm serious. We're frog-tailing it across the pond my dear." Hayden smiled and hauled our luggage through the airport doorway.

"I figured we were going somewhere in the states." I replied following right behind him.

"Why do you think I told you to pack your passport?" He paused before climbing upon the escalator.

"I thought you mentioned it just to throw me off."

"Well, you'd said you always wanted to see Europe. So, I'm taking you to Europe," he beamed. "Our first stop is Dublin."

"Ireland? You're taking me to Ireland? Are you serious?" I was completely taken aback. "Oh, my God!" I squealed and throw my arms awkwardly around him despite the heavy baggage we were lugging around.

***

Our plane landed in Dublin, Ireland a little after ten our time. The eighteen-hour trip to the Irish capital had taken its toll on both of us. I wasn't sure if I was more tired or hungry. The meal on the flight was barely edible and neither of us touched it much.

Hayden was kind enough to relieve me of all the granola bars and fruit roll-ups I'd kept in my carry-on. We were both groggy from lack of sleep and it took a few minutes to gather our entire luggage.

Hayden hailed us a taxi to take us to the bed and breakfast that was expecting us. The sky was cloudy, but the sun was doing it best to make its presence known.

There was a constant breeze that didn't allow much warmth to penetrate the clouds. This was nothing like the humid Midwest June I was accustomed too.

The driver and Hayden loaded our bags into the trunk and we all piled into the car. I leaned my head against Hayden's shoulder trying to fight off the sleep I so desperately needed. I fought to keep my eyes open and enjoy the gorgeous scenery around us.

Dublin was so vastly different from anything I'd ever seen in my corner of the world. Everything looked clean and fresh, but also as if it had been standing there for centuries. I was so impressed and couldn't wait to go exploring once I could look upon it with fresh eyes.

We pulled up to the *Annagh House*. It was an old Victorian estate complete with a cobblestone drive and iron fences. The brightly colored flowers accented the greenery in such a way it almost appeared artificial. A tall man in his mid-fifties greeted us warmly as soon as our cab came to a halt.

"Good mornin', welcome. You must be Mr. and Mrs. Brooks. How nice to meet you. I'm John." He shook Hayden's hand and then mine.

"Pleasure to meet you." Hayden smiled warmly.

"You have such a beautiful place." I stated while the men unloaded the luggage and Hayden paid the driver.

"Thank you, mam'," John helped Hayden carry our things inside.

John escorted us upstairs to our room and kindly acknowledged how tired we were. He told us he would give us a lay of the house after we'd rested and freshened up a bit.

Our room was absolutely breathtaking. The antique furniture and modern amenities had a certain allure that immediately pulled me in as if I was home. I walked over to the oversized bay window and was stunned by the beautiful view of the *Dollymont Beach*.

The colors about the room were a bright butternut cream, fresh sage and pale blue. There was a fireplace on the wall opposite the queen size bed with an antique mantle piece that had the most beautiful design carved into it. I couldn't have imagined a more wonderful place to stay.

Hayden closed the door and walked up behind me taking me in his arms. I leaned back against him and stared out at the bay. I was so exhausted, but somehow, I felt such peace standing there in his arms.

"I can't believe I'm actually here." I said.

"Well, believe it. You're in Ireland my dear."

"Thank you for bringing me here."

"My pleasure. Would you like to take a nap first or shower?" Hayden said softly.

"Why did he address us as Mr. and Mrs. Brooks?" I turned around to face him.

"I wasn't sure how accustomed a privately-owned B&B would be to two adults in such an affair as ours. It's not like the anonymity of a larger hotel. Therefore, I thought it would be best to make our reservations as a married couple." He explained with a slight smile. "And I haven't said Mr. and Mrs. Brooks for almost twenty years."

"Don't look at me with smirk. I will never be a Mrs. again." I tried to pull away, but Hayden grabbed my arm forcing me to look into his emerald green eyes.

"Oh, you don't think you'll ever get remarried?"

"Not today," I teased and gently pulled my arm free.

I stood before him and undressed slowly. His eyes followed my every move. Naked, I walked towards the bathroom and turned on the shower. I was dying to wash off that long flight and feel like myself in my own skin. Hayden stood in the doorway watching me intently.

"Mind if I join you?" he inquired.

"I was hoping you would." Our eyes met in the mirror.

I brushed my teeth over the sink letting the shower steam up the small bath. My eyes watched Hayden removing his clothing in the mirror. I could tell by his movements he was every bit as tired as I and the time difference was weighing heavy on him as well.

Hayden came up beside me and started brushing his teeth as well. I rinsed and climbed into the shower first. The hot water eased all the tension in my joints as it washed over me. I closed my eyes and leaned my head back letting the water fall upon my face.

Then I felt Hayden's hand tilt my head upright and his lips press firmly against mine so soft and tender my knees went weak. I don't know if it was from the fatigue or him, but suddenly I was so light-headed I felt as if I'd float away.

"You look tired." I heard him say in a low voice.

"Thanks," I gave him the best smile I could muster.

"You know what I mean," he leaned down and kissed me again.

"Yes, I do," a small grin slid across my lips. "How about nap first, then food."

"Sounds good. But I must warn you, if you try anything, I'm going to fight you off. A man can only last so long on a diet of pure animal driven passion and fun." Hayden warned.

"Sorry to disappoint you, but I couldn't try anything even if I wanted to. Not without substance and sleep first." I poked his nose playfully. "Afterwards, it's game on."

Several hours later I awoke to the evening sun beginning to sink out of the sky. Hayden was still sleeping beside me, snoring away contently. I slipped out from beneath the covers taking extra care not to stir Hayden. I walked over to the bay window and gazed out at the Bay.

A glow of pink, purples, and oranges were set ablaze over the sparkling calm waters. It appeared as if the water was on fire. A few scattered clouds hovered above in a deep purple hue. I had never seen anything so majestic before.

A warm breeze drifted in through the open window lifting my hair off my shoulders just a bit and raising goose bumps across my arms. It smelled of warm jasmine and sea salts with a hint of clover.

I inhaled deeply still trying to believe I was standing here...in Ireland. I glanced over my shoulder at the man breathing softly with the white sheet draped gracefully over his masculine body. He looked so peaceful, almost angelic-like...and so much like his son.

I tried to push the thought out of my head. After all, they are two entirely different people, but they weren't. They shared so many similarities that it was eerie. Little things, like gestures, facial expressions, overall body language. Small things that only someone who knew them both well would notice. I gently shook my head in the breeze trying to physically shake the recollection from my mind.

I was going to have to if Hayden and I were going to enjoy this vacation. If we were ever going to stand a chance of discovering what was between us, I was going to have to fully let Mason go. I knew in my heart I wasn't in love with him. I knew he was a young man who still had his whole life ahead of him.

Someday he would want to settle down, get married, and have children of his own. I didn't want to be the one responsible for him not having all that. My days of having children were done. I loved my boys more than anything in this world, but I knew I could never give Mason children of his own. And he deserved all of that.

And he certainly didn't deserve to discover that the woman he loves was lying in bed with his father.

I felt horrible.

Why am I here?

I heard Hayden stir and turned around. He stretched, barely conscious of the world around him. He tossed the sheet aside and made his way over to the bathroom. The door closed with a soft click and I turned my attention back to the blazing glory outside. The sun was hovering lowly above the ocean. The brilliant colors streaked across the sky.

Behind me came the soft sounds of footsteps and then strong arms engulfed me. "I love the way you look in that light. Stay where you are, don't move." Hayden went over to his travel bag and pulled out his expensive new camera that he bought before he left Chicago.

I watched him play around with it for a moment before his attention turned towards me once again.

"Hayden, don't. I look terrible." I held up my hand between us. "I haven't even run a brush through my hair."

"You're beautiful," he focused on the camera's little screen. "Trust me." He began clicking away moving around the room trying to capture me from every angle.

So, I stood there in the bay window with the light breeze blowing around me lightly kissing the long silk smoky grey gown with the tiny angel hair straps I was wearing. My hair flowed gently over my shoulders, down my back and lifted randomly by the twilight air.

I felt foolish standing there with him moving about, but in a strange way, elegant and graceful. Hayden made me feel special, beautiful. Something I hadn't felt in years.

Finally, he put his camera aside and took me in his arms. Our eyes locked and that unspoken bond between us ignited. I felt as if all the air was sucked out of my lungs. I couldn't breathe.

A slow grin spread across his perfectly shaped full lips. I could feel myself mimicking his behavior. I leaned up on my toes and gently kissed him.

"I'm starving," I whispered.

"Me too," I rested my head against his chest. "Why don't we get dressed and check out the village and see if we can't find something to eat."

"Sounds good," but I stayed where I was, safe in his arms.

We both freshened up and began the task of locating something to wear in the mess of luggage we brought with us. Hayden put on a pair of Kakis with a white buttoned up casual dress shirt. His sleeves were rolled up to his elbows and he was wearing a pair of brown leather sandals. He looked stunning.

I found a cute navy cotton dress that hugged my body without being snug and a pair of jeweled sandals with a small heel. It was perfect for our first adventure out in a foreign country.

I brushed my hair out until it shinned and left it hanging down loosely over my shoulders. I added a little mascara, a smidgen of eyeliner and a touch of lip gloss.

I looked myself over in the mirror while Hayden waited patiently for me downstairs talking with John about the best places to eat in the area. My reflection stared back at me and I wasn't entirely sure of who I was looking at anymore.

A half an hour later Hayden and I were walking hand in hand down the brick roads of Dublin. I was having a hard time taking it all in. It was so amazing and wonderful and like nothing I had ever witnessed in my life.

The buildings, their architecture was only something I had seen before in movies or television. They were colorful, unique, and picturesque. I wanted to absorb it all.

We found a little bistro that John said served the best cabbage rolls and sat down at one of the little tables on the patio. I let Hayden order our food and blonde ale for each of us as I took in the amazing atmosphere. I felt like I was walking around in a cloud.

The waiter returned shortly with our ale's along with a fat loaf of brown bread. Hayden immediately began cutting into it and I couldn't blame him. We were both starving.

The first piece he cut he smothered in the thick creamy butter from the small dish and handed it over to me. I must admit, it was the best tasting bread and butter I'd ever tasted in my life.

"Oh my God!" I proclaimed while Hayden was busy cutting himself a slice. "This is fabulous! I could live on this."

"Damn," he announced with his mouth half full. "I have to agree." He swallowed a gulp of his ale to wash it down. "It's so moist and tastes a tad sweet. I wonder what's in it."

"I'm not sure. Perhaps John will know." I replied between bites. "I still can't believe we're really here."

"I know," Hayden paused long enough to enjoy the scenery. "It is a bit surreal."

"Yes, and a bit fabulous." I took another drink. "Thank you so much for bringing me here. I always wanted to visit the UK."

"Technically, we're not in the UK." Hayden smiled between bites.

"I thought Ireland was part of the UK." I gave him a confused look.

"Northern Ireland is part of the UK, but we're in Dublin. Dublin is in the Republic of Ireland, so it is a country of its own." He pointed out.

"Seriously? That is so weird. I never knew that."

"Yep, it's true. And did you know that the Republic of Ireland uses the Euro as its currency, has its own stamps and Irish Gaelic is its language although you would hear more people speaking English there than Gaelic. The Gaelic will be more noticeable in the street and motorway signs. Also, the police are not called the police but the Garda. Or to give them their full title, the Garda Síochána!" Hayden explained.

"What did you do while I was taking a nap? Read a quickie link on the history of Dublin?" I laughed.

"No," he laughed. "John told me while I was waiting for you."

The food was amazing. I had never tasted anything remotely close to it in the States. The so-called Irish pups around Indianapolis didn't create delicacies like these.

The spices were deep and rooted, the cabbage rolls crisp and rich favored. I had never been a huge fan of traditional Irish dishes, but this certainly changed my mind.

Between the food and the atmosphere, I lost myself in my surroundings. I believe Hayden did too. We ate most of our meal in silence just absorbing everything around us. The people, the clothing, the cars, the buildings...everything was so different. My brain just couldn't process it all quick enough. There was so much, and it was breathtaking.

After dinner, Hayden and I walked through the streets hand in hand. It was a little cool out and I was glad I brought my wrap. Hayden put his arm around me and pulled me a little closer to him.

The streets were filled with citizens and tourists alike, but they were easy to differentiate. All the tourists looked something like us...gawking at every unique sign, every colorful building, and every cultural aspect of the area. They were oh-ing and aw-ing and pointing — just like us.

Honestly, I could have cared less how touristy we appeared. I was having the time of my life and was going to enjoy every moment of it. Still, it had been an incredibly long day and despite our short nap, I was completely exhausted. I tried to stifle a yawn, but Hayden noticed.

"I saw that," he grinned.

"Sorry," I smiled back. "I guess the flight took more out of me than I'd realized."

"Oh, I'm so glad you said that. I'm so tired, I almost fell asleep in my cabbage rolls." Hayden chuckled. "Would you care if we head back? We can explore all day tomorrow."

"That sounds like a wonderful idea."

A short cab ride and a slip into some comfy clothes later, Hayden and I curled up on the bed with a bottle of wine we'd just purchased at some locally owned shop. It was so sweet and rich and went down a little too smoothly.

Hayden was leaning against the headboard, shirtless and wearing a pair of grey pajama bottoms. One arm was crooked behind his head, the other holding the wineglass.

His eyes held a mischievous grin telling me that despite his earlier claim of being tired, the last thing he wanted to do right now was sleep.

I climbed up on the bed beside him. "Thank you so much for bringing me here. This is more than I could ever imagined." I traced my fingers lightly over his chest while sipping my wine.

"Even with the jet-lag?" he smiled.

"Very much so," I placed our glasses on the nightstand before I reached over and kissed him eagerly.

Hayden wrapped his arms around me and rolled me over. His kisses became more intense as he worked his way down to my neck and collarbone. I entangled my fingers through his short curls. I moaned softly while he removed my shirt between his kisses.

They sent a jolt of electricity through my body and a burning desire for him between my thighs. I wanted him so badly.

I ran my nails across his shoulders closing my eyes and breathing heavily. His fingers tugged my panties down my legs and carefully removed them. His lips caressed the inside of my thighs. The scruff of his shadow beard brushed lightly over my skin. I shivered longingly.

He reached up with one hand and massaged my breast, lightly pinching one of my nipples. I arched my hips towards him.

Hayden's tongue danced teasingly over my clitoris, his fingers gently parting my lips. He slowly removed his hand from my breast and lightly traced it over my abdomen before slipping a couple fingers inside me immediately discovering my G-spot. I gasped out in delight as he increased the pressure ever so slightly.

I rocked my hips with his steady rhythm. My breathing came faster and more intense. A tingling numbing spread throughout my body as I exploded in an intense orgasm. I screamed out as my body shook uncontrollably.

I tried desperately to squirm away from him with all the strength I could muster, but Hayden held on to my thighs, locking his arms around them following me across the bed. I fought my way halfway up the headboard before he finally let go, utterly and completely satisfied with himself.

I grabbed Hayden by his shoulders and pulled him up to me. I wanted him, badly. Needed him, desperately. He slid me back down the bed and entered me with a delightful force that took my breath away.

I wrapped my legs around him and grabbed a hold of his buttocks. The rhythm of our bodies fell into perfect harmony. I loved the way he felt inside me, the way his body moved with mine, the way he filled me.

I nudged him deliberately, rolling him over and straddling him. I sat straight down on him moaning loudly feeling the full force of his thrust deep into me. My nails dug into his chest as I arched my back, throwing my head back.

My hair flung loosely down my back in a darkened veil. Hayden grabbed my hips forcing an increase in our speed and the depth of his thrust. Harder and faster he drove himself into me. His pelvic bone rubbed gloriously against my clitoris sending shockwaves throughout my body.

I could feel myself ready to explode once more. I grabbed a hold of his forearms as my body went an electric numb, consumed with mind-blowing ecstasy.

Satisfied that he had fulfilled his goal, Hayden wrapped his arms around me rolling us over. He hovered over me with a devilish grin on his shapely lips...pride plainly written all over his face. He slowly entered me again loving the feeling as each inch invaded me.

His rhythm was slow and steady, and I matched it with my hips. His lips lightly brushed over mine, his tongue caressing mine softly. But the fire was ignited and would not be ignored. His mouth crushed mine, his tongue probing me imploringly. I loved the way he felt, the way he tasted, the weight of his body on mine.

He lifted my legs and placed them on his shoulders increasing the depths of his thrust. I moaned loudly and ran my nails over his back. His rhythm increased, his kisses overwhelming.

His desire was unquenchable. His body quivered and shook as he exploded inside me. Sweat glistened on his brow; his breathing was labored.

Hayden collapsed beside me, exhausted. Our hearts were still racing. He looked over at me with a cheesy grin.

"That's one way to spend an evening. Now I really need some sleep," He said breathlessly.

"Agreed," I chuckled and rolled off the bed. My legs were still weak, and my knees buckled under me. I grabbed the side of the bed, catching myself before I fell. "I need some water."

I carefully, slowly made my way to the bathroom. I still felt so lightheaded. I couldn't remember the last time I had cum so hard. I shut the door behind me and leaned against the counter. My reflection glowed in the mirror.

I turned the water on and splashed some on my face. It felt so refreshing. My cheeks were red, and my lips slightly swollen from his passionate kisses.

I stepped on one of Hayden's white tee-shirts that were lying on the rug where he must have dropped it before he showered. I casually kicked it aside without a second thought and splashed a little more water on my face. I didn't bother to dry off.

I brushed my hair out and tossed it over my shoulder. As I turned around, Hayden walked up behind me.

He slipped his arms around my waist and laid his head on my shoulder. I leaned back against him and stared at us in the mirror.

He was strikingly handsome. I loved how we looked and fit together. He gently kissed the nap of my neck.

"You look so beautiful." His lips brushed against my cheek. "Your face is wet."

"The cold water felt refreshing," my hands slid around him as I gripped his ass firmly. I pressed my ass against his hardening thick cock.

"You like the cold water?" his breath was hot against my neck. "Do you want me to cool you off?"

"Yes," I barely whispered back.

Hayden reached down and picked up his discarded tee-shirt. He slipped it over my head. I put my arms through the sleeves and the shirt billowed down very loosely around me. His eyes held a devious sparkle as he reached around me and turned the faucet back on. He cupped his hand under the water, holding what he could of it and splashed it upon my chest.

I jumped just a bit from the impact of the cold against my skin but giggled nonetheless. He repeated his action several times until his shirt was soaked, transparent, and clinging to me.

"There. That's better." Hayden leaned over my shoulder kissing me hungrily, his hands fondling my breasts roughly.

"You like that? Do you?" I reached behind me and took a firm hold of his throbbing cock.

I maneuvered it between my thighs being careful not to put it in me. I slide back and forth along his shaft loving how much it aroused him.

"Ah, you want to play that game, do you?" He splashed more water across my chest. I couldn't help but giggle a little more as I wiggled along his cock in a suggestive manner.

"You love it and you know it," I smiled at his reflection.

"And you love this," he abruptly lightly kicked one of my legs further out while leaning me forward just enough to push is big dick into me. My breath caught, and I gasped loudly leaning back into him.

The strength of his thrust lifted my feet off the floor. I caught myself on the counter. Hayden placed his hands on my hips and drove into me. Straightening up a bit, I placed a hand on his thigh before leaning back to kiss him.

He slowed his rhythm up a bit and splashed some more water across my chest then ran his hands lovingly over my breasts. His shirt clung to me like a second skin, my nipples gloriously erect. Haydon took full advantage and pinched them sending a jolt through my body.

He bent over just enough to shove his thirsty tongue in my mouth. I eagerly devoured him running my fingers through his hair tugging him to me. He hungrily moved his mouth down to my neck and shoulders. My hands laid over his massaging my breasts. Our eyes locked in the mirror and embraced. There was a current, a connection between us that I had never felt before in my life.

Hayden gripped my hips and thrust forcefully in to me taking my breath away. He quickly released me stepping back a bit and withdrew from me. I felt his hot cock on my ass as he moaned loudly and spilled his seed up my back.

I held onto the counter to steady myself, my breathing still labored. He crouched over and rested his head on my shoulder, sweat glistening on his brow.

"Damn…," he muttered breathlessly. "You're going to be the death of me woman!"

"I think you have that backwards." Our eyes locked again.

"I love you," he barely whispered.

I didn't know what to say so I did the cowardly thing and pretended I didn't hear him.

Freshly showered, we snuggled up together in bed. Both of us lost in our own thoughts. I rested my head upon his chest listening to his heart beating smoothly with an arm and leg draped over his body. His arms held me securely.

His words haunted me. He hadn't mentioned my lack of reply, but it was obviously noticed. And I couldn't help but wonder if my silence on the matter would dampen our trip.

Yes, I loved him. I knew I did. I loved him in a way I would nor could ever love Mason. I was completely head over heels, mind-numbingly, stupidly, insanely, and blindly in love with Hayden.

I loved him more than any man I had ever been involved with before, including Danny. And nothing but fear kept the words trapped in my throat.

I closed my eyes and tried to focus on the moment and not worry about what tomorrow would bring or about what was going to happen once we returned to the States.

CHAPTER 10

THE SUN WAS BARELY OVER THE HORIZON when I awoke. Hayden was spooned up behind me snoring softly. I slipped out of bed and freshened myself up in the bathroom as quietly as I could. After such an exhausting forty-eight hours, I wanted to let Hayden sleep as much as possible.

I slipped into a long cotton sun dress and grabbed my cardigan before heading downstairs in search of some coffee. The house was still quiet, but there was no mistaking the strong aroma of coffee that greeted me as soon as I stepped out of our bedroom.

The kitchen was spotless and empty when I walked in. There were several oversized mugs sitting beside the coffee maker that must have brewed on a timer, along with a canister of sugar and the choice of French vanilla or hazelnut powered coffee creamer.

Neither would have been my first choice, but without any other options, I poured a mug and added in some sugar and French vanilla creamer.

I walked out the back-atrium door onto the deck. It was a cool morning with a slight breeze. I pulled my sweater a little closer to me and wrapped my hands around the mug absorbing some of its warmth.

The beach was just below the deck and looked so inviting in the early morning light. I looked around and found the beach completely empty.

I climbed down the half dozen steps and sank my toes into the soft, cool, sand. It was exhilarating, and the view was nothing short of spectacular. I walked a short distance towards the water and sat down in an empty wooden beach chair.

The planks were cold beneath my dress. I buried my toes a little deeper into the sand and watched the wave's lap gently upon the shore. The breeze lifted my hair a little off my shoulders and kissed my neck sending a barrage of goose bumps across my body.

It still felt very surreal…being here, being with Hayden. The sound of the ocean filled my ears. It was only enhanced by the powerful smell of saltwater in the air. I reached down and picked up a multi-colored shell out of the sand. I examined the little ridges in it and the seamless mixture of colors.

I enclosed my fingers around it thinking I would take it home with me so that I would always remember the peace and serenity I felt sitting here this morning. I never wanted to forget it.

When my mug was finally empty I headed back up to the Bed and Breakfast. I could hear voices drifting from the open windows even before my feet hit the deck. I paused on the top step with my hand on the railing and turned back towards the ocean for one last view before the moment was lost. I almost hated to let it go.

***

Hayden and I spent the next four days touring Dublin and the outlying area. We visited all the typical tourist traps, historical sites, castles, galleries, and museums. We stuffed ourselves at Bewley's Café on Grafton Street, The Winding Stair, Hatch & Son's, Dax Restaurant and many others.

The Temple Bar was a popular favorite spot of ours and we had a long and fabulous night at O'Donoghue's listening to the live music and drinking more than our share of Guinness.

One night, Hayden took me to the Gate Theatre that had been there for more than 250 years. It was such an amazing place. In fact, all of it was.

***

We left Dublin in our little rental car that was about the size of one of Henry's hot wheels. It was like doing ninety miles an hour down the highway on a skateboard. The scenery was something like out of the Lord of the Rings trilogy although I knew it was filmed in New Zealand.

Everything was just so green and serene. Rocks jetted out along the coastline, trees loomed along the roadways and the periodic rain showers only enhanced the romantic atmosphere that engulfed us.

We drove up to Scotland for a couple days and visited some ancient castles, pubs, and roamed the streets with the friendliest people anywhere in the world. I was sad to say good-bye after only two days, but we were off again only this time on a ferry boat over to the United Kingdom...or rather London for a few days.

At least there they spoke English, but their accents were so thick it was just as hard to understand as if they were still speaking in a foreign tongue.

While London was simply divine, it was not the friendliest of places to visit, especially for an American. Most people were almost rude or maybe that was just the way they were. I don't know, but I wasn't as sad to depart there as I thought for sure I would be before we arrived.

Hayden and I packed up our things once more and took another ferry over to France. I could hardly contain myself about seeing Paris. I thought for sure Hayden was going to tie me down just to keep me somewhat in check. People around us stared as I gushed on about the clothes, the food, the shops, and the little cafes I was dying to check out.

Hayden had a talent of finding the cutest little Bed and Breakfast's in any town or city. Most were adorable, some left a little to be desired and one was downright scary…without intentionally being so. Our new rental car was barely larger than our last one, but it did, thankfully, have a GPS in it.

***

We found ourselves in Amsterdam next after spending the night in a very little and rather charming bed and breakfast. The faded blue paint was peeling off the walls, the hardwood floor boards were well worn, and the entire place reminded me more of my grandmother's house when I was a child, but it was clean, homey, and comfortable.

Amsterdam, itself, was quite spectacular. Of course, I had grown up hearing stories about Amsterdam. It was notorious for their Red-Light District and being legal to smoke marijuana.

I was anxious to explore its seedy underbelly and discover if any of those wild stories I'd ever heard held any truth to them.

Hayden checked us into a hotel in the east district while I stood outside enthralled in the ambiance. It was so bizarre. Even though it was still early evening the place was crawling with tourists from all over the world. Just standing there I heard people talking in languages I wasn't even familiar with.

A group of angry tourists a short way away were arguing with what I assumed was some sort of police over them taking some photos of the women in the window on display. Apparently, doing so was forbidden.

Good to know…

Hayden reappeared looking a little disgruntled. He didn't seem happy about some arrogant British man who apparently wasn't too fond of Americans in general.

Not only did he call Hayden an uncultured Yankee, when Hayden was talking with the desk clerk about certain codes of behavior that had to be followed while in the Red-Light district, he sarcastically asked Hayden if he remembered to pack his Colt.

"He was such as ass. How was I supposed to know it was illegal to take photographs of the women in the windows, or that this place was crawling with pick-pocketers?" He rambled as he carried our bags and I followed him to the elevator.

"Ignore him. Why do you care what he thinks?" I gently rubbed his arm while we waited for the elevator.

"I don't, but why the hell would he say something like that. That son of a bitch doesn't know me from Adam." He hit the button several more times.

"Exactly, so just blow it off. Please, don't let him ruin our evening."

"I'm sorry, but you weren't there. This man was a total ass. How can he make such a statement under the blanket that all Americans are Yankee's toting a gun?" He huffed.

"So, all he did was prove his own ignorance and make a fool of himself in front of everyone in the vicinity. Who gives a shit what he thinks? Let it go." I was already sick of the discussion and pissed that his altercation was ruining our evening.

Thankfully, the doors slid open and we stopped talking. My only hope was that Hayden would cool off enough for us to salvage the rest of the night. I was starving, but certainly didn't want to sit through dinner at a restaurant with him in this sort of mood.

After a short nap, a shower with playful banter, Hayden's mood seemed to have improved. He put on a pair of faded jeans, a cornflower blue tee-shirt and a white casual dress shirt with thin blue and black strips.

He looked so handsome I could hardly keep my hands off him long enough to get ready myself. I slipped into a dark blue slip dress with its tiny straps and mid-thigh length. I put on my three-inch beige sandals whose straps wrapped around my ankles and lower calves.

I brushed my hair out until it flowed across my shoulders and down my back in soft shiny waves.

We emerged from the hotel a little after seven in hopes of finding the least crowded restaurant nearby. We were both starving and anxious to begin exploring the area.

The lights up and down the street were a tad overwhelming reminding me more of the strip in Vegas done up with red hues. People were practically shoulder to shoulder pushing down the cobblestone streets.

With my purse and valuables locked securely in our room and Hayden's wallet in his front pant pocket, he wrapped his arm tightly around my waist as we ventured forward. We found a restaurant a couple blocks from the hotel called *Lombardo's* located near *Rijksmuseum* in the vibrant *Spiegel* quarter.

It was more of a delicatessen than a restaurant, but they served a more traditional menu consisting of hamburgers, and barbeque, and that we were hoping might agree more with our digestive systems.

The outside of *Lombardo's* was unremarkable, yet charming. The handcrafted food shop greeted us with an enticing aroma that immediately made my stomach growl. I perused the menu along the back wall and had a hard time deciding what I wanted. Everything looked so good.

Once we had our food we settled into one of the small tables along the wall. The place was buzzing with people raving about the food. And after I took my first bite, I understood why. It was absolutely the best burger I had ever had in my entire life. I wanted to savor every bite but found myself devouring it quickly. I felt like I hadn't eaten in years.

Afterwards, we browsed the streets and gawked at the shop windows. There was nothing sexual left to the imagination. I was utterly stunned and speechless. I had never seen such a sexual display in all my life, although I believe my Sex and Society professor, Dr. Wilson would have enjoyed studying this place immensely, if he hadn't already.

The shop windows aligning the pathway were riddled with public displays of every sexual exploit my imagination could not comprehend. A combination of men and women performing sexual acts with a variety of utensils was coming at us from every direction.

"Want to check out one of the sex shops?" Hayden nudged me playfully.

"Are you serious?" I tried not to smile too broadly.

"Come on," he pulled me into the nearest shop.

"Oh my God," I muttered with a giggle following along.

I found myself standing inside a shop called *The Golden Fleece* or the *Condomerie*. It was dubbed as one of the largest condom shops in the world. I held tightly to Hayden's hand and tried to take in my surroundings.

There were displays of edible condoms, glow-in-the-dark condoms, condoms with everything imaginable printed on them, and every colored condom ever dreamt of. I picked up a little basket and started making my way about the shop. I picked up a variety of condoms in different colors and print.

"No, absolutely not." The two of us paused in front of the row of flavored edible condoms.

"Oh, come on. Its root beer flavored. You like root beer." He smirked.

"Absolutely not." I took it from his hand and tossed it back in the bin.

"Ok, how about cinnamon flavor?"

"Do you really want something hot and spicy covering your Johnson?"

"Not so much," he laughed and moved down the row. "What about banana flavored? That seems more appropriate."

"You can get whatever flavor you'd like. I'm not putting an edible condom in my mouth, let alone eating one." I shook my head and moved on.

"Why not?" He snuck up beside me and whispered.

"Are you serious? I am not eating a condom."

"If they're anything like edible panties, they probably taste like fruit roll-ups. They're pretty good."

"Really? Then you eat one." I stated in a low voice trying not to listen to numerous other couples around us all having similar conversations.

"Fine," he let it drop and we moved on to the next aisle.

The next shop we went to was the *Casa Rosso Sex Shop* in the heart of the strip. Inside there was a large assortment of sex paraphernalia and a ridiculous collection of DVDs. I picked up a pair of silver nipple clamps and held them out in front of Hayden. "You can't tell me these don't hurt."

"Maybe they aren't for you," He noted taking them from me and playing with the clasp. "They do have a hell of a grip. Ouch!" He sat them back on the table.

They had everything…literally everything. We moved down the aisle where from floor to practically ceiling was every kind of dildo a person, no matter how kinky or what their fetish, could want.

I was certainly no prude, but even I was taken aback by some of the things on display. At the far end of the row was where all the harnesses and strap-on's were kept. Some were fashioned around the waist and thighs, others were like cute little briefs.

"These are…," I wracked my brain for the right adjective and noun to complete the sentence.

"Could be fun." Hayden picked up a box and started examining the back cover.

"Really?" I raised an eyebrow at him, picked up one and gave it a closer look. "Have you ever tried one?"

"No, but after some of the things we've done, it might be fun to try." He shrugged with a mischievous grin.

"I'm game if you are." I couldn't help but be intrigued. "Which one do you want to try?"

"I'm not sure. I don't know enough about these to give objective advice." He chuckled setting the box back down and moving on to the next one.

"If you two are just starting down this road, I would go with something that fits a little snug." A young woman, who appeared to be in her mid-twenties, turned towards us and offered a kindly suggestion, "The briefs work much better than the adjustable straps. They have the tendency to come loose and begin to slide down at the most inopportune moments."

"Wow, okay." I smiled gracelessly.

"And you may want to stop by a bath store and pick up a new loofa to put down the front of the briefs between you and the base of the cock. They have the tendency to severely bruise your pelvic bone." She leaned in closer and added in a low voice. "Trust me."

"I hadn't even thought about that." I replied more to myself than to her. "Thanks!"

"No problem. Have fun," she smiled and bounced away.

Hayden stared at the young lady as she left, "I don't even know what to say about that."

"She has a point. I wouldn't have thought of that." I tried not to laugh.

"Huh? Me neither. What do you think?"

"Let's get…," I scanned over the numerous boxes with all the styles and sizes. "This one." I picked up a box that had a seven-inch detachable dildo made of new skin and little black cotton spandex briefs.

"Are you sure?" Hayden leaned over my shoulder reading the cover.

"Would you like a bigger one?"

"No, thank you," he wrapped his arm around me and walked with me to the cashier.

The night air was stuffy and stagnate when we reached the street. And despite the large crowds that were out and about earlier, it was nothing in comparison to the numbers that were milling about at this hour.

The red lights now seemed much harsher in the atmosphere of the late evening. The easy laughs and charms demonstrated earlier had disappeared and been replaced by a seedier raunchy grime that seemed to leave a layer of filth on the skin that made me want to shower again.

We could hardly make our way through the crowd. I could see how this scene would be a pick-pocketer's dream. I held onto Hayden's arm tightly while he weaved in and out of people. All I wanted to do was get off the streets and hide back in the safety and quiet of our hotel room. This was a little too much for me.

***

We quickly jumped in shower trying to scrub the district off our skin. Our wet bodies pressed together covered in suds, our hands anxiously roaming, our mouths devouring. We stood under the hot water rinsing the suds away and only fueling the fire. Hayden lifted me up, pushed me against the shower wall and entered me with such a force that his thrust took my breath away.

His torso pinned me against the wall, his hands grasped my ass, his breath hot on my shoulder. My arms wrapped around his neck and my nails dug into his back harder with each thrust. I buried my face in his shoulder doing my best not to bite into him.

His grip was almost painful, and the fiberglass shower wall was terribly uncomfortable and harsh against my back and constantly pulling on my hair.

So much for romance…

"Ouch, ouch!" I pushed against Hayden's chest and pulled my hair over my shoulder. "Sorry."

"Oh, sorry." He turned the facet off, shifted my weight, and stepped out of the shower.

I wrapped my legs tighter around his waist and my arms tighter around his shoulders. Hayden held me up with his hands still under my ass and his cock still inside me.

He leaned down and kissed me ravenously. Neither of us bothered drying off. Rather he just carried me over to the bed and laid me down. He gently cupped my breast with his hand, lightly pinching my nipples with his fingers. His lips danced along my collarbone and down my chest.

He sucked on my breast hungrily and teased my nipples with his tongue moving from one to the other. I moaned softly fully enjoying the tingling sensations he sent through my body.

Hayden moved down along my stomach tracing it with his tongue. I grabbed his shoulders and tugged at his hair as he continued his journey down my body. He nudged my legs further apart. His lips tickled the inside of my thighs causing me to squirm in delight.

He wrapped his arms around my thighs holding me tighter, so I couldn't escape. When I finally settled back down, his hands slid around and caressed my ass, massaging it firmly.

I felt his fingers rub gently between my lips and lightly stroke my clitoris. I closed my eyes and relaxed completely.

His tongue danced softly, blissfully teasing my clitoris causing me to physically shutter. His fingers slipped into me stroking my G-spot.

I leaned into him moaning loudly. His technique in giving head needed no improvement of any kind.

My body was enveloped in a tingling sensation spreading outwards from my clitoris. He moved his tongue and fingers, skillfully, artfully.

I reached up and ran my fingers through his short curls tugging them gently. Hayden took his time moving nice and slow, enticing me and bringing me into this slow intense climax that reached the Himalaya's.

I arched my hips and pushed into him a little more. My head fell back, my hair flowing into a tangled mess behind me. I screamed out in delight as my entire body rippled in rhythmic spasms.

I clawed at his shoulders, pulled at his hair, ripped at the sheets. Hayden wrapped his free arm around my thigh and refused to allow me to pull away. But I tried. I tried desperately — my body twitching uncontrollably, thrashing about the bed.

"Stop! Stop...Oh, please God! Stop!" I couldn't take anymore. My head was light and fuzzy and the world around me was fading in and out. I knew I was going to faint. My chest heaved heavily, my lungs couldn't get enough oxygen.

Satisfied he'd completed his mission properly, Hayden finally relented. He rolled over beside me as I collapsed against a mountain of pillows trying to catch my breath.

"Did you come?" A slow wicked grin spread across his lips.

"Damn..." I laid there breathless beside him trying to regain some composure.

"I'm gonna take that as a yes." He chuckled.

"Just remember, paybacks are a bitch." I laughed and rolled off the bed.

I picked up the bottle of wine that had been chilling in the ice bucket and poured each of us a glass. I handed Hayden one and drank mine a little faster than I probably should have. But I was dehydrated so I poured myself another one.

Hayden drank his quickly and got up to fetch himself another also. I walked into the bathroom, splashed some cold water on my face then ran a brush through my hair. The reflection staring back at me in the mirror was beautifully flushed.

When I returned to the bedroom, Hayden was lying against the pile of pillows at the head of the bed still sipping on the wine. He had moved the ice bucket from the dresser and set it in the middle of the bed. He raised his glass to me with a devious smile...the one that I had grown to endear.

I felt a slight chill in the air, so I picked up Hayden's discarded dress shirt and slipped it on, closing it but not buttoning it, around me. I climbed up beside him and helped myself to a third glass of wine.

I snuggled up to Hayden in the little nook beside him as he wrapped his arm around my shoulder. He clinked his glass to mine and took another drink.

"Do you have any idea how sexy you look in my shirt?" he squeezed my shoulder tenderly.

"I bet you say that to all your girls." I remarked playfully.

"Only the ones I whisk away to Europe."

"And how many has that been?" I glanced at him with obvious curiosity.

"Honestly?"

"No, lie to me. I prefer it." I gave him a playful nudge. "What do you think?"

"Oh, we're telling the truth now? Okay," he straightened up a bit and poured himself another glass. "Well, I've had two semi-serious relationships since my divorce and probably half a dozen almost relationships. Only one I took to Europe with me about five years ago. But it turned out she had a better liking of my credit card than of me."

"That sucks, I'm sorry."

"What about you? How many men in your life since your divorce?"

Okay, this is awkward…

"You're the second." I stated quickly and took another drink.

"I see."

A silence fell that left a noticeable gap between us on the bed despite our proximity. I wasn't sure what to say next. I could only imagine the numerous questions that must be flooding his brain. We had never explicitly discussed my relationship with Mason — and for good reason. There were certain details that were better left unknown or not imagined.

"Sorry...," I said in a low voice.

"It's okay, I understand."

The tension remained for several more uncomfortable minutes while each of us attempted to chase away the visions that were creeping into our minds. We sipped our wine and chased away our own personal demons.

I felt Hayden's body relax beside me a bit as he sighed audibly. His grip around my shoulders tightened a little and he leaned over and kissed my cheek.

"Hey," he nudged me a little. "You all right?"

"Of course," I offered him the best smile I could muster.

Hayden set his wine glass on the night stand and cupped my face in his hand. "This is about us, Alex. Just you and me. No one else." He pressed his lips against mine.

I blindly reached behind me setting my glass aside and wrapped my arms around him. My fingers intertwined with his hair pulling him to me.

He slid his arms down around my back and sort of tuck and rolled me under him in one smooth motion.

The wine had gone completely to my head. I felt as if I could float away on a cloud of deviant desires. Hayden's hand massaged my breast firmly before he brought his mouth down to it.

"Wait, wait, wait." I gently made my way out from beneath him. "I'll be right back." I grabbed the little sack of goodies we'd purchased earlier and closed myself away in the bathroom.

I unwrapped the box with the strap-on and took it out of its package. I held the dildo in my hand and turned it over examining it fully.

It was soft but firm, thick without being overly thick, long but not too long. It was perfect. I climbed into the black spandex cotton briefs. They were a little snug.

I then attached the toy in its place and stood back to get a full view of myself in the mirror. I was still wearing Hayden's dress shirt, unbuttoned and hanging with small gap down the front of me but still covering my breasts.

Wow…

I turned sideways to get a better view. I looked so…strange. His shirt covered my body from mid-thigh up and only the toy was visible, sticking straight out. It looked so foreign on me, but I felt amazingly empowered.

I couldn't help myself from smiling. I turned for another frontal view of myself and stroked the penis imposter a couple times before I opened the door.

Hayden was still lying on the bed polishing off the last of the wine. A smile spread across his shapely lips when he saw me enter the room.

I stood at the foot of the bed giving him a full-frontal view with a cocky devious grin on my face.

"Should I even ask what's on your mind?"

"Do you really think it's necessary?"

"You look...," he tried to hide a sneer. "So sexy."

"Thank you," I replied climbing upon the foot of the bed.

Hayden placed his wine glass on the nightstand. I crawled up his body very slowly, taking my time knowing he was watching my every move. I locked my eyes with his in an intense stare down. My arms reached out for his.

His hands lightly traced my biceps and shoulders, stroking them longingly. I straddled over his abdomen and planted my hands firmly on his breast, pinching his nipples a little harshly.

"You're enjoying this," he observed.

"Very much so," I pinched them again with more force causing him to wince just a little.

I leaned over him and covered his mouth with mine, my tongue devouring him. He ran his hands over my back and around to my breast. He massaged them roughly, but not painfully, enticing me to a new level of pleasure. It only made me want him more.

I worked my way down his neck, his chest, and over his abdomen, playing momentarily with his delightful little trail. Hayden had very little hair on his upper body. A tad more than Mason but still, very little. It was subtle, sexy and exactly perfect. I loved tormenting him by playing with it.

I slid my hips down his thighs a little further, resting on the bed between them. I nudged his thighs a little apart and ran my tongue around his pelvic region without touching his throbbing cock.

He rocked his hips back and forth trying to get my attention to focus on his throbbing cock, but I ignored his plight. I was enjoying myself a little too much tormenting him to end it so soon.

My fingers danced featherlike through his scrotum, tracing lightly over his testes. Hayden squirmed and spread his legs a little further apart.

I grinned to myself and ran my tongue along the bottom side of his big dick. It was perfect, pink, thick, and throbbing with just a bit of pre-cum dripping from the head. I lapped it up hungrily. He tasted so sweet.

I took it fully in my mouth and let it glide slowly down my throat. Hayden gasped and lifted his hips to me. I took my time and let my fingers entice his entire groin. I held the base of his cock with one hand and massaged his testes with the other. I moved my mouth and tongue over smoothly, longingly, drawing out his desire.

I reached behind me and picked up some bottle of lubricant I'd left on the end of the bed. I put a few drops on my fingers and rubbed it seductively around his scrotum and anus. Hayden groaned a little louder and edged towards me.

I traced my fingers around in small circles and then slowly inserted a couple into him. His head rolled back as he bent his knees up towards the ceiling. He pushed into my hand and my mouth as I continued to arouse him.

I leaned back a little and took the bottle of lubricant again and poured a good amount down the long length of my imposter cock. I smeared it around thoroughly, locking my eyes with Hayden's and continually working him with my fingers preparing him for my cock. I pushed his knees up a little higher and moved in closer to his.

"Slowly," Hayden whispered, his eyes still locked on mine.

"I will," I smiled down at him.

I steadied myself and positioned myself properly. A knot the size of a bolder grew in my stomach. This was a new adventure for the both of us and I was nervous as hell. I'd never been on this side before in this manner. It felt powerful and controlling.

I pushed forward just a little bit into Hayden. He moaned and reached out for my thighs. The deeper I went, the slower my pace, the louder he became. It was the most amazing feeling to exert that kind of control over him.

I increased my pace fully getting into my role. My lower back and stomach muscles began to scream at me. I had no idea how much work this was. No wonder men who have a lot of sex were in such great shape. This was an extremely strenuous workout. And I hated to admit it, the girl at the store was right, my pelvic bone was screaming. I wished I had listened to her about the loofa.

Hayden closed his eyes and guided the rhythm of my hips with his hands. I could tell by the expression on his face he was lost in his own little world and loving every minute of it.

I began slowly stroking his cock once more taking him to new heights of sexual pleasure he had never experienced before. He gripped my hips harder forcing me to increase my speed. I obliged on both.

He moaned even louder as his hold on me began to become painful. I gave him one good final deep thrust as he came all over his chest. His breathing was labored as he tried to catch his breath. I slowly withdrew my appendage from him and scrambled into the bathroom to remove it and clean up.

Upon my return, I tossed a hand towel at Hayden with a grin. "Thanks," he smiled and wiped off his chest.

"How was that?" I climbed up beside him as he tossed the towel on the floor.

"Damn, woman," he shook his head in disbelief. "I don't think I've ever come so hard. That was intense."

"Good," I snuggled up beside him. "I think I should have listened to that girl in the store. I severely bruised my pelvic bone."

"Is that why you were walking funny?" He leaned down and kissed the top of my head.

"Oh, God," I covered my face with my hands. "Was it that obvious?"

"Just a smidge." He laughed at me.

"How do you feel?"

"Honestly? When we sort of discussed this earlier at the store I was half kidding around thinking you'd never try something like that. But you called my bluff." Hayden talked in a low voice while he rubbed my hair as I lay with my head on his chest. "I admit I was more than a little skeptical about it, but wow! It was so intense...amazing. I've never experienced anything like that before. I mean I wouldn't ever want to try that with anyone other than you. You were slow and let me adjust. You made it passionate, loving."

I didn't know what to say. I knew it was a compliment but had no clue how to appropriately respond to something like that. So, I simply nodded and closed my eyes. A short while later I heard Hayden whisper; 'I love you' or at least I think he did. I may have been dreaming by then.

CHAPTER 11

WE WENT FROM AMSTERDAM, back to Southern Germany and traipsed all about these little towns I'd never even heard of before. Hayden and I checked out numerous historical sites from World War II, villages that haven't changed much and witnessed little things such as half bombed out buildings that were never rebuilt and bullet holes in the sides of concrete buildings. It was like walking through a dream I heard my grandfather talk about from my childhood.

We moved on about every other day trying to take in as much as we could in the time we had. I was amazed with how small Europe felt in comparison with the United States. But what I loved the most was the feeling of relaxation it brought.

It wasn't hurried, the people weren't rushed. They weren't fiddling with the latest gadgets and seemed mostly unfazed by the technological advances everyone in the States was so obsessed with. It made me want to buy a little cottage in the village and stay here forever in some quiet little town where the people were friendly, the food was sowed, and meals were cooked rather than purchased at a drive-thru window.

This was exactly where I'd always dreamed of living.

The architecture was unbelievable. I had seen pictures of Europe my entire life, but they were nothing to walking the streets.

The colors were so vibrant, the craftsmanship so stunning. Everything felt so homey and welcoming. And the food, oh my God, the food was amazing!

I had gotten to Skype with my boys about every other evening and tell them about my fabulous European adventure. Of course, Hayden was never in view of the screen, but would listen across the room and read or watch television during my little conversations with them.

I missed them so much and at times felt guilty for having such a good time without them. They seemed to be enjoying their time in Phoenix with Danny and even Max was getting along with him a little better these days. That, at least, somewhat helped lessened the guilt for being away from them.

From Germany we visited Austria and Italy. We spent three very short days in Austria and two in Italy. I felt like I was on a whirlwind tour and had done nothing but eat, shop, have mind-blowing sex, and occasionally slept for over two weeks straight. We needed at least another week minimum to do all the things we were both still dying to do before we left.

But unfortunately, Hayden had to get back to work. We wound our way back up to Germany for our last couple of days in Europe. We were both mentally and physically exhausted given all the places we'd been, things we'd seen and the wonderful people we'd met along the way.

Our last night in Europe had finally caught up with us and as much as neither of us wanted to return to our crazy lives waiting for us across the pond, we both knew we had to go home.

On our last night in Europe we shared a lovely intimate dinner at this elegant little bistro. The food literally melted in our mouths and was so full and rich in flavor I ate until I almost made myself sick.

Hayden was silent through our meal and I could tell he wasn't looking forward to our return to reality. Neither was I. For the last three weeks we had spent every minute of every day together…and I couldn't remember the last time I was so happy.

Now all those unanswered questions that loomed before us and between us were demanding responses. And I didn't know if I had them.

Chapter 12

WE LANDED ON AMERICAN SOIL at three o'clock in the morning. Even at that hour the O'Hare airport in Chicago was buzzing with people. We had another hour and a half layover until our flight to Indianapolis left. We had been from Tegel Airport in Berlin to Dusseldorf International Airport in Dusseldorf to Chicago, Illinois and only one more stop on our long journey home.

At this point I didn't even know how long we'd been traveling or what time or day it was. Between layovers, switching planes, airlines, and time zones, I was happy to even remember my own name.

I rested my head against Hayden's shoulder in one of the lounge chairs. I could barely keep my eyes open. But somewhere in the back of my mind, I couldn't help but wonder how far we were from Hayden's home or office. I was so curious about both and this life that he'd created in this town.

I couldn't help but wonder if the man I had just spent the three most amazing weeks of my life with was the same man he portrayed himself to be around others in his world here. Somehow in my gut, I knew he wasn't showing me a false face.

We took a cab from the airport to my house, arriving just before the sun came up. Neither of us bothered with the formalities.

We barely got our suitcases inside my front door and the door locked behind us. We fumbled our way down the hall, stripped beside my bed and collapsed until late afternoon.

I woke up to the sweet aroma of coffee and bacon. I crawled out of bed and felt all the hours of grime from every airport sticking to my skin. I felt disgusting.

***

I jumped into the shower and then put on a pair of sweat shorts and a tank top before I made my way to the kitchen. I found Hayden freshly showered and standing over my stove cooking blueberry pancakes and bacon.

I walked up behind him and wrapped my arms around his waist leaning my head against his back.

"I could get used to this." I gave him a tender squeeze.

"Me too. I hope you're hungry. I got up a little while ago and ran to the store. You had nothing here to eat." He patted my hands lovingly before he flipped another pancake.

"Aren't you ambitious?" I let him go and helped myself to some coffee.

"Not really, just starved." He flashed me a cocky grin.

"Can I help you with anything?" I offered.

"Nope, just relax. It's almost ready."

I sat down at the already set table with my coffee and watched him put the finishing touches on our breakfast for dinner meal. The smell was intoxicating, and my stomach rumbled. I couldn't remember the last time I'd eaten.

Hayden came over a plate full of bacon and another loaded down with more pancakes than we could eat in a weekend.

"Dig in," he grinned clearly proud of his masterpiece.

"Thanks," and I did as he asked.

Neither of us said anything until we were both on our second helpings. We were too busy shoveling the food in our faces to converse. I never imagined that traveling could have taken such a toll on me both physically and mentally.

"What are your plans for the rest of the week?" He broke the silence.

"Huh?" he had caught me taking a bite of bacon.

"Do you have any plans before the boys come home?"

"Not really," truthfully, I hadn't given it any thought beyond picking up Billy.

"Want to go to Chicago with me?"

"Are you serious?" I almost choked.

"Sure. There's still three days in the work week left. I thought we'd drive home tonight. I can work the next three days and see how things are going up there and we can spend the weekend visiting the museums and such." He seemed to already have things well planned out and I had to admit I was seriously curious about his life there. But he was forgetting one serious obstacle...

Mason.

"What about...?"

"Mason? Not to worry. He's staying at his mother's remember?" How could I forget?

"And you think he wouldn't want to see you after you've been on vacation for the last three weeks? Does he even know where you've been? Who does he think you've been with?" The questions came pouring out of me.

"He knows I was on vacation in Europe with a lady I've been seeing. That's all I told him." He chuckled.

"What if he comes by when I'm there?"

"Well, we can either be honest with him or you can hide under the bed. Which do you prefer?" I almost wanted to smack the smirk off his face. I truly don't believe he understood the situation I'm in.

"Very funny. I'm being serious?"

"So, am I? We need to talk with him don't you think? There's only four weeks before the semester starts, and all of his winter clothes are still hanging in your closet, he still has several drawers in your dresser." He pointed out. "Hell, Alex. His shoes are still sitting by the front door as if you're waiting for him to return."

"I know. I know. I know." I took a drink of coffee trying to gather my thoughts. "What do you expect me to do?"

"I expect you to be honest, with both of us. Who do you want to be with Alex? Me or Mason?" I was thankful he didn't say 'my son', but it stung just the same.

"It's complicated, Hayden. I have to talk with Mason. My boys have gotten really attached to him and it's going to be hard on them to lose him. Especially after all the shit their dad has put them through. And I don't have a clue how I'm going to explain you to them."

"You're over thinking this, as usual, Alex. It's simple. Yes, you had a fling with Mason. But it's over. You've both moved on. That's life. Your boys are still young enough. They won't care. They'll like whoever you like." He reasoned, but I knew Max better than that.

"Please, don't push me on this. I promise I will talk to them. And to Mason. But I have to handle this in my own way. This isn't exactly a normal situation." I pleaded. I hated it when he pushed this subject.

"So, I guess I'm driving back to Chicago alone." He put his fork down and got up from the table.

"Hayden…," I got up and followed him to the sink. I wrapped my arms around him. "Please, don't be like that."

"I don't want this to end." He said softly.

"Then don't go," I looked up into his deep green eyes.

"I have to. I've been away too long. I need to answer some emails and check on a few accounts." He leaned down and kissed the top of my head. "I have responsibilities too, ya know."

"I know," I said softly. "Can you come back this weekend?"

"Of course, but you know we'll be right back here on Sunday." He paused. "I hate long distance relationships." I felt my stomach twist into the biggest knot. I was terrified of what direction he was going with this. "You do know we have Universities in Chicago, some very good ones, in fact."

"I know," I didn't know what else to day. I just wanted him to drop the subject.

"I know you're not ready for something like that, but just give it some thought."

"I will," was all I could mutter. Every fiber of my being was terrified.

Thankfully, Hayden let the subject drop. But when I walked through the family room I noticed his luggage wasn't there. He must have already put his things in his car. For some reason, those missing bags that I was so accustomed to seeing beside mine made me sad.

I truly didn't want him to leave. I wanted him to stay with me. But I knew I was now facing what I truly never wanted to face.

Reality.

A short while later I walked Hayden to the door. I didn't want him to leave and the little bubble we had spent the last three weeks in to burst, but then I realized it already had by just landing in the States. Reality had returned with us and now we both must face it.

I rested my head against his chest and wrapped my arms around him. I knew he was only leaving for three days but after being with every second of the last three weeks, three days felt like an eternity. Hayden held me close to him and kissed me on the top of my head. "I'll call you as soon as I get there."

"Call me from the road if you get bored." I smiled up at him. "Are you sure you don't want to leave in the morning instead?"

"No, I can't. I need to be in the office early and catch up. But I'll be back Friday evening as soon as I can."

"You'd better." I squeezed him a little tighter. "I'm going to miss you."

"I'll miss you too." His hand traced the side of my face bringing my lips up to his. He kissed me softly. "I'll talk to you soon."

"Bye," I reluctantly let him go.

And without another word, Hayden left.

CHAPTER 13

I ARRIVED AT MY PARENT'S HOUSE shortly before eight in the evening. It was muggy, and the lightening bugs were out in full glory amongst the thick line of trees around my parent's house. I climbed out of my car and paused for a moment listening to the lazy sounds of crickets. It was incredibly peaceful out here. I was so excited to see Billy again that I almost didn't mind that my mother was there and would surely play twenty questions with me about my trip.

I knocked twice on the screen door before letting myself in. Billy leapt off the couch and pounced on me, nearly knocking me off my feet.

"Hey girl, how are you?" I hugged her tightly and fought against her attempts to lick my face. "Oh, I missed you!" I rubbed her ears and hugged her again.

"Hello stranger, I thought I heard you come in." I stood up and hugged my dad. "How was your trip?"

"Fabulous. I had the best time." I looked around for my mother, being careful not to reveal too much in her presence. "Where's mom?"

"Out on the back deck talking to her sister on the phone." We walked into the family room and sat down, my dad in his recliner, Billy and I on the couch. "So, tell me about your trip. Where'd ya go?"

"Everywhere," I laughed. "He took me all over Europe. It was amazing. We stayed in Dublin, Ireland, Scotland, London, Paris, Italy, Germany, and Austria. I cannot describe what an experience it was. I never wanted to come back."

"Are you serious? Wow! I'm impressed." He leaned a little forward in his chair. "Did he pay for your entire trip?"

"Yes," I couldn't stop smiling. "I couldn't believe he did. I can't even imagine what it must have cost.

"This guy must really care about you. I'm guessing this guy is more than just some guy?"

"Yes, but it's complicated." I admitted.

"How so?"

"It's a long story. Let's just say it's challenging at best. And I'm not sure how to work this out." I tried to be as vague as possible.

"Are you in love with him?"

"I could, but I won't let myself." I reluctantly confessed.

"Why not?"

"Because I can't." I absentmindedly petted Billy.

"Because it's complicated," he sighed heavily. "I don't understand you, Alex. If you truly care about this man, there's nothing you two couldn't overcome if you really wanted too."

"Not this time. Love has nothing to do with it and certainly can't fix this." I shrugged.

"Why don't you explain to me why?"

"I can't. I wish I could, but I can't."

"You know, you used to confide in me." My dad pointed out.

"I know, but I can't this time. Please try and understand it's just something I have to work out myself."

"Okay, but if you change your mind I'm a good listener." He smiled.

"I know. Thanks!" I patted Billy and stood up. "I'd better get going. I still have to unpack."

My dad got up and helped me gather all of Billy's things and load them in my car. "Thanks again for watching her for me. I appreciate it." I hugged him tightly and gave him a kiss on the cheek.

"Anytime," he smiled. "You call me if you need me or want to talk." He said as Billy and I climbed in my car.

"I will. Thanks Daddy."

Billy was clearly happy to be home. She bounced around the house and wouldn't let me get anything done.

I finally had to put her in the backyard, so I could finish unpacking. I turned on some music just to block out the silence. It didn't take me long to get things organized and I was done in record time.

Now what do I do?

I am not accustomed to having spare time on my hands. I sat down on the deck and called Danny just to talk to the boys. Henry seemed to be having a good time, but Max was miserable and couldn't wait to come home.

His only concern was rather or not I had remembered to sign him up for football and I assured him that sign-ups were this up-coming weekend and I would make sure he was registered. We talked for a short while, and I hated getting off the phone with them. I missed them so much it physically hurt inside.

Billy and I went back inside, and I changed into my pajamas. She had finally settled down and curled up in her favorite spot on the couch. I joined her and flipped on the television and began surfing the channels.

I considered calling Lisa and telling her about my trip, but I knew she was already in bed and had to get up early for work. I'd have to wait and talk to her tomorrow. Finding nothing good on, I turned it back off and went to my bed.

***

I spent the next day lounging around in Debbie's pool. My mind kept playing our European trip over and over in my mind. I wanted so badly to go back there where things were simple, and it was just Hayden and me. It seemed like forever ago and not just a couple days.

I felt so torn and still didn't know what to do about the two men in my life. Each had their pros and cons and while it was true, that Hayden's pros severely outweighed Mason's with one exception...one extremely important exception and the only one that mattered. I'd met him first, slept with him first, and let my boys get attached to him.

That one small detail determined everything. And there was no escaping it. I couldn't reason the situation out myself let alone explain it to people...especially my sons. They loved Mason and were so attached to him.

I was already dreading his graduation because I knew he'd be moving back to Chicago and our little affair would be over. I had casually talked with my sons about this little fact and both knew that he would be leaving. However, knowledge wouldn't make it hurt any less when the time came and we all knew it.

I showered and put on a pair of shorts and tee-shirt before I went to the kitchen to rummage up some dinner. I fixed myself a peanut butter and jelly sandwich simply because there was nothing to eat. I desperately needed to go to the grocery store sometime this evening.

Instead, I found my car headed in the direction of Lisa's house. My house was just too quiet, and I wanted to escape the silence for the comfort of chaos that lived at Lisa's.

However, when I arrived Brian was there picking up the kids for their Wednesday evening visit. I barely got to say goodbye to them before they drove away.

"Hey, I was just getting ready to call you. How was your trip?" Lisa said as I followed her into the house.

"Fabulous, I didn't want to come home." I watched Lisa grab her purse, cell, and keys.

"You hungry?" she paused for a moment.

"Starved, I haven't gone to the store since I got home and there's nothing to eat at my place."

"Good, let's go get something and you can tell me all about your trip."

We chatted about our kids during our short drive to *O'Charley's*. Lisa was looking a little hazard this evening. She was still wearing her work clothes and her hair was falling out of the bun she had put it in this morning. She had dark circles under her eyes and her make-up was less than stellar.

"Are you all right?" I asked as we slid into a corner booth in the bar.

"Yeah, I'm fine." She gave me a halfhearted smile.

"Bullshit," I looked her squarely in the eye.

"Brian told me this weekend that he's getting married again. He proposed to Kyra." She shook her head. "I can't believe that bastard. He cheats on me with her and now he's going to marry her!"

"I'm sorry, Lisa. That sucks!" I sympathized.

"Yeah, well, who cares?" She shrugged. "So, tell me about this trip. Where did he take you?"

"On a European tour." I couldn't stop myself from smiling.

"You're kidding me?" But I was still smiling from ear to ear. "Seriously? Oh, my God! You lucky bitch! Where did you go?"

I spent the next ten minutes going over our full itinerary of where we'd gone, places we'd seen, food we'd ate and so on and so forth.

"Is that all?" She shook her head in dismay. "I'm so jealous."

"It was so beautiful. It was like walking around in a dream. It was so romantic." I pulled out my phone, clicked on the photo gallery and handed it to her.

I sat there quietly while she flipped through over a hundred photos I'd taken and answered questions she had and responded to her comments over this or that photo. I enjoyed watching her expressions over the various photos. Finally, she handed me the phone back.

"I can't believe you got to tour Europe. I've always wanted to go." She remarked.

"We had the best time. Hayden is so incredible. I didn't want to come back. But you know the sad thing is, I had the time of my life over there and I can't show anyone else these photos. Well, not the ones that have Hayden in them anyway."

"That sucks. I'm sorry. Have you thought about what you want to do?" she asked.

"I haven't got the faintest." I sighed heavily and ran my fingers through my hair. "How in the hell did I get myself into this?" I rested my head down on the table.

"You slept with your beanie boy's dad? And then toured Europe with him." She giggled a bit.

"You know what I mean?" I rolled my eyes at her. "Why does everything have to be so complicated?"

"Alex, you know I love you, but what did you honestly expect to happen?" Lisa asked.

"I don't know." I muttered.

"You just wanted your cake or rather to eat your cupcake and your cake too." She snickered.

"Very funny…," I couldn't help but laugh too.

"Didn't you?"

"Okay, fine. But you saw him!" I raised my hands for emphasis.

"Yes, and he's edible. They both are, but that doesn't mean you're supposed to be stingy and keep them both all for yourself." I couldn't help but notice the twinkle in her eye.

"Hayden dropped the 'L' bomb on me." I admitted.

"Are you kidding? The 'L' bomb?" She took a long sip of her drink. "Oh, my God! What did you say?"

"Nothing," I put my head down on the table. "I couldn't say anything. And believe me, my silence spoke volumes."

"And by your reaction, I'm guessing that didn't go over well?" I looked up at her with raised eyebrows.

"What do you think?"

"Well, do you love him? Okay, let me rephrase that. Are you in love with him?" She inquired.

"I could be, easily. But I'm not going to allow it."

"I'm surprised you said that with a straight face." Lisa rolled her eyes at me again. "You can't control who you fall in love with. You know that."

"I beg to differ. If I don't allow it to happen, it won't. We don't have to always give into our baser desires." I tried to state with as much conviction as I could.

"You're so full of shit, you know that Alex? You really are." She laughed at me. "You already slept with him — all over Europe for that matter. You can't sit there with a straight face and tell me you're not in love with this man?"

"I'm not saying I don't have feelings for him. I'm simply stating that I'm not going to allow myself to fall in love with him." I clarified.

"Whatever," she took another sip of her drink. "Deny all you want, but you have very strong feelings for this man. You may not be in love with him as of yet, but you're damn close to falling hard."

"You're a lot of help." I muttered and took another long drink.

Lisa and I continued to debate for the rest of our dinner. She stood firm on her stance about Hayden and I wouldn't budge on my belief that we could consciously control whom we fall in love with. I wasn't even sure if I believed anything I was spouting off about, but I was not about to admit that to her. I think I was trying to convince myself more so than her and we both knew it.

***

Later that evening after I'd spoken to the boys and crawled into bed, I couldn't get Hayden off my mind. Every time I closed my eyes I kept picturing him walking barefoot along the water's edge on the beach in Dublin.

His short hair blowing in the breeze, his white casual dress shirt untucked, and his eyes sparkling in the early morning light. He was a breathtaking sight to behold and I physically ached for his touch.

It had been over three weeks since I'd slept alone and as much as I'd hated to admit it, I'd gotten used to falling asleep in Hayden's strong arms. I'd come to rely on the safety and security his very presence allotted me, especially in a foreign country.

I couldn't figure out what had come over me in the last year and a half. I had spent five years asserting my independence, proving to myself that I could survive without a man in my life and in such a short amount of time, all that hard work had been for not.

Now I was lying here alone and missing Hayden more than I ever wanted too. Even in some small way I sort of missed the childish and playful antics of Mason.

Plus, I still had to figure out what to do about him coming back before the start of the term which was rapidly approaching.

I rolled over and wrapped my arms around my pillow. I knew I was going to have to end things with Mason once he returned. I had accepted the idea before I ever got on the plane with Hayden and I knew it was coming. Even though I knew he'd moved on and technically so had I, I was still dreading it.

CHAPTER 14

HAYDEN ARRIVED SHORTLY BEFORE DINNER on Friday evening. I literally bounced out my front door to meet him and leapt into his awaiting arms in my driveway. He looked so irresistible and I couldn't believe how much I'd missed him. I pressed my lips fully over his. He wrapped his strong arms around me and lifted me up squeezing me tightly.

"Well, hello!" Hayden laughed putting me back on the ground. "Did you miss me?"

"Just a smidgen," I demonstrated a short distance between my thumb and index finger for emphasis. "Did you miss me?"

"Very much so," he kept his arm around me as we walked back into the house. "I got spoiled waking up beside you every day. I miss it."

"Me too," I confessed.

Hayden followed me into the house and closed the door behind us. "How were things at the office?"

"Fine. Busy. Everything went smoothly while I was gone…well almost." He chuckled. "Nothing I couldn't fix."

"That's good."

"So, what have you been doing since I've been gone? Anything exciting?" He sat down on the couch and pulled me down beside him.

"Not so much." I shook my head. "Laid around the pool. Solved the earth's energy crisis…the usual stuff."

"That's my girl," Hayden wrapped his arm around me and pulled me closer to him. He leaned down and kissed me again. His smile broadened. "I hate to admit how much I've gotten attached to you since our trip. I hated being away from you."

"I know, I hated it too."

"Are the boys coming home on Monday?" he asked.

"Yes. And I cannot wait to see them. It feels like they've been gone forever."

"I'm sure they'll be happy to be home."

"I know I will be. Are you hungry?"

"Starved. What are you in the mood for?" Hayden squeezed my shoulder gently.

"That little pub in Austria by the lake. I am craving one of those cinnamon cake muffins thingies. They were so good."

"Cinnamon cake muffin thingy?" he laughed at me. "You're so cute."

"Don't laugh at me. I can't remember what they're called." I shoved him playfully, but he refused to let me go.

"And where do you think you're going?" he tried to tickle me.

I squirmed and twisted trying to get away from him, but he was too strong for me. It felt good to be with him again and to laugh with him. He pulled me beneath him and tickled me until I had tears running down my face and was screaming for release. "Stop! I'm gonna wet my pants!" I hollered, but Hayden just laughed. "Please! Please! I give!"

"Say pretty please," Hayden pinned me down.

"Pretty please!" I squeaked.

He leaned down and pressed his lips over mine. The scruff on his face brushed against my chin. I smiled to myself at the strange comforting feeling it brought about in me. I could taste the lingering flavor of mocha coffee on his lips. He tasted so sweet.

Hayden cupped the side of my face and then slid his hand behind my head gently entangling his fingers in my hair. I leaned into him missing the love and security I felt in his arms. His grip on my hair got a little stronger and intense. His tongue stroked mine hungrily.

With a little nudging I rested back on the sofa cushions. Hayden hovered over me for a moment, a coy twinkle in his eyes.

He relaxed on top of me careful to keep his full weight off me but letting me enjoy the feel of his body on mine. The scent of his cologne filled the air and was intoxicating. The smell only enhanced my desire for him.

I ran my hands over his muscular chest and ripped abdomen. His skin was hot beneath my fingers, as was his breath on my neck. I closed my eyes and covered my mouth with his. Hayden's hand glided down my thigh smoothly slipping back up beneath my skirt. His fingers wrapped around the side of my panties and roughly pulled them down ripping them in the process.

My hands gripped his back while his mouth consumed mine with such intensity I couldn't catch my breath. Hayden unfastened his pants without hesitation, yanked them down crudely and tossed them to the floor before I even realized it.

My legs wrapped around his waist and he entered me with a deep thrust. I moaned out in pleasure and a deep desire for more. I loved the way he felt inside me.

I arched my hips into him and tightened my legs around him. The fire between us raged uncontrollably; the lust that had to be satisfied before we could play our little games with each other exploring our sexuality uninhibited.

What we normally spent hours on was over within a few moments. We had exceeded our limit and had to satisfy the desire born deep within us. Hayden came before I could and collapsed upon me breathing heavy. His face was buried in the nook of my neck and shoulder, his breath hot against my skin.

"I'm sorry, but I had to have you."

"Me too," I replied.

"I couldn't wait. When you came running out and jumped in my arms I would have taken you on the hood of my car if I could have gotten away with it." Hayden leaned up and smiled. A bead of perspiration glistened on his forehead.

"I would have let you."

His smiled broadened. "No, you wouldn't have, you little minx."

"I may have surprised you." I taunted. "Don't think you know everything about me, Mr. Brooks."

"I'm sure your neighbors would appreciate that."

"Who cares? Most of them probably wouldn't know what to do with a hard dick if it was put in their hand." I laughed.

Hayden laughed and climbed off me taking a seat on the edge of the couch and put his boxers back on. "You're sweet. And if that's true then I'm sure they would just love calling the police on you for defiling the hood of my car in broad daylight."

"Trust me, they would have enjoyed it very much." I sat up and straightened my clothes while looking around for my panties.

Hayden stood and pulled his pants up. "Are you hungry? I'm starved. What do you say to getting something to eat and then we can play for the rest of the night?" A devilish grin slipped across his lips.

"I'd love too," I stood up beside him and wrapped my arms around his waist.

We drove into town and had dinner at the little pizza joint where we'd shared our first meal together. It seemed rather fitting or more like returning to the scene of a crime. We dined on the same toppings, same drinks, and extremely different conversation.

Our relationship was growing stronger, not just sexually, but intellectually and emotionally. That much was obvious. And as strong as my attachment was to Mason, it was easily twice as strong to Hayden. I tried to push all thoughts of Mason, the future and what tomorrow may bring out of my head and focus solely on the man I truly adored sitting before me.

On our way back to my place I gave Hayden a brief tour of the small town I grew up in. He seemed really intrigued and wanted to know everything about my childhood and how I had managed to spend my entire life centralized in this community. A fact that I both loved and hated equally.

We returned to my house at the edge of twilight with the windows down and letting the air awaken our senses fully. It was warm with just a hint of sticky humidity in it. The sky was cloudless, and the stars were beginning to twinkle overhead. It was a night of romance that could be felt in the air like a warm blanket covering over us and keeping us safely in its grip.

Being the true gentleman as always, Hayden opened the car door for me and took my hand walking me up to the house. I had long forgotten what it was like to be romanced and had thought it was a concept that now only lived in my overly active imagination. However, it was here holding my front door open for me and I blushed at him for no reason whatsoever than my own mischievous thoughts as I crossed over the threshold.

"What was that look for?" Hayden raised an eyebrow at me.

"No reason," I played innocent.

"What's going on in that pretty little head of yours?" He closed the door behind us and took me in his arms.

"I was just thinking about romance and how it might not be dead after all." I confessed.

"Romance isn't dead," he leaned over and kissed me gently. "It may have taken a nap for a while, but I can assure you it's alive and well."

"Oh really," I stared into his deep green eyes. "You think so?"

"I know so," he pulled me closer to him and kissed me more firmly.

"It's a good thing you're cute," I taunted.

"You don't think I can be romantic?" A slight smile turned up on the edges of his shapely lips.

"I didn't say that. In fact, I know you can. You've proven it many times. That's not really what I meant. I was thinking about how gentlemanly you are...opening doors, taking my hand, putting your hand on the small of my back, the little things that seem rather trivial, but honestly mean a great deal." I confided.

"You can thank my father. He always told me to treat a lady the way I'd want someone to treat my mother, my sister, or my daughter...once she was born. I guess that's when it really hit home for me. I never knew really what it was like to love someone so much or be so fiercely protective of someone until I held my kids for the first time."

"I know what you mean. My boys are everything to me. It's hard for me to imagine there ever being a girl good enough for them." I chuckled and led him over to the couch.

"I think I'll plead the fifth on that one." Hayden sat down beside me. "But I will say my son has excellent taste in women."

"You're a sick man. You know that don't you, seducing your son's girlfriend. You should be ashamed." I playfully smacked his chest.

"Oh, I am," he grabbed my wrist and pulled me to him. "Very much so."

"I can see that." I giggled as he buried his facial stubble in my neck.

"You realize some of this blame rests on you as well?" He moved back and looked at me. "You seduced your boyfriend's dad. What kind of twisted malicious lady are you?" He smirked.

"Oh…I seduced you! You wish," I stated jokingly.

"You were just helpless against my stunning personality and irresistible charm." Hayden gloated.

"Witless charm," I muttered loud enough for him to hear.

"Ouch! That was below the belt." He chuckled.

"I thought you liked showing off what you have below your belt." I teased.

"Only to you and every chance I get!" He countered.

"That's what I thought."

"But you loved my cock…"

"I do, but you'd better not be showing it off to anyone else." I grabbed a firm hold of it through his pants.

"You're the only lady in my life." Hayden leaned forward kissing me sweetly. "I promise."

"What am I going to do with you?" I rolled my eyes at him.

"I can give you some suggestions if you'd like. For instance, you can take me back to your room and have your way with me or…" I cut him off with another kiss and squeezed his thick cock that had hardened at my touch.

"And you think you deserve that?" I taunted.

"I've been good," he pointed out.

"How good?" I questioned.

"Very," Hayden stood up and scooped me up in his arms.

He headed down the hallway towards my bedroom. I felt so small in his muscular arms, safe and secure, protected and dearly loved. I rested my head against his shoulder inhaling the intoxicating smell of his cologne. I closed my eyes wishing silently that I could have this feeling, this man, this love for the rest of my life.

***

The weekend passed all too quickly. It seemed that no sooner had Hayden arrived he was preparing to leave. And I hated it. I missed him so much when he was gone. It amazed me how in such a short time as our trip to Europe had made me so attached to him.

Sunday evening Hayden and I curled up on the couch with Billy watching reruns of *The Walking Dead*. I felt so comfortable and relaxed. I was trying hard not to think about him leaving in the wee morning hours to make the drive back to Chicago to work. I wanted us to stay just like this, every evening, forever. But I knew that would be difficult at best, if not impossible.

"You're being awful quiet tonight." Hayden mentioned during a commercial break.

"Sorry. I'm just trying to think of all the things I need to do before the boys go back to school next week. Danny rarely gives me a lot of time to get their supplies and clothes." I repeated what was on my mind earlier.

"You know that Friday's Mason's last day at the firm. I would imagine he'll be driving back to Indy shortly thereafter. You guys go back to school in what two weeks?"

"Yes," I told him.

"Have you thought about what you're going to say to him?"

"Not really. I haven't talked to him since before we went on vacation." I looked up at him. "Who does he think you went to Europe with?" I knew Mason wasn't stupid. He'd likely put two and two together since the boys knew I went to Europe.

"He doesn't know where I went. I told everyone in the office I was going on vacation and if they needed to reach me, they had my number." He stated.

"Didn't anyone ask?" I'd never seen his office but for some reason I pictured it as the office from *Mad Men* just because it was a marketing firm. And it was hard for me to imagine his co-workers or employees not being curious enough to inquire as to where he disappeared to for three weeks.

"Actually, it's been sort of fun. There's been an office pool going since I left trying to figure out where I've been. And the rumors and speculations have been spectacular." He chuckled.

"Really?" Now that was more along the lines of what I envisioned.

"I'm not kidding. One of the girls, Abbie, she's a junior partner, created a destination board and hung it in the conference room. It's complete with a world map, little pins with name tags of workers stuck in their location guess and a cash chart beneath it.

It's sort of the office joke now. I've had to change all my passwords on my office computer, laptop, and phone. And they are a relentless and sneaky bunch." He laughed.

"That is hilarious," I giggled. Now I really wanted to see his office and meet these employees.

"Oh, believe me. I've been having fun with them. I'll drop subtle little hints about something I ate or saw, something very nondescript just to screw with them and sure enough within a few hours some of the pins are rearranged and more monies are placed."

"Don't they know you're just messing with them?" I shook my head in disbelief.

"Yes, but they don't know what to believe. They're just hoping that there's some truth in something I say." A devious smile spread across his shapely lips.

"You're just mean."

"It's all in good fun. And it's not like they don't deserve it. They've tried hacking all my electronics since I've been back. More than once, so don't feel too sorry for them." He explained.

"It sounds more like high school than a marketing firm." It sounded like a fun environment to work in.

"Sometimes it is, but it's all in good fun. I think it's important to break the monotony of a long work day with harmless humor."

"I think that's great. I hope I find an environment like that to work in after I'm done with school. I think it's crucial for people to love their professions and they tend to be more productive if they enjoy being around the people they work with."

"I do too. That's why I don't get upset about these types of antics. They are a great group. I'm very fortunate to have them working for me. I've learned through trial and error the hard-knocks of running a marketing firm."

"You should be so proud of how much you've accomplished. I think you're amazing." I brushed his cheek lightly.

"I think you're amazing…going back to school, raising two sons alone, and balancing it all. It's impressive." His gaze locked onto mine and I just stared into his beautiful green eyes.

"No, it's insane." I sighed heavily. "Half the time I have no clue what I'm doing. The other half I feel like a dog chasing its tail."

"Why do you say that?"

"Are you kidding? Look at how much you've accomplished in your life and where you're at in comparison to where I am. You've done so much and here I am starting all over again in my thirties. It's pathetic."

"You should be proud of yourself. It takes real guts to do what you're doing." His eyes gleamed.

"Aw, you're sweet, but I think you're mistaking guts for naivety. I had no idea what I was getting myself or my sons into when I made the decision to return to school. College is so much harder than I ever dreamed it would be. I feel like I've had to sacrifice so much with my sons because I'm always studying." I tried to explain.

"I'm sure you're not giving yourself enough credit. Your sons love you so much and I am positive they are proud of how hard you are working to give them a better life." Hayden smiled.

"How can you say that? I'm doing exactly what you did only a decade behind you and I know that Mason blames you for missing out on so much of his childhood because you were working all the time trying to build your firm. Even though he's old enough to understand that, he still…"

I couldn't admit what else his son had told me about how much he didn't like him because he felt he was never there for him.

"Kennedy doesn't feel like that. I have a wonderful close relationship with my daughter and she's proud of me. Mason is a good man. He's kind and caring, but he was also born with certain frustrations and has always blamed me for them. Your boys are different." He assured me.

"Not always, but I hope so." was all I could say.

We sat in silence for the remaining half of the show. He kept his arm draped loosely around my shoulders and stroked my arm with one finger as if he was doing it absentmindedly, completely content with the world. I rested my head against his chest and tried to focus on the television.

CHAPTER 15

I WAITED ANXIOUSLY at the end of the terminal for the boys to walk into the common area. Their plane landed ten minutes ago and there was still no sign of them…just hordes of nameless, faceless people walking by. Finally, I heard Max's voice before I saw either of my boys.

"I don't need a babysitter!" He declared in an angry voice.

"I'm not a babysitter. I am a flight attendant and it's my job to make sure you find your mom." I could tell the young woman probably in her mid-twenties was struggling to keep an even disposition with my son. I hated to think how Max had tormented her on his long flight from Phoenix.

"Momma!" Henry took off at a run and leapt into my arms.

"Hey little buddy," I wrapped my arms around him. "Oh, I missed you so much!" I kissed his cheeks.

"I missed you too. Phoenix was hot. I don't like it there." Henry rambled.

"Hi Momma," Max halfheartedly waved. "This is our mom…obviously." Max glared at the flight attendant.

"Mrs. Rose?" The exhausted young woman inquired as she approached.

"Ms. Rose. And yes." I smiled and glanced over at Max. "Should I even ask how you were on the flight?"

"Not if you want to remain in a good mood." Max muttered.

"I need to see your driver's license, please. Just for verification." She offered me the best smile she could muster, but really looked like she'd rather strangle my son.

"Of course," I set Henry down and dug my wallet out of my purse. "Here."

"Thank you," She glanced at it quickly. "Sign here, please." I scribbled my name down on the line and handed the board back to her.

"Thank you," I shook my head slightly at Max who rolled his eyes at the girl.

"Good luck," I heard her say as she walked off in the other direction.

"Come on, let's get your luggage." I tasseled Max's hair with a smirk.

***

We got back to the house a little before nine in the evening. Henry fell asleep on the way home, but Max chatted up a storm. He complained about the weather, his Dad's new girlfriend, Jennifer, and the extreme boredom he said he had to suffer through. I listened intently and commented accordingly being as sympathetic as I could. Max was on a roll and all keyed up. I could only imagine how difficult he must have been on the flight.

That poor woman.

I carried Henry into bed and tucked him in. He was so tuckered he didn't flinch a muscle. I brought his things to his room and set his bags beside his bed.

He looked so peaceful, like a little angel. I wished he could stay my little boy forever. I leaned over and kissed his forehead and ran my fingers lightly through his hair. A slight smile spread across his lips.

"I love you, Momma." He said in a small voice.

"I love you too, little man."

"I'm so glad I'm home." He whispered and then rolled over on his side.

"Me too," I kissed him once more before leaving his room and shutting his door halfway. "Sweet dreams."

***

The next morning, I took the boys out shopping for new school supplies. For once I didn't have to buy them any clothes. Danny had at least this year bought each of them an entire new wardrobe for school before they came home and for that I was extremely grateful.

But I still had the challenge of finding their supplies, backpacks, and the other ten million little things they needed. And the two of them kept arguing and shoving each other. I was ready to break out the duct tape and Taser.

I had planned on taking them out to lunch and spending an enjoyable day with them, but I guess they didn't get the memo. They were going at it before we even left the house and it only got worse.

We made it to Target and Max made a snide comment about the backpack that Henry wanted. I quickly gathered up the absolute necessities to get them started, paid, and took them straight home.

I fixed them lunch and sent them both to their room to chill out for a while. I was so disappointed. I slumped down at the kitchen table and put my head down. I had missed them so much and wanted to make this day something special for the three of us.

Instead, it had turned into a screaming match between the two of them and then me intervening, only to succeed in making them both made at me.

Unfortunately, the boys were hitting that stage where their age difference was more pronounced. Max was on the verge of being a teenager and trying desperately to grow up. He wanted to leave all the things from his childhood behind and surge towards the next phase of his life.

Henry was also noticing the changes in his brother and was doing everything he could not to let them happen. I hated watching the two of them growing further and further apart and even though I was speculating, I was pretty sure it had started growing more prominent over their summer vacation.

***

Thursday morning after I got the boys off to school I got myself ready to make the trip to campus to get my textbooks. I finally had my schedule for the upcoming semester and printed off the syllabus for each of my courses.

I threw on an old pair of jeans and a baseball tee-shirt, put my hair in a ponytail and grabbed my flip-flops. I was excited to get back to campus. As much as I had enjoyed this summer, the long hours spent doing nothing before and after our European vacation had been excruciatingly boring.

I rolled the windows down and pointed my car towards campus. I turned the music up and relaxed as David Bowie belted out *Heroes* on the radio. The warm breeze flooded my car and splashed my face with the smell of jasmine and fresh cut grass. The sky was a bright robin-egg blue with little wisps of white fluffy clouds scattered about. It was such a beautiful day.

I parked in the lot across from the student center and locked up my car. It felt so great to be back here. It was almost a strange home-coming of sorts. I walked over to the bookstore and went in search of the multiple books I needed for the semester.

The aisles were packed with students and it was like playing Jenga, but where the students had replaced the blocks. They were stacked up to the ceiling and ready to tumble over at any moment. I almost felt bad for those tardy souls who waited until the first day of class to try and find their books. I knew from experience they were going to be SOL.

Six hundred and forty-seven dollars poorer, I dropped my new books in my trunk and thought I'd take a trip over to Michelle's office. I wasn't sure if she'd be there or not since this was the only time she had off between teaching summer classes and the beginning of the fall semester. But I wasn't ready to head home yet.

Campus was starting to come alive again. Over by the dorms I could see students carrying large trunks up to their rooms followed by concerned parents struggling to let their kids enter this scary world and take their first steps towards true independence.

I swallowed hard thinking again about Max trying to push his way into his teen years. I hated to think about that far-off day looming over me in the distance when it would be me dropping Max off at his new dorm room on some college campus.

Micelle's office was across campus in the science building. It was so nice to see some familiar faces that smiled and waved in my direction as I walked across the quad. The smell of fresh cut grass filled the air and made me sneeze several times. Some students passing by called out 'bless you' with a friendly smile.

"Thanks," I hollered back to them.

The science building had the air conditioner on full blast and was freezing when I entered. I shivered as I wound my way through the long hallways back to Michelle's office. I found her buried behind a pile of paperwork at her desk.

Her glasses were halfway down her nose, her long blond hair barely held up by a clip on the back of her head and she looked half-hazard. It was the first time I had ever seen her in such a state.

"Are you all right?" I knocked lightly on her open-door frame.

"Alex?" She looked up and smiled. "Hello, come on in?"

"What's going on?" I asked sitting down in one of the chairs across from her desk.

"You wouldn't believe me if I told you." She sighed with a half-smile.

"Try me."

"Well, you know Dr. Johnston, right? The Dean of the psych department." She tapped her pencil on her desk.

"Of course," he was the one who had hired me to tutor a couple of the football players in the introductory psychology course.

"He managed to get himself into hot water last week with a couple of female students." Michelle shook her head slightly.

"What? You're kidding me." I couldn't believe it. He was such a sweet man and had always been very professional with me.

"I wish I was. Now he's suspended and under review by the board of the University and I'm stuck trying to figure out all this crap." She motioned to the piles of paperwork on her desk.

"What'd he do?" I couldn't help but be curious.

"Apparently, he thought it was okay to take a couple female students — underage female students boating last weekend out at Turkey Run."

"Underage?"

"Yes, well, sort of. They were legal at least but underage for drinking. They were both twenty." She rolled her eyes in disbelief.

"Seriously?" I couldn't help it, I laughed.

"Yes, and they were all drinking heavily. And they got caught by the police having a threesome on the boat. Needless to say, they were all arrested." She smirked.

"I can't imagine him doing something like that." I giggled.

"Not me," Michelle chuckled. "I've been around him long enough to know he has a wild streak in him that survived his youth."

"Wow, I never would have guessed." *Sometimes people can surprise you.*

"The University has done their damnest to keep it out of the news. The fallout for the school would be a disaster."

"I'm sorry, but that's too funny." I tried to reign myself back in.

"I know it is," she finally let her pencil drop to the desk and folded her hands. "So, tell me. How was Europe?"

"Fabulous! We had the most amazing time."

"And does Mason know about this yet?" Michelle inquired.

"No, but it doesn't really matter. I spoke to him before we left, and he was already seeing another girl in Chicago. I told him I was also seeing someone else."

"And how did he take that?"

"Not so well. Seemingly, it's okay for him to date someone else, but it's not for me too. I haven't spoken to him since and he's returning soon. I don't know exactly when but the last day of his internship is tomorrow and classes start next week."

"Is he heading to your house?"

"I have no idea. His things are still there. I'm not sure if I should pack them up or what, so I've left them exactly the way they were when he took off." I shrugged.

"So, you know he's going to come by at least," she stated.

"I guess if he wants his things he will."

"Have you considered what you're going to say to him?"

"Hayden wants us to be together and that's just unrealistic if not impossible." I told her.

"Are you in love with him?"

Damn, I was so sick of that question.

"I could be, but I'm not letting myself. I mean, I can't. This could never work. How could we ever explain this to his son and my boys, my family? No one would ever understand how this happened. Hell, I'm not even sure how this happened."

"So, you met a man and hit it off. Yes, it sucks that you were involved with his son first, but hey, shit happens." She shrugged her shoulders slightly.

"It's not quite as simple as that I'm afraid."

"Why not? Don't you think you're making more out of this than necessary?" she asked.

"You don't think this is sick and twisted on some level?"

"Have you tried explaining it?"

"I did to my friends Lisa and Debbie and they were not really judgmental. Well, maybe a little bit, but they are still struggling with it. They like Hayden, but they also like Mason. This would be so much easier if one of them was a complete bastard."

"Would it be?" a slight smile curved across her lips.

"Stop shrinking me," I laughed. "I'm not one of your patients."

"I'm not practicing anymore. I teach now." She smirked.

"I know," I playfully rolled my eyes. "But seriously, I don't know what I'm going to say to Mason when he returns. I've been trying to figure it out ever since we got back from Europe and I still don't have a clue." I complained.

"Have you considered telling him the truth?"

"The truth? Yeah, that should go over well. Hey Mason, by the way, I'm the one who went to Europe with your dad for three weeks and screwed his brains out. That should go over well." I chuckled.

"Who knows, maybe you'll get lucky and things between him and this other girl got serious over the summer and he'll opt out first."

"And how do you propose I explain my relationship with his dad?"

"I wouldn't say anything just yet. Wait a while, like six months or more and then you can say you casually ran into each other, had coffee and hit it off. Will he have a hard time accepting it? Maybe, but at least that way he won't feel like you left him for his Dad and his ego won't be nearly as damaged."

"Do you really think that could work? That Mason wouldn't hate me. Us?" I tilted my head and studied her expression.

"I think if you and Hayden really want to make a go at this relationship, that's your best option."

"And my boys?" I asked.

"Same approach. Lay low for now, give it time, and approach it later after an acceptable amount of time has passed."

"I see what saying. It might work." I said in a low voice more to myself than Michelle. I glanced down at my watch. "I'm sorry. I've got to get going if I'm going to beat the boy's home." I stood up and gathered my things. "Thanks for the talk."

"Anytime. It was nice to see you. You look good." Michelle rose from her chair and walked around her desk. "I almost forgot to ask, would you like to be my assistant again this semester?"

"Of course," I smiled and shook her hand. "I was planning on it."

"Wonderful, I'll see you next week."

I thought about Michelle's words all the way home. Could it really be that simple? Could there be a way that would be *acceptable*? I still had my doubts, but I had to admit I was feeling a little more optimistic than before. The passing of time would make things better for everyone involved, Mason and my boys included. I wasn't so much worried about my family or rather my mother. I was used to being a disappointment to her in every aspect of my life.

So why should this situation be any different?

I found myself smiling and turning up the radio, loving the feel of the hot breeze blowing across my face through the car windows. For the first time in a very long time, I breathed a little bit easier.

CHAPTER 16

TUESDAY MORNING after I'd gotten the boys off to school I cleaned up the kitchen and took my coffee out on the back deck. I sat down on the swing in my pajama bottoms and university tee-shirt and watched Billy roam about the backyard. It was a beautiful morning and the fresh dew glistened off the grass. The gardens were alive with color and fragrance filling the air with the distinct smell of tiger lilies. I breathed in the fresh damp air and enjoyed the silence.

"I thought I'd find you back here." I looked over towards the side of the house startled by the sound of his voice and Billy's sudden barking.

"Mason! I wasn't expecting to see you." He looked stunning in a pair of dark blue gym shorts and an old grey baseball tee.

"I rang the doorbell. When you didn't answer, I knew you'd be back here with your coffee." He smiled and walked up on the deck. He leaned down and kissed me briefly before taking a seat beside you. "How are the boys? Did they already leave for school?"

"Yes, about twenty minutes ago. They'll be sorry they missed you."

God, he looks good!

"I've missed them," he smiled. "And you."

"How was your summer? Did you enjoy your internship?" I asked.

"A lot. It was really fun. I learned more in less than three months working there than I did sitting in a classroom for the last three years."

"That's usually the way it works. Hands on experience is always more valuable." I took a long sip of my coffee.

"It was so great. I can't wait to go to work there after graduation. The people were great too, so funny." He lightly touched my hand. "I've got the funniest story to tell you, but before I do, do you care if I get me a cup of coffee?"

"No, help yourself." Mason hoped up and disappeared into the house.

I leaned back in the swing and swung my legs back and forth. Hayden had told me last night that Mason had left for Indy Sunday morning. I couldn't help but wonder why it had taken him two days to come see me. A part of me wanted to inquire, but the other part honestly didn't want to know. Most likely he had been hanging out with his buddies at the dorm bragging about their summer adventures.

"Anyway," Mason came back out and plopped down beside me once more. "My dad took off for like three weeks or so. Nobody, and I mean nobody, knew where the hell he went. So this girl, Abbie — she's this junior partner or something, she created this map-board and office pool in one of the conference rooms. Everyone was making bets on where he went and even when I left, it was still going. I've got twenty down on St. Thomas." He chuckled and took a drink.

"That's strange." I awkwardly took a drink myself. "So, no one has a clue?"

"Nope. It's weird. I'd put money on it, he's seeing someone. He's been all happy and chipper." Mason shrugged. "He's definitely getting laid."

"Did you ask him about it?" I couldn't stop myself from asking.

"Are you kidding? I grilled him repeatedly. He wouldn't cough any information up. I have no idea what's going on with him. I went by his place the weekend before last and he wasn't there. I have a key, so I let myself in and thought I'd wait on him, thinking he was out running errands or something, but he never came home and just showed up in the office on Monday. I asked him where he was, and he just smiled and said it wasn't my business…that I was old enough to understand that. Then he smiled this goofy grin and walked off into his office. I'm telling ya, he's definitely getting laid."

"At least he's happy, right?" I said uncomfortably.

"Sure, I guess." He shrugged. "I'm glad he's happy, but I wish I knew why he was being so secretive about her."

"I'm sure he will tell you at some point. Maybe he just isn't ready yet and wants to see where the relationship is going first." I offered.

"Maybe," he leaned back against the seat. "I could care less."

"You two didn't make amends over the summer?"

"Agh…," he crinkled his nose up a bit. "I guess so. We really didn't spend that much time together. He kept disappearing all the time. I saw him a little at the office and we had lunch a couple of times."

"Well, at least it's a start." I half-smiled. "What else did you do over the summer?"

It was now Mason's turn to shift awkwardly. He was silent for a minute and ran his finger over the rim of his mug while searching for the right words to say. "I stayed at my Mom's. It was great spending time with my siblings, but my mom kept treating me like a little kid and we argued a lot."

"I'm sorry."

"After the first week I was ready to move in with my Dad and at least with him gone all the time, I was able to crash at his place." A devious grin spread across his lips.

"Did he know you were there?" Hayden never told me Mason was staying at his place.

"I don't think so. We texted back and forth a couple times and he kept in contact with Abbie, so we had a pretty decent idea of his comings and goings after that first weekend he disappeared. I always picked up after myself and kept the place clean. Besides, he said I could crash at his place whenever I wanted too. So, I don't think he'd care even if he found out." Mason explained.

"Well, I'm glad you two are getting along better." I stated casually.

"I suppose so. It helps that he's finally seeing someone." He shrugged.

"Your dad doesn't date much?" I slipped out of curiosity.

"Hardly ever. In fact, I can't remember the last time he got involved with someone. And I don't understand it. Women flirt with him relentlessly. The girls around the office talk about him and how good-looking he is. They even remark about how he rarely dates. I know he goes on the occasional date, but they never develop into anything." Mason rambled.

"I wonder why?" I wondered aloud. "Any ideas?"

"I don't know. He's always been a workaholic. His whole life's been devoted to building his firm. Maybe now that it's established he'll find someone to settle down with." I could tell Mason was getting bored with the topic.

"How are things with Megan?" I had to ask.

"Alex, I'm so sorry about all that." He looked down at his mug and was quiet for several long seconds. "I kind of found myself...well, you know."

"Yeah, I do know." I lightly touched his arm. His skin felt just as warm as I remembered.

"Did you ever go out with that other guy?" I looked up at me with this sheepish look.

"Yes, I did." I admitted.

"And are you still seeing him?" His words echoed loudly through my brain. I looked up at him and stared into his beautiful sea-blue eyes and half considered bluffing, but immediately decided against it.

"Yes, but it's complicated."

"Why is that?" He reached over and touched my leg with one finger.

"So, are you still seeing Megan?" I tried to turn the tables on him.

"No, not really. She goes to Northwestern. Long distance flings don't exactly work so there's really no use in attempting it. Besides, it wasn't anything. We just hung out because we were the youngest people at work, both stuck there for the summer doing internships." He explained nonchalantly.

"Is she going to be working at the firm after college?" For some reason the idea just clawed at my brain.

"Doubtful. My dad wasn't exactly thrilled with her performance. He commented more than once that it was a good thing she's pretty." I accidently snorted in my coffee recalling Hayden saying that expression more than once on our European vacation.

"Oh," I squeaked.

"Are you going to answer my question? Why are things complicated with this new guy? Is he married or something?"

"No, he's not married."

"His kids don't approve?" I physically bit my lip to keep from laughing.

"Yes, he has kids. I've met one of them and his son likes me, but I'm not sure if he'd be too thrilled to know we're dating. The same can be said for my boys as well." I cautiously chose my words.

"Are you two exclusive?" His eyes pierced mine and I was rendered speechless.

"I don't know what we are." I whispered.

Mason leaned over and placed his hand on the side of my face. "I missed you so much." His voice was as smooth as milk chocolate.

"Mason...," but before I could finish he pressed his lips firmly over mine and pulled me closer to him.

His arms enveloped me, his body pressed against mine. I could feel the rate of his heartbeat increasing in his chest pressed firmly against mine. His lips felt so familiar and tasted so sweet. I wanted to let myself go and melt into him just like I used to love doing, but my brain...and my heart started screaming at me.

"Mason...," I reluctantly pulled away from his. "We can't do this."

"Are you sleeping with him?" his eyes implored.

I stood up and walked over to the deck railing. I looked down at the empty coffee mug in my hand. "I need a refill. I'll be right back." I bolted into the house before Mason had the chance to utter a response.

"Oh, my God. Oh, my God. Oh, my God." I muttered repeatedly while moving from the counter for sugar, to the coffee maker, over to the refrigerator for creamer and back again.

What the hell am I going to say to him?

I took a deep breath and walked back outside. I leaned against the railing and looked at Mason fidgeting with his own mug.

"Well?" He asked eagerly.

"Yes, I slept with him." I answered honestly. "Did you sleep with Megan?"

"Sort of," his eyes dropped.

"Sort of? How do you sort of sleep with someone?"

"It means I tried to but couldn't." His cheeks turned a bright red at the admission.

"What does that mean?" I crossed over the deck and sat down beside him.

"It means I had a few unexpected difficulties." He refused to meet my eye.

"I'm not trying to be dense here. Are you saying that you couldn't get it up or couldn't get off?" I asked with as much compassion as I could muster for such a topic.

"Both, if we're being honest."

"Both? How is that possible?"

"What it means is I had difficulty achieving lift off and when she finally got me somewhat hard, I couldn't get aroused enough to have sex let alone get off." He quickly took another drink to keep from looking at me.

"Oh," I didn't know what to say.

"It's nice to know you didn't have any performance issues." Mason's voice dripped with sarcasm.

"Mason, that's kind of an unfair thing to say." I lightly touched his arm, but he pulled away from me.

"It's true, though. Isn't it? You didn't have any problems sleeping with someone else."

"I don't exactly have the same equipment as you to have those kinds of problems. Where you drinking when it happened? Cause alcohol can sometimes...," he cut me off before I could finish.

"The first time, yes and that's what I blamed it on. But the three other times...I was completely sober. Explain that?" he said a little hotly.

Perhaps I'd trained him better than I'd thought.

"Why are you getting upset with me?"

"I'm not upset with you. It's just, well...," he looked back down at his mug for a moment than looked back up at me with pleading eyes. "I didn't want to have sex with her. That's why I couldn't do it. You're all I could think of. You're the woman I love. The only one I want to be with."

"Mason," I put my hand over his and this time he didn't pull away.

"Please, Alex. Please don't say it." He brought his finger up to my lips. "Just don't. Give me a chance. I know we can make this work. I know you believe I'm too young to make a serious commitment, but I'm not. I love you and I love your boys. We're a family."

Okay, that hurt.

"Mason," but he leaned down and pressed his mouth over mine.

He wrapped his arms around me and pulled me closer to him. I found myself kissing him back, my arms around him, my resistance melting away. I missed him too, more than I realized. I allowed myself to be picked up and carried into the house and back to my bedroom. Mason gently placed me down upon my bed and climbed up over me. His hand brushed my hair away from my face as he gazed into my eyes. His lips brushed mine lightly, then with more force, his tongue searching for mine hungrily.

My hands reached out and began pulling his shirt over his head. I tossed it aside and ran my fingers over his smooth muscular chest. It was so warm to my touch, so perfect, so familiar. My fingers slipped down to the top of his shorts and under the waistband.

I grabbed a firm hold of his thick cock and felt it throbbing in my hand. Mason gasped and placed his hands on my breast, massaging them roughly, pinching my nipples through my clothes.

In one swift motion my shirt was tossed across the room followed immediately by my bra. Mason brought his mouth to my breasts. His tongue teased my nipples playfully.

I closed my eyes and ran my fingers through his thick blond waves. He traced his tongue down to my abdomen while keeping one hand on my breast, the other working my shorts down.

Once those were discarded, Mason slid over the side of the bed until his feet touched the ground. He reached up, placed his hands on my hips and slid me over to him. He pushed my legs a little further apart. His tongue gently stroked my clitoris.

I relaxed and brought my knees up to my chest. Mason slipped his fingers into me and immediately found my G-spot. He rubbed it firmly making me gasp loudly. The strokes by his tongue became harder, more intense. He sucked on my clit and moved his fingers in and out of me, teasing me delightfully.

I wanted him. I arched my back loving every stroke he made, every movement he made with his hands. I grabbed his shoulders and pulled him towards me.

"Fuck me," I moaned.

Mason scrambled across me reaching for the nightstand and his supply of condoms. He put one on eagerly and positioned himself between my legs. I wrapped my legs around him, craving him so badly. My hands traced over his shoulders and down his arms. He hovered over me staring into my eyes with such an intense love it took my breath away.

"I love you," he whispered.

"I love you, too."

"You're the only one I want. No one will ever take your place in my heart." I gulped down the large golf ball in my throat as he leaned down and kissed me sweetly.

I wrapped my arms around his neck and pulled him closer to me, because one, I wanted him. And two, I had no idea how to respond. All his words did was make me feel horrible. I tried to push them out of my mind and focus all my attention on the moment. But it was difficult. I closed my eyes and all I could see was Hayden.

Mason kissed me again, thankfully breaking my train of thought. He barely touched the tip of his tongue to mine. He tasted sweet like caramel mocha coffee. He kissed the nap of my neck softly sending a way of shutters through my entire body. He adjusted himself and entered me slowly with a low, deep-throated moan.

***

I excused myself afterwards and jumped into the shower. I felt horrible. I couldn't believe what I had done. I felt so incredibly guilty. I stood under the hot water and let my tears wash down the drain with the rest of the hatred I felt towards myself. Images of Hayden haunted me.

I knew he would be livid if he'd known what I'd just done. And I hated the thought of seeing that disappointment in his eyes and knowing I was the one who had caused him pain.

And as much as I cared about Mason, even loved Mason, I could no longer deny to myself or anyone else that I was in love with Hayden.

I sat down on the bottom of the tub and wrapped my arms around my knees. I rocked back and forth crying softly to myself. I heard Mason knock softly on the bathroom door, but he didn't try and open it. He didn't call out to me. He just went silent.

When the water went cold, I toweled off and threw on my robe. Mason was sitting on the bed when I came out of the bathroom. He was dressed and looking uncomfortable. He fidgeted with his hands and gave me a weary smile.

"Are you all right?" He asked.

"Yes," I lied walking over to the dresser.

"Your eyes are red, and I heard you crying in the shower. I'm sorry. I shouldn't have…," his voice trailed off.

"Mason, I don't know what to say." I set my panties on my dresser and sat down beside him. I placed my hands over his and squeezed them gently. "I shouldn't have."

"You've fallen in love with him, haven't you?" His deep blue eyes glistened with fresh tears.

"Yes," I couldn't deny it. "I love you, Mason. I honestly do."

"But you're *in* love with him." He stated softly.

"I don't know what to say."

"Is he in love with you?"

"Yes," I stared down at our joined hands.

"What about the boys? Have they met him?"

"No, and they're not going to, at least for a while. They love you so much and I don't want to hurt any of you." I tried to explain.

"Then don't do this." Mason slipped off the bed and got down on his knees in front of me, our hands still locked together. "Alex, we're great together and you know it. I love you so much. And I love your boys. You three are my family. Please don't do this." Tears rolled down his cheeks and my heart ripped in two.

"Mason, I know this isn't fair." I hated myself for the tears that began falling down my face all over again.

"I love you, Alex." Mason reached up and wrapped his arms around my waist and buried his face in my lap. His tears fell on my thighs as I slowly stroked his hair.

"I love you, too." I whispered.

"Please don't give up on us. I know I can be the man you need me to be."

I didn't reply. I didn't have one. I silently continued to stroke his hair and brushed my own tears away with the back of my hand. I hated myself for this. I hated hurting him. He was such a loving and kind young man with a huge heart. And he was the one who had brought me out of my solitude and breathed life back into my world. I owed him more than this.

"I know, and you're right. You're right." I hugged him tightly. "I don't want to lose you. I'm so sorry."

He looked up at me with these big puppy dog mourning-full eyes. "Do you mean it? We can try to work this out?" I nodded through my tears. "Oh, baby, I promise I'm going to make you so very happy." Mason buried his face in my chest and squeezed me even tighter.

CHAPTER 17

THE BOYS STORMED into the house full of excitement after seeing Mason's car parked in its old spot in our driveway. They practically jumped on him after bursting through the front door. I sat on the couch and watched their reunion.

I laughed at their excitement but was also filled with a tremendous guilt for all of it...the boy's happiness over being reunited with Mason, for my own feeling towards him and most of all, for having sex with him.

A short while later the boys — all three of them, were playing Xbox while I started dinner. I could hear them hollering and screaming at each other over whatever game they were playing. I put the cheesy potatoes in the over and set the timer. Then I stepped outside to fire up the grill for the steaks when my cell went off in my pocket.

It was Hayden.

I swallowed hard and swiped the screen. "Hello," I did my best to sound chipper.

"Hi darling, how was your day?" His voice was as warm as hot coca and my heart began to ache all over again.

"Mason's here." I said and sat down on the swing.

"Really? I'm surprised it took him so long to drop by. I figured he would have gone straight to your house when he left."

So had I.

"He's inside playing Xbox with my boys."

"And did you two get the chance to talk?" Hayden nudged with little subtlety.

"Yes," I was at a complete loss for words.

"And?"

"And he cried, Hayden. I made him cry. I feel like complete shit right now." I explained.

"Does he know I'm the other man?"

"No, of course not." I assured him. "I would never do that."

"I know you wouldn't. How is he handling things?"

"Not well. I feel horrible. He cried and said how much he loves me and my sons." I started crying all over again. "He called us a family. He begged and pleaded for me not to end this."

"Alex, I'm so sorry. I know this must be hard on all of you." I could hear the genuine empathy in his voice.

"This is an impossible situation." I hastily brushed my tears aside. "I don't know what to do."

"Are you wanting to end things with me, Alex?" The nervousness was evident in his voice.

"No," I answered immediately. "No, not at all. I wish," I swallowed hard. "I wish I could see you right now." I desperately longed for the security I felt in his strong arms.

"Can I see you this weekend?"

"I don't know. My sons are home. I can see if Lisa can take them for the night, but what about…"

"Is he staying there?"

"I don't know. He was here when my sons came home from school today and they were so happy to see him. I don't know what to do. They've gotten so attached to him." I answered him honestly.

"And let's not forget the parental guilt you feel from them having an absentee father." Hayden muttered more to himself than to me. "So, you don't want them to lose someone else they love. I understand. As much as I hate it, I understand."

"Please, don't…" I began but Henry's voice cut off my words.

"Momma? What's wrong? Why are you crying?" My little boy came over and put his arm around me.

"I'm fine." I wiped the tears from my cheeks and smiled up at him. "What'd ya need?"

"Mason said he's gonna take us to *Orange Leaf* after dinner. Is that okay?"

"Of course, buddy." I tousled his hair a bit. "Can I call you back in a while?"

"Sure, attend to your sons. I'll call you later. I love you." And before I could say anything else he was gone.

I stuffed my phone back in my pocket and followed my son back into the house. Henry returned to his game and I finished up the preparations for dinner. Thankfully, the boys were so excited to have Mason home no one noticed my silence. Max and Henry talked nonstop about their summer in Phoenix and Mason regaled them of his misadventures in Chicago. The three of them were so happy and I felt like an intruder at my own dinner table.

*****

I finally got the boys to bed after Mason had sugared them up at their favorite ice cream parlor and joined Mason on the couch. He was playing on his laptop and barely looked up when I sat down beside him.

"So, how are the guys? Did they have a good summer?" I figured it was a safe topic.

"I don't know. I haven't seen them yet."

"Oh, I just thought you've been staying at the dorms. Didn't your internship end last Friday?" I asked confused.

"Yeah, but I hung out with my family for a few days and drove down to Indy this morning. I came straight here to see you. I haven't even been by the dorms yet." He answered casually.

"Oh, I see." I turned my attention to the television and tried not to question whether Mason was lying or hiding something from me.

He seemed so engrossed in messaging someone on facebook he barely noticed when my phone rang a few minutes later. I looked down and saw Hayden's name, got up and walked outside to the back deck to answer it. My head was still spinning from Mason's lie.

"Hi," I was thankful I'd caught him before he was sent to voicemail.

"You sound better." I closed my eyes inhaling the sound of his voice.

"Not really, more confused than anything." I went on to recount my brief conversation with Mason.

"That doesn't make any sense." Hayden remarked when I'd finished. "Where has he been for the last few days?"

"If I had to guess, I would say Northwestern with Megan." I speculated.

"But why would he lie to you about that?"

"Guilt would be my guess. His tearful pleas wouldn't have been nearly as believable if he'd admitted he's spent the last several days in sexual bliss with Megan, don't you agree?" Now I was pissed.

"That's pretty devious. Do you really think he'd lie to you like that?"

"At this moment, I don't know what to believe. And there's really no way for me to ask him without him knowing I had spoken to you or his mother. And well, we both know how that'd go." I said sarcastically.

"What are you going to do?"

"I don't know, but I am going to call Lisa tomorrow and see if she can watch the boys on Saturday night. I miss you so much." I confessed.

"I miss you too, sweetheart. Call me tomorrow."

"I will. Sweet dreams."

"Good night," and the phone went silent.

I looked out over the blackened yard. Only the shadows of the trees could be seen swaying slightly in the warm breeze. I wasn't ready to go back inside. A matrix of emotions was washing over me. I wasn't sure if I wanted to laugh, scream, cry and go pound on Mason. I wanted to believe there had to be a reasonable and rational explanation for the timeline discrepancy.

I leaned back in the seat and swung my legs back and forth. I sighed deeply and ran my hands through my hair. The warm air suddenly felt stifling. A part of me wanted to turn the clock back six months.

The other part of me wanted to speed it up six months just so I could land in a place where Hayden and I were together and happy.

I closed my eyes and drifted off to the little beach in Dublin. Hayden was holding my hand as we walked along the beach, the surf splashing around our feet and kissing our calves. The wind was blowing softly, but steadily.

I could still picture the love in his piercing green eyes when he looked at me; the dimples in his cheeks when he smiled. I could almost feel the light scruff on his face when he kissed me. I missed him so much I physically ached deep inside my chest.

I got up and went back inside. Mason was still sitting on the couch exchanging messages with someone. If I had to venture a guess as to with whom, there was only one name that rang in the back of my mind...Megan. I pushed the thought out of my head and walked into my bedroom.

I got myself cleaned up and ready for bed. Six months ago, I would have been out there sitting beside Mason. Six months ago, it wouldn't have even occurred to me to go to bed without him unless he was up studying for an exam. Six months ago, my life my sense.

I turned off the light on the nightstand and crawled into bed alone.

CHAPTER 18

FIRST DAY OF MY JUNIOR YEAR IN COLLEGE.
Mason and I drove to campus together in his Camaro. The
sun was shining brightly in the cloudless August sky. The
aroma of fresh cut grass hung heavy on the morning air. He
reached over and placed his hand upon mine and gave it a
gentle squeeze.

I looked over at his profile. He was strikingly
handsome with his shadow stubble, dimples, the soft waves
in his dirty blond hair and sunglasses. He was certainly a
sight to behold.

I had managed to hold my tongue since my conversation
with Hayden. Mainly because it was easy to keep silent on
the subject when I saw how happy my boys were to have
Mason back in their lives.

I knew there was nothing I wouldn't do for my boys
and if having Mason in their lives made them happy, then I
would have to let go of Hayden and embrace Mason with
my whole heart.

If it were only that easy.

The fact that we'd not had sex again since the first day of
his return was never mentioned. Mason had not even tried
although he was sleeping beside me every night. He stayed
up late into the night chatting on his laptop with someone
and I never inquired about it.

Instead, I would go to bed alone and pretend to be asleep when he finally came to bed. It was clear we things had changed over our summer apart and our little fling had come to an end.

Now it was only a matter of burying the corpse and walking away from it. But I wasn't sure if either of us knew exactly how to do that.

***

My classes flew by. It seemed the entire campus, especially the psychology department, was consumed with Dr. Johnston's indiscretion. Everyone was buzzing about it openly and speculating on the Dean's future.

It was so distasteful that I had a couple of Professors address it openly in class. Each apologized for his behavior and stated that it was not a subject to be discussed in their classes.

However, that certainly did not deter the gossips from doing what they do best and by the end of the day, Dr. Johnston himself, would have laughed at the wild stories that had been circulating about him.

One student told me they were all found naked and smoking everything but their shoes. Another disagreed and said they were snorting cocaine as well as drinking heavily.

Still, I overheard someone telling another student that Dr. Johnston had been busted with over a pound of marijuana on him. It truly was comical how stories got embellished and took on a life of their own.

However, I knew somewhere, Dr. Johnston, the extremely kind man that I had come to know under his employ, was probably doing anything but smiling at this moment. Or maybe he was?

Even Mason, who spent most of his time in the business building, had heard all the rumors and even a few I hadn't throughout the day. He excitedly told me about them on our way home. I half listened to him, but the other part of my brain was more focused on the fact that not only did I have a ton of studying to do, but both Max and Henry had football practice this evening.

After hearing about Dr. Johnston's exploits all day long, I was more concerned with how I was going to get dinner on the table, my boys and my homework completed and make it to practice.

Mason pitched in helping the boys with their schoolwork while I fixed dinner. It was amazing how we all fell back into our old routine from spring. It was almost as if the summer never happened.

But in the back of my mind and in the far corners of my heart, Hayden lingered. His smile haunted my every waking minute. His piercing green eyes pleaded with me to end this with Mason. His voice as comforting as smooth chocolate, beckoned me to him. I missed him dearly.

Two hours later I found myself sitting in the bleachers beside Henry's practice trying to focus on the first chapter in my psychopharmacology class when Lisa sat down beside me. Mason and Max had taken off across the field for Max's practice.

"I see beanie boy has returned." Lisa remarked sitting down beside me.

"Yep," I looked up from my text. "He returned a few days ago."

"What about Hayden? Does he know?"

"Yes, and he's not too happy about it." I drummed my fingers on my text. "I don't know what to do. The boys are so happy he's back."

"Are you?" She gave me a sympathetic look.

"Honestly? No." I looked down trying not to say what I knew was going to roll off my lips. "I'm in love with Hayden."

"I *knew* it!" Her face brightened.

"But I can't be."

"Have you told him?"

"No. I didn't realize it until the day Mason arrived. I want to tell Hayden, just not over the phone."

"You knew it when Mason kissed you didn't you?"

"Yes," I admitted.

"When are you going to see him again?"

"That depends. Can you keep the boys on Saturday night?" I looked at her hopefully.

"Of course," she grinned. "But what about beanie boy? How are you going to get away from him?"

"I have no idea. Any suggestions?"

"There's a Billy Joel concert in St. Louis this weekend. Tell him you're going to that."

"With who?"

"Me," she smiled.

"Not if you're watching the boys. They'll definitely blow my cover."

"Oh, I know. Does Mason ever talk to that Professor you're friends with? You know, the one you work for? Michelle something," She asked.

"That's perfect. Mason never talks to her. He says he always feels like she's analyzing everything he says." I laughed.

"Then I'd go with that. Plus, she'd alibi you in a heartbeat. You said she knows all about Hayden, right?"

"Yes, and she was the one who suggested that I break things off with Mason, bide my time for a season or two and then announce my relationship with Hayden."

"I think she's right. You'd be much happier if you were with the man you truly love...and not his son." She reiterated what I already knew.

"I know, but what about my boys? They are so attached to Mason. They'll be heartbroken if they lose him too."

"Him too? Lady, you've got to quit letting Danny's mistakes run your life. It is not your fault he cheated on you and it is certainly not your fault that the asshole moved across the country from his sons."

"I know. I know." It was hard to argue when I knew she was right.

"And as much as I like Mason, and I do Alex, he's not exactly a father figure to the boys. He's more like an older brother and you know it."

"I hate it when you're right." I muttered. "But that's not going to make it hurt any less when he's gone."

"Children are resilient. They will be fine." Lisa reassured me.

I, however, was not so sure. I knew how badly Max behaved after Danny moved. Plus, how he returns to that behavior every time something occurs with his dad that he believes is wrong or affects his world. Henry, on the other hand, would just cry and withdrawal.

Either way, I knew they would both react negatively in their own ways. And I didn't want to be the cause of them being hurt or disappointed again in their young lives.

After the boys were asleep and Mason was busy studying in the family room, I sat out on the back deck and called Hayden. His voice was as warm as a blanket. I told him my cover story for the weekend and that Lisa was going to keep the boys Saturday night.

We made plans to meet after Henry's noon game, Max luckily played the first game at eight. Lisa was going to take the boys directly after our sons' game and I was going to be free to spend some alone time with Hayden.

I almost felt like a teenager sneaking around to see the boy my parents had forbidden me to date. It was almost comical that at my age, I had to do this.

CHAPTER 19

SATURDAY AFTERNOON I was in my car heading north to meet Hayden in a little rinky – dink town with a big ol' smile across my lips. Mason was staying at my house to keep an eye on Billy. He never blinked an eye when I told him my cover story. He was either that trusting or didn't care. I wanted to believe in the former rather than the later.

I rolled the windows down and let the warm afternoon August breeze flood over me. My hair was flowing in the wind and the sun was warm on my face. I was wearing a pair of black shorts and a teal and black tank top that accented my tan perfectly.

I wanted to appear casual but also look nice for Hayden as well. I was so excited to see him I was practically bouncing in my driver's seat to the beat of the music blaring from my car stereo.

My mind was a whirlwind of thought. I ran through the last two and a half years of my life and thought about everything I'd done, every decision I'd made, every choice that had brought me here today. I couldn't and didn't regret getting involved with Mason. He may not ultimately be the right man for me, but because of him I'd met the man who was. Even as sick and twisted as this all seemed to me I was certain I had made the right decision.

Thirty minutes later I was pulling into a Holiday Inn off the side of the highway. I couldn't help but feel weird about having to meet Hayden in such a place.

As if we were doing something wrong. I suppose we were in a way, depending on who you asked.

I found myself on the fourth floor knocking on room 423 that Hayden had sent me in a text. He had arrived almost an hour ago and had been waiting impatiently for me to arrive. I stood outside the door with my overnight bag tossed over my shoulder and felt the fluttering's of butterflies in my stomach. I reached out and knocked lightly on the door.

"Hello darling," Hayden opened it before I finish knocking. "Come in." He wrapped his arms around me before I even put my things down. "Oh, I've missed you." He kicked the door closed with his foot.

"I've missed you too," I kissed him with all the fire that had been building in me since the last time I set eyes on him.

"I know it hasn't been that long, but it feels like it's been forever. I got spoiled being with you every day on vacation. Now it's unbearable being apart." He said in-between kisses.

"I know. I hate this situation. I just want to come clean, so we don't have to sneak around like this." I reluctantly pulled away from him and set my things down on the dresser.

"Did Mason question your story?" He sat down on the edge of the bed.

"Nope," I shook my head in disbelief. "I don't know if that makes me feel better or worse. I hate lying to him, but I didn't know what else to do. I don't even think he's been back to his dorm room since he's been back."

I leaned against the dresser and looked at him. "Have you spoken to him?"

"He called me about ten minutes after I got here. He wanted to know if I would reconsider Megan's position. He claims it was his fault that she messed up some projects she was working on. I explained to him that I knew better. They worked in different departments on different projects. The girl was completely incompetent and screwed up everything she touched. I explained to him that just because she's cute and built does not mean she's employable."

"And what did he say to that?" I was curious as to how much this young girl was aware of my relationship with Mason. I imagined she knew nothing.

"He wasn't happy. But this girl was such a disaster that I couldn't even give her a form recommendation letter." He explained.

"Ouch!"

"I did ask him what his plans were for the weekend. I also asked him if he'd made up with Alex." He raised his eyebrows at him.

"And what did he say?"

"He said that he and Alex were working on it. He thinks she fell in love with someone over the summer. Apparently, she's been really withdrawn. I asked if he's tried talking with her and he says he has.

He said he knows this other guy is closer to her age and the only reason he's still there right now is because her sons are attached to him. I asked him if he thought that was a good enough reason, but he swears that he'll be able to win her back."

"You're kidding," my shoulders slumped forward. I felt horrible. Mason knew all along but believed he could win my heart back to him.

"I wish I was. I'm sorry, Alex." He walked over and took me in his arms. "What do you want to do?"

"I need to let him go," I whispered.

"And your boys?" Hayden's eyes held mine.

"They'll be upset at first, but they will be fine." I assured him. "I think we should do as Michelle suggested. I end things with Mason, we lay low for the time being, bide our time for a while and give everyone a chance to move on with their lives. Then, next spring, we can accidently run into one another."

"Next spring? That's eight months away minimum. Do you really think we have to wait that long?" He brushed my hair away from my face with such tenderness it gave me chills.

"I think we do if we don't want people to freak out over us. I need to put a substantial distance between my relationship with Mason and my relationship with you."

"I hate this. I understand what you're saying, and I guess you're right, but I was hoping I could meet your sons and we would be able to spend the holidays together." His eyes held such sincerity it broke my heart.

"I wish we could. I truly do. And I want you to meet my boys, just not like this, not yet."

"What happens next spring after we come out?"

"What do you mean?"

"You've just started your third year of school, right?" He took me by hands and led me over to the bed. We sat down on the edge and kept our hands locked as one.

"Yes," I knew where he was going, but I didn't want to venture there just yet.

"Have you considered transferring?"

"No," I answered honestly, but it pained me to see the look on his face when I said it. "Hayden," I lightly touched the side of his face. "We will figure this out. Don't worry. And you know how I know we will?"

"How?" Hayden whispered.

"Because I'm in love with you." I looked him in the eye and said softly.

"You are?"

"Yes, very much so. I can't deny it any longer, to myself, to you or to anyone else." Hayden leaned over and kissed me so sweetly.

"I'm in love with you, too!" He kissed me again with a little more intensity. "Oh, Alex, I love you so much. And yes, we'll make this work." He grinned from ear to ear.

Hayden leaned me back on the bed and pressed his mouth firmly over mine. His hand cupped the side of my face tenderly. Our eyes locked and we held each other's gaze for a moment neither of us saying anything.

This wasn't about the sex. It wasn't about lust. It was about two people connecting on a level that was spiritual; a bond that a few seldom find with another. Something that I never believed existed outside of a Danielle Steele novel.

One night was not nearly enough. A lifetime wouldn't be enough.

***

I drove down the highway feeling so alone. I had spent the last twenty-three hours in the arms of the man I loved, only to leave him to travel back to the humble existence I must maintain for the time being for the sake of my sons. Hayden and I had discussed it at length and there was simply no other way.

Mason would be graduating in May and then moving back to Chicago to take his position at his dad's firm and our relationship would be over. I knew it. He knew it. Even my sons were aware of the situation as it was discussed openly since Mason's summer internship.

It was only logical for the sake of my boys to remain on our present course. Especially since I still had another year of undergraduate school to complete my bachelors and transferring at this point was not even an option. Hayden and I would just have to keep our relationship hidden until next fall or winter.

It wasn't going to be easy, but it would be easier for my boys and they were my first consideration.

My heart was filled with sorrow and the weight of my decisions was lying heavily upon my soul. I wished desperately that I'd met Hayden under different circumstances, but there was nothing I could do about it now. Still, I felt horrible.

I dearly cared for Mason, I loved him. He was truly an amazing young man and we'd been so happy together once upon a time. I could only hope that I could keep Hayden out of my thoughts long enough to allow Mason back in them.

But my heart, my heart belonged solely to Hayden and there was nothing I, nor Mason, could do about that.

Chapter 20

BRIGHT AND EARLY ON A SUNDAY MORNING the second week of October the four of us piled into Mason's Camaro and headed south to Brown County to enjoy the last remnants of fall. We left the house with dew still wet on the ground. I was happy it wasn't frost.

The boys climbed in the backseat of Mason's car and I in the passenger seat. Max was none too thrilled about the prospect of spending the day walking around in some 'girlie tourist trap'. When I finally told him to stop complaining, he slumped in the corner of the backseat and stared out the window for the remainder of the ride.

We headed south towards Bloomington since that was the only way I knew how to get there. It was a gorgeous fall day, bright and sunny and the leaves were in a spectacular array of golds, auburn, crimson, and orange.

The air was warm with just a hint of a cool breeze that kept it from being hot. The day required a sweatshirt, but nothing along the lines of a coat was necessary…yet.

Mason was in a particularly chipper mood and insisted on singing along with *Train* at the top of his lungs. Max and even Henry joined in before long. All were slightly off key and despite my best efforts, I found myself in the mix as well.

We only touched on the outskirts of Bloomington before turning onto SR 46, but we did get to pass alongside the Indiana University Stadium, fraternity row, and several other academic buildings.

Even from a distance the campus was everything a classic Ivy League college campus idealization in a hundred movies had made it to be from the tall columns, the endless rows of gardens, fountains, to the limestone and red bricked buildings. I silently envied the young students that milled about getting the full experience of what college life was like.

The further we traveled from the city limits the curvier the road became, and the foothills covered with trees in their full colorful foliage was nothing less than breathtaking. Mason slowed down just a bit, so we could all render in its beauty.

Henry thought it was 'really neat' the way the leaves changed colors in the fall, but Max kept asking how much longer until we get there. I shot him a dirty look before I told him we were close. He shut up and slumped back down in the corner of the backseat.

We parked in the side lot next to the CVS where there were still a few spots left to be found if you knew where to look. The streets were already filled with people. Apparently, everyone in Indiana had the same idea we had to lavish the final remains of fall.

Max quickly fell in pace with Mason while Henry lingered behind with me, thankfully taking my hand on the overcrowded sidewalk.

The two in front started in immediately about being starved so we set out with one goal in mind...food.

We stopped at several of the restaurants and all we packed with forty-five minute to an hour wait list. But for my starving men, that was not going to suffice. So, we ventured on trying to find something to satisfy their manly appetites.

We ended up at some barbeque joint that was only a very small upgrade from a street vender wheel cart. Fortunately, I sadly underestimated the place because they served the best pulled pork sandwiches I'd ever eaten. Henry and I stuffed ourselves with one while Max and Mason consumed two apiece and still complained that they were hungry.

By mid-afternoon my oversized purse was stuffed with salt-water taffy, rocky road fudge, chocolate mint fudge, peanut butter fudge, roasted cashews, and cinnamon almonds along with various other trinkets.

All three of the boys had stuffed themselves on caramel apples, ice cream and kettle corn. Max had finally relented and even enjoyed himself. I caught him smiling more than once and I smiled to myself thinking that perhaps, just maybe, things were going to be all right.

The packed couple mile radius of shops was difficult at best to maneuver through. I caught myself several times watching Mason, enjoying our time together. We occasionally held hands or in a mess of people, he would protectively put an arm around my waist, or simply just smile at me.

The ride home was much more pleasant than the ride down. Most likely because the three of them were on an endless sugar high that would cause them to crash and burn within the next hour or so.

But for now, the radio was turned up, there was a nice breeze through the windows and the four of us sang off key all the way home. It was about as perfect day I could ask for.

***

The fall semester was moving steadily along and before I knew it, midterms were upon us once more. The boys, football, student teaching, and trying to keep the house running smoothly were difficult on a good day. My classes had become more challenging and required a great deal more time than my previous ones. Most nights I felt lucky if I got three hours of sleep.

Mason was fairing much better than me. He was enjoying his courses and the material seemed to come easily to him. I envied the fact that most days he had his homework completed before the boys made it home from school. That one small thing allowed him the freedom to run the boys to football practice four nights a week while I was stuck buried in books.

He was also spending a lot of time helping them with their homework before practices and on those rare evening when they didn't have practice with their teams, Mason would toss the football around with them in the backyard, so the house would be quiet for me.

It was very sweet and considerate of him to help so much and I truly don't think I could have gotten through the semester without him. But I also knew he had an ulterior motive.

Mason was trying desperately to step into the shoes of a man two decades older than himself and be a role model for my sons. I loved him for it and I was impressed by his efforts.

However, it did little to remove Hayden from my heart. I thought about him every day and missed him terribly. I spoke with him daily and with each passing day it became harder and harder…on the both of us despite our good intentions for our sons.

***

Halloween crept up on us and both boys were excited to go out for the evening. Max dressed up as a *Walker* from *The Walking Dead* while Henry and Logan had decided to go out together dressed as *Minecraft* zombies. Lisa was gracious enough to offer to pick up Henry to spend the night and take him trick or treating with her kids.

Max was staying over at Aaron's with several other guys, all of whom were dressed up as *Walkers* too. And despite his insistence that they were all trick or treating as well, I had serious doubts that they would be.

Mason was staying home with me to pass out candy while I was cramming for a psychopharmacology exam. He seemed a little disappointed in not being able to take the boys out himself, but he did slip into his old prison inmate costume from last year.

He urged me several times to put on my police uniform too, but he finally dropped it when I showed him the material I was responsible for learning.

Halloween was my favorite holiday and I truly wanted to dress up and spend the evening with my boys too, but it simply wasn't possible. I still had three of the six chapters to read that were going to be covered on the exam on Monday. The material was overwhelming, and I found it fascinating. This was easily my favorite class this semester, but it was also by far, my hardest.

After my sons left I curled up on the corner of the couch with a notebook, highlighter, pen, and my text. I flipped through the chapters to find the place I'd left off earlier and got comfortable. I chewed absentmindedly on the end of my highlighter, a bad habit I'd picked up since going back to school, absorbing the words as my eyes scanned the page.

I was on the fourth page when the first trick or treater rang the doorbell. Mason rushed over and answered it immediately. Then shortly thereafter, he didn't even bother closing the door. The children came in droves giving Billy the perfect excuse to act like she was on crack.

I sighed heavily and put my study material on the coffee table. It was pointless. Even if I locked myself in the bedroom I still wouldn't be able to concentrate with all the racket both inside and outside my house.

I put on another pot of coffee, helped myself to a couple of fun sized Milky Ways from the bag on the counter, and made my way back to Mason in the family room.

He was standing just inside the screen door holding a plastic pumpkin filled with candy. I slipped up behind him and wrapped my arms around his waist.

"Are you having fun?" I gave him a gentle squeeze and rested my head against his back.

"A little. I'd rather be out with the boys." He muttered before greeting the next group of kids who arrived on our porch.

"I know, but Max wanted to hang out with his friends and Henry really wanted to go with Logan."

"But we had so much fun last year." Mason complained.

"Yes, we did. But I would imagine you were just like Max at his age. You'd rather spend Halloween with your buddies than with your mom and her boyfriend." I leaned around him and grinned.

"True," he muttered.

"He's just growing up." I sighed. "As much as I hate it, he keeps pulling further and further away from me. And that's the way it should be. But as long as he knows I'm still here when he needs me then we should be all right."

"He knows," Mason leaned down and kissed the top of my head.

Max was getting ready to celebrate his twelfth birthday in a couple days and Henry had recently celebrated his eighth. It was so hard for me to believe my boys were growing up so fast. Henry wanted to make a big deal about his, so we'd had a sleepover with five of his friends.

Mason had been a huge hit with his buddies and everyone had a blast. Max, on the other hand, found it necessary to fight me over having a cake.

He didn't want one, or a party, or anything else like a special dinner. He was adamant about it. However, when I pointed out how he'd declined everything about his birthday except his gifts, he just smirked and left the room.

I had a bad feeling I was in for a *baptism by fire* lesson on the teenage years with him.

A few hours later after all the sugared-up children had returned to their homes Mason and I had the entire house to ourselves. He got comfortable on the couch watching *The Conjurer* and pigging out of the Halloween candy we still had left. Seeing him content I snuck into my bedroom and slipped into my officer uniform from last year.

I took a few extra minutes to pin my hair up and add the accessories for the final touch. I wanted to surprise Mason and see if I couldn't make his Halloween a little better despite the boy's absence.

A broad smile spread across Mason's lips when he saw me enter the family room. I leaned against the wall at the end of the hallway with one hand on my hip and bent my knee, foot against the wall. "I heard you made parole." I licked my lips. "So, this will be our last night together. We'd better make it count."

"Anything you say Officer, mam'."

I walked over to him and crawled up on his lap, straddling him facing him. I ran my fingers gently through his curls and down his jawline over his scruff, a wicked smile on my lips.

"And you'd better do what you're told." I told him with an authoritative tone.

"Yes, mam'."

I lifted Mason's face gently in my hand and brought his lips to mine. I kissed him firmly caressing his tongue with mine.

Slowly, while still kissing him, I climbed backwards off his lap. Our lips parted, both of us smiling. I held onto his hand and without a word led him down the hallway to my bedroom.

I backed Mason up against the bed with my hand in the center of his chest. My lips pressed firmly over his while my fingers unzipped the prisoner jumpsuit. I pushed it back off his shoulders and watched as it fell to the floor.

He was wearing nothing but a grey tee-shirt and dark blue boxer briefs. He stepped out of the jumpsuit and kicked it aside with his foot. Taking my time to entice him fully, I gently pulled his tee-shirt over his head and dropped it on the floor.

Mason attempted to put his hands on my hips, but I brushed them off and shook my head. He immediately put them back at his side. I pointed my index finger in the center of his chest and pushed gently.

In one smooth move he hopped up on the bed. I went over to the nightstand and took out one of the white silk scarves. I joined Mason on the bed and placed his hands together, one on top of the other and wrapped the scarf around them. The other end I tied loosely around the bedpost.

I crawled slowly up his body and straddled him. Mason smiled deviously. I held eye contact with him moving my hips in small circles grinding on his with light force. I could feel his hard cock twitching, eager to break free from his boxer briefs.

I traced my nails over his chest, pinching his nipples firmly making them stand erect. I bent down and took them into my mouth taking the time to suck and nibble on each of them.

Mason squirmed beneath me, but I continued along my journey ignoring his bodily pleas. I scooted back a smidgen along his thighs and playfully traced the light trail of hair down his sculpted abdomen. I ran my fingertips over his hot skin and then switched to my tongue just to heighten the intensity. He struggled beneath me letting a low moan escape from deep within his chest.

I ran my tongue over the top of his boxer briefs, teasing him slowly, deliberately. Mason quivered. I looked up into his eyes and smiled softly at him. I traced my fingertips along the inside of his thighs, back and forth repeatedly, fully enjoying the torment it aroused in him.

He writhed about beneath me and tugged at the scarf binding his hands above his head. I playfully, but firmly smacked his thigh and shook my head at him to show him I disapproved of his misbehavior.

Mason settled, but his breathing increased. I made my way down his thighs taking his boxer briefs with me and dropping them off to the side.

Slowly, I crawled back up his body and traced my tongue over his abdomen around his belly button down his little happy trail.

I purposely bypassed his throbbing cock and instead ran my tongue over his testes and all around his dick without paying any attention to it.

Mason tried shifting his hips towards me to move his cock closer to my mouth, but I continued to ignore it.

I spread his legs enough for me to fit in between them. I sat up on my feet and wrapped my fingers around his beautiful purple cock. I smiled up at Mason with a devilish grin and ran my tongue over the head of his dick lapping up the pre-cum dripping down the side.

I hungrily took it in my mouth and slid it down my throat massaging it with my tongue and sucking firmly on my way back up. He groaned loudly and arched his hips towards me.

I tightened my grip and increased my speed loving the reaction it brought about in Mason. I could tell he was close, but I wasn't ready to let him reach it. As his thick cock throbbed intensely between my lips I let it drop gently back to his stomach.

I maneuvered my way up and straddled over him. I glided my hips over him sliding lightly, teasingly over this rock-hard appendage.

Mason wriggled his muscular torso beneath me. I grinned deviously down at him, loving the way I drove him crazy. His brilliant blue eyes gleamed back up at me. I ran my fingers slowly over his sculpted chest.

His skin was so warm and smooth to the touch. I playfully tweaked each of his nipples before leaning down and sucking on each of them again in turn.

I reached over and took a condom out of the nightstand drawer and carefully slipped it over Mason's purple dripping cock. I moved my hips up in deliberately slow movements above him and maneuvered myself over his.

I glided my hips over the head of his thick cock feeling it rubbing teasingly between my lips. Gently and slowly I lowered myself down on it. His dick filled me gloriously inch by beautiful inch.

I rocked back and forth, grinding down on him, my hands firmly on his chest. Mason arched his hips pushing up into me. My pace increased as we fell into a perfect rhythm.

I leaned back placing my hands on his thighs as my body reached full ecstasy. I screamed out in pleasure, my body spasmed in pure frenzy, my lungs gasping for air. Mason moaned loudly joining me in my delight.

I collapsed down on his chest, hot and sweaty, my body numb and completely spent. I could feel Mason's heart pounding in his chest, his breathing was labored. His skin glistened beautifully, his hair a tangled mess of curls.

I don't think I'd ever seen him look so incredibly sexy before. I closed my eyes and felt an overwhelming sense of guilt. My heart belonged to Hayden and I had to let Mason go.

I untied Mason and scampered off the bed heading into the bathroom.

I started the shower and stared at my reflection in the mirror. I didn't like the person who looked back at me.

I wanted to scream at myself for what I was doing to both of them. I knew this situation had to end. I was living a lie and all of us were aware of it to a certain extent. Some more than others, but all knew we were existing in a false reality.

I was ready to open my eyes, I simply didn't know how.

CHAPTER 21

OUR BRIEF FALL ENDED RATHER ABRUPTLY. A cold front moved in and our temperatures dropped forty degrees overnight. Bitter winds tore down from the north and brought us temperatures typical for January and February, not the first week of November. I had no other option but to kick on the furnace and dig out the winter coats from the back of the hall closet.

The cold air also brought us to basketball season by the end of the month. The two weeks break between sports had been a nice reprieve and a much-needed break from all the running around almost daily. I took full advantage of the extra time to catch up on my reading and even get ahead on it in a couple of my classes.

Mason used the time to play *Minecraft* with the boys. They were taking turns engineering some medieval castle and fortress surrounded by motes, forests, and mountains. I would check in with them occasionally and see the progress they were making. I had to admit it was pretty awesome and was thrilled that it was something the three of them could do together as a team.

But the strain between my boys seemed to be growing larger and it was getting harder to find common interests between them.

Yes, they both played the same sports, but now that Max was starting a growing streak, the gap in their playing level had increased dramatically in the last several months. I felt bad for my little Henry as I watched him struggle desperately to keep up with his older brother.

Another downside of the early onset of winter was that it ended my evening chats with Hayden. It was too cold to sit outside on the deck and talk. So, our conversations were now limited to between classes on campus or the rare occasions that I got five minutes alone.

However, it didn't lessen my feelings for him nor my desire to be with him. But the more time I spent with Mason, the more confused I became.

Lisa had grilled me about it numerous times since Mason's return. She said she couldn't understand why I didn't end it with one or the other. She urged me repeatedly to just let Mason go. I tried. I truly did, but my boys loved having him at the house and I did feel guilty that Danny was an absentee father.

I knew how much they needed a male role model in their lives and although Mason wasn't the perfect solution, he was there, he tried, and he loved them both and that meant everything. I looked at all the pros and cons from every angle and was still torn between the two men...and the fact that they were father and son only made it a hundred times more difficult.

***

The weekend before Thanksgiving Mason took the boys home after their games on Saturday afternoon so I could go shopping with Lisa to pick up all the necessities for Thanksgiving dinner. It was her ex's weekend with the kids, so she was free as well.

We decided to take full advantage of our temporary relief from life's little responsibilities and have an actual sit-down lunch at a restaurant that had servers instead of a line and cashier.

We stopped at *Granite City* on the north side of the city. It was a cloudy grey day and light flurries were floating down from the sky and disappearing as soon as they landed. The weatherman had said it was 33 degrees out this afternoon, but accounting for the wind chill factor, the air was a balmy 24. It felt more like the weekend before Christmas than Thanksgiving.

The hostess put us in a corner booth near the kitchen. She handed us our menus and scurried off before either of us could say anything to her. Shortly thereafter a cute young waiter came by for our drink orders.

I asked for an ice tea and Lisa got her usual diet coke. I started skimming over the menu not really sure of what I was in the mood for when Lisa placed her menu on the table, folded her hands-on top of it and looked directly at me.

"What?" I crinkled my eyebrows at her. "Why are you looking at me like that?"

"So, when is the little man heading home?" I didn't have to ask who she was referring too.

"Tuesday after his morning class," I dropped my eyes back to my menu and tried to ignore the look she was giving me.

"And Hayden…?"

"What about him?"

"Where is he going for Thanksgiving? Isn't Mason having it with his mom?" She tapped her index finger impatiently.

"Hayden is going to his sisters for Thanksgiving with his family. And yes, Mason will be at his mom's." Having decided on the grilled chicken spinach salad I set my menu aside. "Why are you grilling me on this?"

"And have you decided where are you spending Thanksgiving?" She tilted her head to the side with a slight smile.

I sighed heavily. "I thought we covered this already. The boys are I are fixing our own version of Thanksgiving dinner. Plus, Samantha and her fiancé, Oliver are stopping by for desert after they have dinner with our folks." I faked a smile and rolled my eyes.

"You really should go by your parents. I thought you and your mom were getting along better these days?"

The cute waiter returned, and we placed our orders. "We are," I assured her. "Mainly because I only deal with her when I absolutely have to."

"I admit your mother's difficult on a good day, but considering how Danny's family is, it's important for your boys to have your family." She pointed out.

"I understand that, believe me I do. But you have no idea what it's like to grow up with a bipolar mother who periodically goes off her meds because she hates the insomnia side effect it sometimes causes. Which of course leads to another psychotic break and trust me, those are always entertaining."

My voice dripped with sarcasm. "At least your mom is the kind that bakes cookies and does things with you and doesn't criticize everything you do. I love your mom." I'd only met Lisa's mom a couple times when she was visiting Lisa and she was the kind of mother I'd always wished I'd had.

"My mother's far from perfect I can assure you." Lisa chuckled. "But we are close, and I hope that I can be that way with my daughters when they grow up. She's been an amazing role model for me. I don't know how she did it, raising us alone after my dad passed away."

"I've never been close with my mom. She was never really a mom in the sense that moms are loving, caring, nurturing…understanding. Mine was more cynical, negative, full of manipulation and hatred. She used to love to tell us how we ruined her life while she beat her head against the kitchen cabinets."

"Your mom has a mental illness. You're studying psych, you should understand that." She tried to reason.

"Sure, now I do, but try living with it while growing up. It wasn't easy. And just because I understand it now, doesn't mean I have to ruin my holidays. But I do make sure that she's never alone with my boys. My dad is always with them. I don't want them subjected to what I had to endure as a kid." I informed her.

"Is she taking her meds now?" she inquired.

"Who knows? Some days she's almost normal, but then twenty minutes later she grows claws and horns. So, I just stopped trying."

"I'm sorry." The waiter dropped off our lunches.

"It's hard to miss something you've never had," I lied and shrugged.

"Well, she must have done something right because you're an amazing mom to your boys." Lisa reached over and placed her hand comfortingly over mine.

"You know I was scared out of my mind when I got pregnant with Max. I was terrified of becoming a psychotic bitch like my mom or an alcoholic like my dad. It was then that I decided that if I was going to raise my children right, I was going to be the exact opposite of them in every possible way." I explained.

"Damn, a little harsh, but understandable."

"I'm guessing you're going to your moms for Thanksgiving?"

"No, I'm hosting it this year because Brian is picking the kids up at four to go to his family's dinner. So, my mom is spending Wednesday night at my house to help me prepare everything and my brother and his family are going to be over by eleven. Dinner's at one." She rolled her eyes. "I guess no family's perfect."

"True, but that's the reason why I want to start building holiday traditions with my boys. I want them to look back someday with great memories instead of the screaming holiday matches that I grew up with." I could only laugh because it was true.

"Should I even ask if you're going to see Hayden over the long weekend?"

"Not a chance. Danny blew off the boys again for Thanksgiving, so I'll be with them the entire four days. I just feel bad. Max expected it, I hate to say, but Henry was crushed…again. But it's all the more reason for me to make it extra special for them both."

***

We took our time and perused through Costco. They had already decked the halls from top to bottom in Christmas and the placed looked like elves on crack had their way with it. I was searching desperately for my holiday spirit.

Thus far this season it had been escaping me. I picked up the gingerbread kits for a house, a train, and a Christmas tree placing them all in my cart. I figured the boys would enjoy assembling and decorating them. Well, at least Henry would.

I browsed around picking up baking ingredients for the various cookies and candies I planned on making over the next several weeks. I had planned on putting together several large baskets of goodies for the students I worked with for Michelle. I figured it would help lift their spirits while we went over the material that was sure to pop up on their final exams.

Lisa stopped at the large frozen display of turkeys and picked up a twenty-four-pound bird. Mine was a little more difficult to select. I checked dozens of tags shifting and moving birds about the bin trying to find one for the three of us.

"Gee whiz, Alex. Just pick a damn bird." Lisa tapped her foot impatiently.

"The smallest one I can find is fifteen pounds. If I do that we'll be eating turkey until Easter." I complained.

"Then just get a large chicken and tells the boys it's a turkey." She suggested. "It's not like they'll know the difference."

"I'm not going to lie to them about our thanksgiving dinner." I gave her an annoyed look. "This would go much faster if you'd help me."

Reluctantly, she joined me. It took us over five minutes to dig through a countless number of birds until we finally stumbled upon a twelve-pound bird hidden in the far corner at the bottom.

Together, she and I made a comical pair trying to pull the buried bird free from its comrades. But with a lot of wiggling, a lot of under-the-breath swearing, we did it.

I picked up the rest of the necessities for our small holiday feast. A small can of yams, a bag of white sweet corn, the fixings for green bean casserole, several other various items, and the ingredients to make a batch of yeast rolls from scratch were added to my cart.

It all looked rather meager in comparison with Lisa's overflowing one and it was a sad reminder of things I'd rather forget.

I grabbed several more Christmas decorations I thought would enhance my ever-growing seasonal décor. My goal was to make the house as festive as possible. I had a horrible feeling that my boys were going to have another difficult holiday season yet again because of Danny's recent excuses which only felt like another rejection to his sons.

After fighting through the long lines at the check-out Lisa and I finally headed home. Unfortunately, it seemed the entire city and all the surrounding suburbs had also decided to get a jump on their holiday shopping and therefore, we were headed no way fast. The cars were lined up in every direction.

It was going to be a long ride home.

CHAPTER 22

MASON MADE IT HOME LATE Sunday evening after the boys had fallen asleep. He looked worn and tired from the long Thanksgiving weekend. He dropped his bags in the foyer and plopped down on the couch beside me. He leaned over and kissed me briefly and let out a deep breath.

"Everything okay?"

"Yeah," he ran his fingers through his curls looking older than his twenty-two years. "It was just a long weekend. Not much of a break." He smiled over at me. "I'm happy to be home. I've missed you."

"I missed you too." I lightly placed my hand over his.

"My family is crazy, in a good way, but crazy nonetheless. Thanksgiving at my mom's is just nuts with aunts, uncles, cousins, and grandparents. I swear, you couldn't move," he chuckled.

"That sounds fun." I smiled and traced my finger lightly over the top of his hand.

"Yeah, well, it wasn't." He shifted towards me. "There was arguing over how to prepare dishes or deserts or the proper way to carve the damn bird. They even bickered over how to set the table. It was ridiculous." He shook his head. "I spent half a day with them and by midafternoon I escaped to my Dad's, but he wasn't home. I imagine he went to his sisters for Thanksgiving."

"Why didn't you go over to your aunt's house and see him?" I asked.

"We had an argument the last time we spoke, and I didn't feel like getting into it again with him."

"Argument? About what?"

"I asked him to write a recommendation letter for a friend of mine and he wouldn't do it. He said she didn't fulfill her duties in a manner that he felt comfortable writing one for her. He was being a real ass about it and I told him so." Mason shrugged it off.

"And you haven't apologized to him? That was business, not personal." I tried to explain.

"Yeah, that's what he said," he rolled his eyes. "I call it 'helping someone out'".

"You have to understand, Mason. If your dad writes a letter of recommendation he's personally endorsing her. He's saying that she knows what she's doing and is not only competent, but good. You're asking him to put his name and his business' reputation on the line. That's hardly fair if he doesn't believe it to be true." I attempted to explain it as plainly as I could.

"You sound just like him." He got up and went to the kitchen. I remained on the couch, but I could hear him fixing himself a drink.

Sometimes he truly acts his age.

"Mason, please try to understand. You put your father in a difficult position. I don't believe he refused your request for any other reason than professionalism." I said as he reentered the room.

"I am his son and he refused to do me a favor." Mason spat as he flopped down on the couch.

"It was a favor that could bring into question his personal and professional integrity. That wasn't right of you to put him in that position." I said gently.

"My dad expects everyone to be perfect and when someone falls short, he can't give any leeway." His arms gestured with emphasis.

"Perhaps in business he may be that way, but it's also made him very successful. I'm sure he's not like that in his personal life."

"Oh, yes he is. He's always been that way. I was hoping that since he finally got involved with someone, he'd lighten up a bit. But he hasn't. I'm going to guess that the relationship is over since he spent Thanksgiving alone...again." Mason rolled his eyes with a deep sigh.

"Did he tell you that?"

"No, like I said, I didn't see him, but my sister told me. He told her they're still together, but she had some sort of family obligations out of state. Neither of us is buying it though. If he was still in a serious relationship, why wouldn't he have gone with her?" He questioned.

"You don't know the nature of their relationship. Don't make assumptions because more often than not, they turn out to be wrong." I cautioned him.

"I know my dad, you don't. He's an extremely persistent man. If he wants something or someone, he goes after it until he gets it." I couldn't come up with a response to that.

Instead, I put my hand back over his and patted it gently. "Well, I'm glad you got to spend some time with your family."

"How was your Thanksgiving?" Mason finally leaned back and relaxed.

"It was great. The boys and I cooked a bird and all the trimmings and desserts. It was fabulous. We stuffed ourselves and there are still plenty of leftovers. Samantha came by with her fiancé and my dad. They stayed for a couple of hours and helped us decorate the tree."

"This place looks like it got hosed down my Santa's elves." His eyes scanned over the room. "It's beautiful, very festive."

"I know we kind of over did it." I looked around at all the greens, gold's, and reds that clung to every surface. "I guess I was trying to compensate for Danny's brush off again this year." I shrugged.

"I'm sure they love it." Mason squeezed my hand. "I'm glad you had a relaxing weekend. We're both going to need it with finals coming up."

"Damn! You had to bring that up? I haven't even opened a book since Wednesday. It's been nice." I playfully smacked his arm. "I'm so jealous of you, you're almost done."

"Yeah, but right now I still have finals to prepare for," he complained. "But let's not worry about those tonight. I've missed you." He leaned over and kissed me softly.

"I missed you too." I rose up to meet him and wrapped my fingers in his hair.

Mason scooped me up in his arms and carried me back into our bedroom. He placed me up on the bed and closed our door.

Without pause he climbed up on the bed and laid down beside me. He lightly brushed my hair away from my face, our eyes locked. I stared at his deep blue eyes and remembered the first time I saw them in that lecture hall. It was hard to believe that was almost two years ago.

"I love you," Mason whispered before bringing his lips to mine.

"I love you too."

Mason pulled his hooded sweatshirt over his head and tossed it off to the side. Then he removed his tee-shirt in the same manner. I ran my fingers over his sculpted chest admiring the definition of each individual muscle.

His skin felt hot and smooth to my touch. He lifted my torso barely off the bed and pulled long-sleeved shirt off over my head and dropped it on the floor. His hand then slipped underneath the elastic waist of my fuzzy fleece pajama bottoms pulling them down and tossing them aside.

My body responded eagerly to his touch, but my mind was focused on Hayden. I closed my eyes and suddenly I saw him…looking at me with his emerald green eyes on the beach in Dublin. The image was haunting me. I couldn't shake it.

I kept my eyes closed and bit my tongue, so I wouldn't cry out for him to stop. I had to find a way out of this. But how?

Chapter 23

AS ALWAYS FINALS WEEK WAS HELL. I was completely exhausted. My courses were challenging and packed full of details that cluttered my mind to the point that I was forgetting things that were everyday trivial matters, such as on the last day of finals I realized after almost bursting into tears from pure exhaustion after my last final, I'd also forgotten to put on deodorant that day. And that silly little thing broke the camel's back. After the classroom had cleared, I rested my head down on the desk with tears rolling down my face.

Finally, I pulled myself together and made my way down the hall to Michelle's office. Her door was cracked open and I could see her buried behind stacks of papers. Her blond hair was swept up in a pencil on the back of her neck, she had another pencil tucked behind her ear and her glasses were resting crookedly upon her head. She was living evidence of finals week.

"You busy?" I knocked softly.

"Alex?" She looked up and smiled. "No, come on in. Have a seat if you can find one."

I walked in a moved a pile of papers off one of her chairs and set in on the floor beside me. "How are you?"

She let out a short chuckled. "I'm getting there. How are you?"

"I just completed my last final." I let out a deep breath and slumped back into the chair. "Thank God. This semester has been hell."

"Your classes or your personal life?"

"Both," I shook my head. "But I did email you the final papers from our class. The kids did great."

"Thank you for taking care of that for me. You were a huge help this semester. Are you staying with me for the spring?"

"Of course," I rubbed my eyes. I knew they were red and puffy, but I didn't care.

"Good. I really enjoy working with you." She reached into her desk. "I got you a little something for Christmas." She handed me a small beautifully wrapped box. "I thought you could use it."

"You didn't have to do that." I unwrapped the gift and pulled out a soft brown leather case. Inside was a beautiful sterling silver flask engraved with my initials on one side. "Thank you, Michelle. It's perfect. I love it." I had to laugh. "It's exactly what I needed."

"I know you don't drink whisky, but I figured it would work for wine as well." She said.

"I got you a little something as well. It's not much but I figured you and your hubby could use it for a night out without the boys." I handed her an envelope from my purse.

She opened it up and pulled out the two movie gift certificates. "Yes, we would love this! Thank you so much. God knows we need a night out by ourselves."

She reached over and tucked it into her purse. "Now tell me, how are things going with Mason and Hayden?"

"The same really. Nothing has changed. We're all still stuck in the same situation until Mason graduates I guess." I shrugged. "It sucks, and I don't know what to do about it."

"Yes, you do. But you don't want to rock the boat with Mason or your sons." She smiled gently. "You realize Alex, it doesn't matter when you and Hayden come out, the end result is going to be the same whether it's now or next spring or even next Christmas. Mason is still going to be hurt. Your boys are still going to be shocked, and you know your family and Hayden's are going to speculate how long this has been going on between you two."

"I know. There's no way to win this situation." I agreed.

"Are you sleeping with them both?" Michelle raised an eyebrow at me making me blush.

"Yes, sometimes. Things with Mason have slowed down to a crawl. And I haven't seen Hayden very much. I miss him terribly."

"Do you really think Mason is fooled? He knows something is wrong." She pointed out.

"I know. He's questioned me numerous times and I'm running out of excuses." I shrugged again. "I don't think it matters anymore. He knows it's over and he's only around because of my boys. I know it and so does he."

"That's screwed up." She sighed.

"And for Christmas? Where is everybody going to be spending it?"

"Mason is going back to Chicago and is supposed to spend Christmas with Hayden, but I don't know if he'll see his dad while he's home. They had an argument before Thanksgiving and I don't think they've spoken since. But I'm staying home and relaxing with my boys. I want to spend the next three weeks enjoying them, reading some trashy romance novels, and eating too many Christmas cookies. Are you traveling this holiday season?" I asked.

"Yes, we're leaving Saturday morning and heading out to Denver, Colorado. It's going to be ten fun-filled days of skiing, presents, and arguing with my mother-in-law over everything from how I wash her son's clothes to how I spread peanut butter on my son's bread. The woman is a nightmare, and every year it's the same thing. I've given up trying to get out of it and just make sure I have plenty of wine stashed in my suitcase." Michelle rolled her eyes with a smirk.

"Sounds fun. That's one thing I do not miss at all...Danny's mother. That was a true blessing when our divorce was finalized. I don't miss her meddling in my life telling me how she was such a better mother and wife than me and how everything I did was wrong." I chuckled. "If she's such a great mother, how did she raise such a prize as her son?"

"I understand. I want to tell my mother-in-law the same thing. I love my husband more than anything but there are days when he dances all over my last nerve and the very sound of him chewing his food makes me want to reach across the table and smack him." She laughed whole-heartedly.

"You know what's really funny is they probably say the same things about us to their friends." I giggled.

"No, because that would involve them revealing they have feelings and anything other than 'she pissed me off today or last night'," she mocked a male voice. "They don't discuss it."

"True," I shook my head slightly. "Well, I'd better let you get back to work. I know you've got a lot to get done before grades are due in." I rose from my chair and put the papers back on the seat. Michelle got up and walked around her desk.

"You have a great Christmas and try not to worry so much. It will all work out the way it's supposed too." She wrapped her arms around me and hugged me.

"I know, and I'll try. Thank you for everything. Merry Christmas." I embraced her back. "You travel safely."

"We will. I'll see you next year." She squeezed my arm lightly and walked back to her chair.

"Yes, Happy New Year!" I closed her office door behind me as I left.

The frigid air smacked me in the face as soon as I exited the science building. It had turned bitter cold so early this year. There was little doubt that we'd have a white Christmas.

It had been snowing on and off for the last couple weeks. And here we were a week away from Christmas and I was already hating the cold weather. I closed my eyes briefly and saw Hayden and me lying on the beach in Spain.

I could almost feel the hot sun blazing down upon us, goldening our skin. Oh, how I wanted to be back there on that beach with him rather than walking across this concrete quad in the vicious wind and snow flurries.

Later that evening and after a long afternoon nap I showered and slipped into a lovely emerald green dress for the Christmas party over at Debbie and Mark's. The material was snug without being tight, flowing down to rest a couple inches above my knees.

The neckline was low and elegant. I enhanced it a bit with a silver chain holding a small silver gold locket in the shape of a heart. I added a little make-up to my face and then pinned my hair up in a French twist.

Max whistled at me as I entered the family room. "You look beautiful, Momma."

"Thank you," I smiled back at him. "You remember the rules, right?"

"Yes, Momma." It was only the second time I'd left him and Henry home alone. It still made me nervous even though Max had been insisting he was old enough to take care of his brother and didn't need a babysitter.

"Just making sure, buddy." I leaned over and tasseled his hair playfully.

"You're going to be across the street. Do you really think I'm going to have some wild party of my own or burn the house down?" He smirked.

"Knowing you...nothing would surprise me." I chuckled.

"Me neither," Mason agreed as he entered from the kitchen. "You look beautiful, Lexie." He smiled over at me.

"And you clean up rather well yourself." Mason looked edible in his dark grey slacks with a soft grey and white sweater. Very few men could really pull off wearing a sweater and look stunning in it. And Mason was one that certainly could.

"Are you ready to go?" Mason asked.

"Yes, just let me say good night to Henry." I touched his arm lightly as I passed him by on my way to Henry's room.

I found my little man sitting on his bed playing *Mario Kart*. He always played the *Baby Mario* character and was the best player in the house. No one, not even Max could beat him at *Mario Kart*. Henry paused the game when I knock lightly on his partly opened door. "Hey lil' man, we're getting ready to leave." I sat down on the bed beside him.

"Okay," he smiled and resumed his game.

I sat there for a moment watching him race around the ice track dodging penguins and throwing shells at his opponents. "Bedtime at ten, okay?" I patted him on his leg.

"I know, Momma." He said with his eyes still glued to his television.

"Be good. Holler if you need me. I have my phone." I leaned over and kissed his forehead. "Good night, sweetheart." I got up and made my way to his door. Right before I left his room, he paused his game again and hollered.

"Kisses!" I turned around and saw him up on his knees in the middle of his bed with his arms stretched out towards me. "I want kisses and hugs!" He smiled.

An instant smile spread across my face as I hurried back into his loving arms. He wrapped them around my neck and squeezed me with all the strength he had in him. "I love you, Momma. Have fun tonight."

"I love you, too." I kissed him again before letting him go.

***

Mason and I arrived at Debbie's around eight thirty. There were already dozens of people crowded into her house, mainly co-workers, friends, and a few of our least annoying neighbors.

Luckily, Debbie and Lisa had become friends through me and she and Erik were there as well for which I was truly grateful because standing in the foyer and gazing around the room, there were only a couple of faces I recognized.

Debbie had done a beautiful job decorating the house for Christmas. Her tree was over twenty feet tall topped with a moving porcelain angel. It looked stunning in her two-story family room beside the fireplace.

She had placed a pine garland dressed in little clear lights and red bows around the mantle and through the spindles up the staircase and around the balcony.

Even the stockings were hung on the fireplace each with the names of her children sewn in. It truly looked like a little winter wonderland created with style and elegance.

As I scanned over the crowd, I realized that Mason was by far the youngest one there. I spotted Lisa over in the corner with Erik and walked over with Mason to join them.

Lisa was wearing a burgundy velvet dress that was mid-thigh with matching heels. She looked beautiful. Even Erik was dressed up in navy slacks and a red sweater. His hair was starting to get a touch of grey at his temples and it only enhanced his natural good looks. Lisa was indeed a lucky lady to have found him.

"Merry Christmas," Lisa beamed as we approached. She leaned in and hugged us both, as did Erik.

"Merry Christmas! Have you been here long?" I asked helping myself to some of Debbie's famous punch.

"No, we arrived shortly before you. This is my first." She held up her glass. "The first of many."

"Amen!" I clinked her glass with mine and took a drink.

The evening ticked on slowly and calmly...a direct contrast to every party Mason and I had attended together before. Of course, all of those, except for our last Halloween party, everyone we had gone to together had been with his crowd of friends.

The conversations were mildly interesting, in a sad pathetic and demented sort of way. Thank goodness there was Lisa and lots of alcohol.

CHAPTER 24

FRIDAY AFTERNOON MASON LEFT FOR CHICAGO for two weeks to spend the holidays with his family. The boys and I had made plans to go over to my parent's house to have an early Christmas with them before my siblings invaded. I had made it clear to them I was not going to ruin my holiday by sharing it with my brother and that stick he was married too.

Plus, I wasn't about to subject Mason to an evening with my mother. He and my dad got along well, but my mother was still very condescending with him and went out of her way to make him uncomfortable every opportunity she got.

By four o'clock I had the boys packed and loaded into the car. Henry was still at the age that he really enjoyed staying at my parent's house, but Max got bored easily, especially in the winter time. During the other three seasons he absolutely loved it because he and my dad would take the dirt bikes out to the woods and ride the trails.

But with the snow on the ground and the freezing temperatures it wasn't a possibility. So, he basically hung out with my dad watching stupid comedies, played games on his phone, and posted 'I'm bored' messages on his facebook.

Max grumbled and groaned all the way over there while Henry sat in the backseat talking a mile a minute about all the things he was going to do over Christmas break.

Billie was curled up beside him sleeping soundly before we ever made it out of the neighborhood. I was so jealous.

My mom had baked a small ham for our Christmas dinner and the aroma hit me as soon as we opened the front door. It smelled marvelous. My stomach immediately started growling.

We dropped our things in the living room and found my dad sitting in his recliner in the family room watching an old black and white Jimmy Stewart movie.

"Oh, Merry Christmas," my dad tried to climb out of his recliner with Billie hopping all round him. "I didn't hear you guys come in."

"Merry Christmas, Dad." I hugged him tightly and kissed his cheek. "It smells wonderful in here."

"I know and your mother has banned me from the kitchen." He pouted.

"Then keep your fingers out of the damn food, Mister." My mom entered the room and playfully smacked my dad with a kitchen towel.

"I'm hungry." He complained.

"You're always hungry." My mother and I said in unison and laughed.

"Help me boys, they're ganging up on me." My dad reached over and hugged both my sons. "Merry Christmas guys."

"Merry Christmas, grandpa!" Henry returned.

"Merry Christmas," Max muttered as he walked over and flopped down on the edge of the couch.

"He's pleasant these days," I smiled at my parents.

"And he's just beginning the teen years. You've got a lot to look forward too." My dad put his arm around my waist and we followed my mom into the kitchen.

"Don't remind me." I added.

"Where's Mason? I thought he'd be joining us." My mother asked setting the final touches on the table.

"He left for Chicago this afternoon. He was trying to beat the traffic." We both knew it was a lie, but it sounded so much nicer than the truth because the truth was Mason hated my mother every bit as much as she hated him. He avoided coming over here if possible every chance he could. And I couldn't blame him. My mother was nasty to him every time he was around.

"Well, I suppose that's for the best. This is a *family* Christmas dinner." Mother added sarcastically.

"Seriously, mother. Don't start." I stopped midway into the kitchen and stated flatly.

"I didn't mean anything." She tried to smile innocently.

"Can I help you with anything?" I took a deep breath and inquired.

"No. No. Everything's done now. You could have if you would have shown up two hours ago like you were supposed to." She gave me a coy look. It took everything in me not to walk out the door right then and there and take my boys with me and never come back. The woman will never change.

"Ignore her," my father whispered softly and patted me on the back.

"I'm trying," I told him in a low voice. "It's not easy."

"I know." He agreed.

"Well, are you two just going to stand there while the food gets even colder or are you going to get the boys, so we can eat?" My mother said in a rough voice.

The five of us sat down together and enjoyed the delicious food. My mother continued with her typical sarcastic quips. My father did everything he could to reign my mother in and keep her mouth under control. She picked at my boyfriend, she complained about the money I was wasting going back to college at my age, she even went as far as saying I could have tried harder to forgive Danny for his transgressions.

I sat there silently fuming trying to remember why I had bothered to come over here at all and that I would be leaving this year, once again, with my boys and before presents were opened.

It seemed to be a power struggle between my parents on who thought what an appropriate comment was to fall out of my mother's mouth. Max and I sat there uncomfortably while Henry hardly noticed anything going on. He was stuffing his face with stuffing, ham, and deviled eggs and yammering on to anyone who would list about what he was hoping to get for Christmas.

Finally, my dad interrupted my mother's latest rant over how I take on more than I can handle with my sons, school, student teaching, the boys' sports, their homework plus my own, and still keeping my household running efficiently. I had already drawn blood on the side of my tongue from biting it so hard.

"I say we open some Christmas gifts." My dad said in a cheerful voice with his eyes resting on me.

"Good idea," I muttered and rose from the table. I quickly began clearing all the dishes, rinsing them and putting them in the dishwasher. I wasn't about to listen to her complain about that one too.

Once everyone was gathered in the family room around the tree I couldn't help but look at my watch. I was shocked that it was only six in the evening. It felt like we'd been here for hours rather than less than two. I couldn't wait to go home.

The boys opened their gifts with little enthusiasm after the first couple where my mother had bought them shirts I knew they'd never wear and toys that were clearly for children much younger than them. But they were gracious and tried their best to fake enthusiasm while they thanked both my parents for them.

I had pretty much gotten the same treatment...clothes I'd never be seen dead in and household items that, I believe, had previously adorned the halls of a nursing home facility.

We went through this every year. My mother was notorious for buying the worst possible gifts. I honestly believe she went out of her way to do it because no one could be that wrong all the time by accident.

She'd been to my house countless times, raised me, and known my sons since birth and knew our styles, our tastes. Yet, every holiday, every birthday, she would come up with the ugliest and most bizarre crap she could find for all of us.

We took it home kindly, stuffed in the back of the hall closet or in the corner of the garage and then each spring cleaning it managed to find itself in the trash bin or the annual neighborhood garage sale.

My father loved his new black and red motorcycle helmet the boys and I had gotten him. It matched the new motorcycle he had bought last summer.

His old helmet was solid black and had a few scratches from general wear and tear on it, so I wanted to surprise him with something I knew he'd really like. And fortunately, I was right in letting Max pick it out.

We had debated back and forth between two helmets and Max insisted his was the right one for grandpa. He was correct, my dad was thrilled.

Mom even seemed to like the new bread maker we got her and was anxious to try out the variety of breads packages we'd gotten her to go with it. Normally, I would get some backhanded compliment from her.

One that was almost a compliment but was in fact simply a snide insult dressed up in sequins and glitter. She was an expert at them. I was waiting for her to thank me for giving her a gift that would certainly add to her and my father's waistline or something of the same, but instead she seemed genuine for the first time since I couldn't remember when. In fact, she was speechless. If I'd known that's all it took I would have gotten her one years ago.

"Okay, I have a small surprise for the boys." My dad got up and went to the hallway closet. "I couldn't help myself when I saw them I knew I had to get them for my boys." He set down two very large boxes in front of my sons.

They both looked a little hesitant, but curiosity got the best of them. My father rarely bought gifts himself. He typically always left that up to my mother. But when he did it was almost always something spectacular and expensive.

My dad never seemed to grasp the concept of moderation. Which is exactly why my mother never let him go shopping unaccompanied.

"Oh my God!" Max squealed lifting a thick riding snowsuit out of the box followed by a ski mask, goggles, winter riding gloves, and boots. I couldn't believe it. My jaw quickly hit the floor. I couldn't imagine what that gear must have cost. And buying it for both boys, plus a set for him? I was stunned.

"I just thought the boys and I would have more fun this weekend if we could take the bikes out in the snow." My sons were already climbing into the gear.

"Not tonight," I informed them. "It's already dark outside and you know how I feel after you riding after dark. There's no headlights on those bikes."

"We know, mom." Max said back rolling his eyes at me. "We're only trying them on."

"Just making sure."

My mother sat there silently fuming. I knew how frugal she was with money and I could almost see her estimating the cost of each item in her each and multiplying it by three in her head. I tried not to smile as I watched her for a second.

"These are awesome! Thanks grandpa!" Henry hugged my dad tightly.

"Yeah, these are great. Thanks grandpa! Can we ride tomorrow?" Max chimed in.

"I don't see why not."

With this wonderful turn of events, I don't think I could have bribed my boys to come home with me for the weekend. I hadn't seen them that excited in a long time. I stood up and hugged my dad. "You nailed it, Dad. Thanks!" I whispered in his ear.

"I understand them," he smiled back at me. "I didn't want them…Max, to be bored senseless this weekend. Plus, it's not like we won't use them all winter."

"True."

I stayed over at my parent's house until almost nine in the evening. Once my mother was on her third glass of wine she was much more tolerable to be around. And despite all her comments and the aggravation she caused me, I dearly loved my dad and enjoyed spending time with him.

Plus, it was wonderful to see my boys so excited. They couldn't wait to get up tomorrow morning, throw on all their gear, and take off on their bikes. It had been almost six weeks since they'd been able to ride, and they were addicted to it.

***

Billie and I locked up the house, turned off the lights and made our way back to our bedroom. It was after ten and the house felt so cold and quiet. I hated it when the boys were gone. The silence was deafening. Billie curled up beside me on the bed and I turned on the television for some background noise.

I checked my phone one last time before I turned out the light. Mason had sent me a text saying he'd made it to his mom's and he'd call me tomorrow. I smiled and put my phone on the pillow beside me hoping that I'd hear from Hayden before I fell asleep.

I didn't.

CHAPTER 25

SATURDAY MORNING, with the boys staying at my parent's house for the remainder of the weekend, I took full advantage of the opportunity to finish up some last-minute Christmas shopping for the men in my life. Lisa and I had combed through the mall downtown and bought our weight in retail. We had lunch at *The Ram Brewery* and enjoyed their Indy Blonde Ale.

The weather had turned bitterly cold in the last several days and a dusting of flurries was steadily falling from the sky. I was so relaxed, and it was such a relief to finally let go of all the stresses from the semester. It had felt like such a long semester between Mason and I, not to mention trying to figure things out with Hayden. I just wanted to enjoy this break free from all the stress and drama and spoil my boys a bit.

Lisa turned down our street and I immediately noticed the black BMW sitting in front of my house. My stomach jumped with a tinge of excitement I couldn't ignore.

"Is that Hayden's car?" Lisa noticed the look on my face.

"Yes," I couldn't take my eyes off it.

"I didn't know he was coming down?" She remarked.

"Neither did I."

"When was the last time you spoke to him?"

"Right before finals, but we've been texting. I told him this morning that the boys were spending this weekend with my parents and you and I were spending the day shopping. He just said told me to have fun and he'd talk to me later. He never mentioned anything about coming down here." I explained.

"I'm guessing he knows Mason is back in Chicago," she pulled into my driveway and Hayden climbed out of his car.

"I would imagine so," I remarked before opening my door.

"Surprise darling," Hayden rushed up and threw his arms around me lifting me out of Lisa's SUV. "Ah, I've missed you so much!"

"Oh, my God! What are you doing here? I wasn't expecting you." I wrapped my arms around his neck and kissed him eagerly.

"I couldn't pass up an opportunity to see my girl. When you said the boys were staying with your parents for the weekend I had to come down." He pressed his lips against mine once more before setting my feet on the ground. "Hello Lisa," he called over the top of her car.

"Hello, Hayden. How are you?" she smiled over at him and climbed out of her vehicle. She went around back to open the hatch for me.

Hayden helped me gather my gifts and bring them into the house. We both hugged Lisa and wished her a Merry Christmas before she headed back home again. We left all the presents in the family room next to the tree.

Hayden started to build a fire and I retreated into the kitchen to retrieve some glasses and a nice bottle of merlot I'd bought last week when I thought I'd be wrapping Christmas presents alone this evening.

"Would you like a glass of wine?" I offered taking a seat on the couch.

"Please," he had the wood and kindling already crackling in the fireplace. The smell of the burning wood was intoxicating and the chill in the room was beginning to disappear.

"I'm so happy you decided to come down." I poured our glasses and set the bottle aside. "I was afraid I wasn't going to see you over the holiday."

"I couldn't not see you." He took a long sip of his wine and leaned in to kiss me again. "I cannot tell you how hard these last four months have been on me."

"I know," my eyes dropped to the floor. I wasn't sure what to say to him.

"So, what did you get today?" Hayden took advantage of changing the subject. Some things were just too painful to discuss.

"Gifts from Santa for the boys. A couple things for my family and such." The 'and such' meant both he and his son but I couldn't bring myself to say it.

"Would you like me to help you get them wrapped?" he offered taking a seat beside me on the couch.

"You want to wrap Christmas gifts with me?" I gave him a funny look.

"Yes. Let's just say I'm in the holiday spirit. Do you have any Christmas music?"

"Of course. But I'm afraid it's not the more modern versions. My collection consists of Bing Crosby, Nat King Cole, and Mitch Miller." I smiled. "My grandparents used to play them all the time when I was a kid and we'd make Christmas cookies together, so that's what I prefer now. It just makes it feel more like Christmas to me." I explained.

"My grandparents listened to them too." Hayden said as he helped himself to a little more wine.

I got up and turned on the old records that my grandmother had given me shortly before she'd past away. The covers were showing a little bit of age, but despite their age, they were in excellent condition. *Jingle Bell Rock* rolled softly out of the speakers.

I closed the lid and went over to the hall closet to gather up the wrapping paper and bows for the gifts. I set all the wrapping accessories down on the floor between the Christmas tree and the fireplace.

The white lights on the tree glowed off the gold and red trimmings that greatly enhanced the ambiance along with the warmth from the embers of the fireplace.

I crawled over to the coffee table and saw that Hayden had also refilled my glass. I took a small sip and brought it with me setting it down on the stone around the hearth. I started emptying the numerous bags I'd brought home and sorting the gifts into categories of whom they were for.

"I'll be right back. I left my things in my car." Hayden rose and walked out the front door.

I paid him no mind figuring he was grabbing his overnight bag. I nodded to him and continued softly singing to myself along with the music. I was completely happy.

"Please don't be mad at me, but I couldn't help myself." He said upon his return closing the front door and locking it behind him. He was carrying several packages himself and had his overnight leather duffle bag hoisted over one shoulder.

"Why would I be upset? What did you do?" I playfully eyed him suspiciously.

"It's been so long since I got to buy toys or stuff for younger kids that I picked up a few things for your boys." He set his things down and began pulling out wrapped packages and set them under the tree. "So, these are from Santa," he smiled.

"You shouldn't have done that." I was truly surprised by his gesture.

"I wanted too," he smiled.

"What did you get them?" Curiosity filled me.

"You'll just have to wait and see on Christmas morning," he said with a devious grin.

"That's not fair. I'm not a child." I laughed.

"I know that, but it's more fun this way."

"But you don't even know my boys." I wagered. "How would you know what they like or want?"

"I've listened to you talk about them for the last eight months. Plus, I've seen their bedrooms. I think I've got a fairly good idea of the kind of things they'd like." He put the last gift under the tree and came over beside me.

"You really shouldn't have." I told him again.

"But I wanted too," he kissed me softly on the cheek and finished off his glass of wine.

Hayden and I spent the next couple of hours wrapping presents for about everyone in my family. We managed to put a good dent in the bottle of merlot while we laughed, teased, and tormented each other trying to make the gift wrapping look presentable.

We sang along to the music together and I couldn't help myself from wondering if this is what it would be like to be solely with him and perhaps, someday, married to him. I caught myself several times just watching him as he'd tie a bow or line up the edges of the paper so that the wrapping appeared seamless.

He took such great care in his work and attention to detail. He was so sweet, considerate, and loving. A part of me couldn't stop thinking about what it would be like to be his wife. Something I never thought I would find myself even contemplating again.

I stood up and immediately felt the full effects of the wine going straight to my head. I steadied myself and walked into the kitchen for another bottle of merlot. Hayden got up and followed me in.

"Hey sweetheart, let's go grab some dinner before we start on the next bottle. I'm starving." He slipped his arms around me while I stood looking in the open frig.

"Sounds good," I closed the door and turned around the face him. "What are you in the mood for?"

"Italian. I want some of that pasta we had that night on the bay." He gave me a gentle squeeze.

"Oh, that was so good. I want some of that bread. It simply melted in your mouth. I could live on that bread." I looked up into his beautiful green eyes. "Granted, I'd be three hundred pounds, but I'd be so happy." I grinned.

"You'd still be beautiful." Hayden leaned down and kissed my forehead.

"How about the Claddagh Irish Pub over at the mall. It's about as close to the food we had over in Ireland but not nearly as good. It's not bad though." I shrugged.

"Okay, that sounds good. Do they do carry-out?"

"I believe so. Why?"

"I just thought I could go pick it up while you set the table, maybe light some candles..." He raised his eyebrows at me in a comical manner.

"I can do that. But you don't know where it is."

"That's why they made GPS darling," he chuckled and pulled me back into the living room. "Can you pull up their menu, please?" We sat down on the couch together and I opened my laptop.

"Let me see," I typed in the name and address pulling up their page. I clicked on their menu and browsed through. "I'll have the Spinach Chicken Melt, please."

"Okay, I'll call it in." Hayden continued to browse through the menu even as he dialed the number.

I excused myself while he was busy on the phone. I began picking up all the wrapping material and accessories and put them all back into their storage box to hide away in the closet for another year.

Shortly thereafter, Hayden left to pick up our dinner. I tidied up the kitchen from the boys and my breakfast that morning, loaded the dishwasher, and set the table for dinner.

Then I straightened up the living room and put on a fresh record. My mind was racing with all my earlier thoughts no matter how hard I tried to dismiss them. They were haunting me.

I went into my bathroom and looked at myself in the mirror. I quickly brushed out my hair and pinned it up into a French knot. I touched up my make-up just a bit and decided to slip into something a little more comfortable.

I stripped out of my clothes in the middle of my walk-in closet and stood there naked and freezing trying to find something sexy but warm, which was almost impossible in the middle of winter in the Midwest. I tried my best to ignore Mason's clothes hanging up behind me where once upon a time, Danny's had been. "God, this is so fucked up!" I declared loudly to myself.

I finally gave up on sexy lingerie and slipped into my silk bright pink and white polka-dotted pajamas I'd gotten at Victoria Secret's last month. They were sexy in a cute sort of way.

The flowing bottoms and long-sleeved, collared, buttoned down shirt were more of a wife sexy than girlfriend sexy, but at this moment I didn't care. I was freezing, and he was going to return any minute with dinner.

I hurried back into the dining room and took out two tall silver candle stick holders and a couple of red tapers out of the hutch. I placed them on the table and lit the tapers.

They burned beautifully giving just enough light between them and the garland lights along the top of my cabinets. It was very romantic.

I heard a car door shut and I hurried over to the front door to open it for him. Hayden came walking up the freshly snow-covered walkway with his arms loaded down with our dinner.

"My goodness, what did you order?" I laughed.

"Dinner," he came in and slipped off his snowy shoes in the foyer.

"I know you said you were hungry, but this is ridiculous." I lifted the bags out of his arms and carried them into the kitchen setting the down on the island. "What did you get?" I asked as Hayden joined me at the island.

"You lit some candles," he noticed. "And I love the pajamas. Very cute." He started emptying the white carton boxes out of the bags.

"Cute," I muttered. *Not exactly what I was going for.*

"I like it much better than some silky nightie. This looks like you. Sexy and sweet."

"Looks like enough food to feed ten people." I observed trying to ignore his last comment.

"Let's see," he started opening containers. "I got some Corned Beef and Cabbage Rolls for an appetizer. For an entrée, some Gaelic Chicken for me and one Spinach Chicken Melt for you. And for dessert, two Irish Car Bomb Cheesecakes."

"Wow, this looks wonderful." I helped him set everything out on the table and then poured us each a glass of sweet tea.

"I know it's not that little pub in Dublin, but I hope you like it," he sat down in the seat across from mine.

"It smells wonderful. Thank you."

"You're very welcome," he reached across the table and placed his hand over mine. "I've missed you so much."

"I've missed you too." I whispered in reply.

"How much longer do we have to go on like this?" his eyes pleaded in conjunction with his words.

"Hayden, please. I'm so happy you're here. Don't spoil it." I pulled my hand back and placed it in my lap.

"You never want to talk about it. All you ever say is 'it's complicated'. What's so complicated? Why are you still living with Mason after you know what he did last summer?" He questioned.

"Oh, I'm supposed to judge him for dating someone I don't know his age when he was under no obligation to me and I was busy running around Europe sleeping with his father? Good Lord, Hayden. Seriously?" I inquired trying to do my best not to roll my eyes at him.

"Alex, I know it's unconventional, but…"

"Unconventional? That's a slight understatement isn't it? How in the world do you honestly expect me to explain this to my family? To my sons? They know and love Mason. I can't just tell them that I'm trading him in for his father because you're closer to my age and there's a possibly for a future with us. And let's not even mention what my ex-husband could do with this information in a courtroom if he so choses too. I'd look like a whore to a judge for sleeping with both the father and the son. Damn, Hayden. Why can't you understand that?"

I got up and left the table. I was no longer hungry at all.

I walked back to my room and closed the door. Billy looked up from her nap on the center of my bed. I walked over and sat down on the edge scratching her behind her ears. "How in the world did I get myself into this mess, ol' girl?" She crawled over and rested her head on my lap. "Don't ever fall in love, Billy. It sucks." I muttered.

"Alex?" Hayden knocked softly on my door. "Can I come in please?"

"Yes," I replied.

Hayden opened the door slowly and walked over to sit down beside me. "I'm sorry. I know how hard this situation has been. I didn't mean to put more pressure on you. I just don't understand why you can't explain it to people."

"Explain? To my sons? How? They love Mason. There's no way to explain this to them. If you were any other man perhaps, but you're Mason's father. That one's hard for even my best friends to comprehend."

I stood up and walked over to the dresser. "Hell, I'm struggling with it myself and this has been going on since last summer." I turned to face him.

"But Alex…" Hayden approached me with his arms out.

"Don't," I backed up into the dresser as he engulfed me in his arms.

His mouth came crushing down on mine. My arms automatically drew him in. I wanted him. There was no denying that. But I was also so tired of having this same argument with him. It was always the same, always the same words, the same positions on each side. That part of me wanted to scream, lash out irrationally and somehow make him look at things from my perspective.

All the information I understood about men could fit on a post-it note.

Hayden had become a drug to me and I was in desperate need of rehab. He saw me. The *real* me. He possibly understood me better than anyone else in this world. But this situation was bad for me and I knew it. I was going to have to let him go. It wasn't a matter of my own heart. It was a matter of my son's love for Mason.

But for tonight, tonight I was going to be with him.

I closed my eyes and let myself melt into him. He was air and I was slowly dying without him. I loved this man more than I'd ever loved any man in my life and the thought of living without him physically ached in my chest.

Hayden lifted me up and carried me over to the bed. His mouth crushed over mine, his tongue dancing seductively with mine.

He tasted of sweet red wine and a hint of the cigar he must has smoked while he was out. I knew he occasionally indulged when I wasn't around.

The soft stubble on his face brushed lightly against my skin. His breath was labored. I could feel his heart pounding in his chest as he fell upon the bed beside me. Our legs intertwined, our hands groping, grabbing, pulling each other's clothes away.

We quickly discarded them to the floor. Our mouths devoured one another. We were like two horny teenagers fumbling through our first sexual experience.

It was hot. It was heavy. There was no foreplay, no teasing, no romance. It was pure frustration, pure lust, pure aggravation with the entire situation.

Hayden rolled over on me. I could feel his hard cock throbbing against my thigh. His breath was hot on my neck. He nudged my legs apart and I wrapped them around his waist.

He entered me with such a force that it literally took my breath away. I could feel him pulsating inside me with each deep forceful thrust. My nails dug into his back as my body clung to his. He had never been this way before with me, nor I with him.

I wanted him. I didn't want to play. This was exactly what we both needed. A moment of release, un-waivered unadulterated release from everything that was pent up inside us since we returned from Europe.

There would be time for romance, time for wine, time for hand-holding and gazing into each other's eyes in front of a blazing fire in the hearth while soft fluffy snowflakes fall outside our window. There would be plenty of time for that later. This was not that time.

Hayden's cock thrusted deeply into me hitting my G-spot perfectly every time. My grip on him tightened. My legs wrapped around his neck. My head fell back, my eyes closed, the intensity of his rhythm rocked through my body.

The light-headedness took over, electricity coursed through my veins. I screamed out in ecstasy as I exploded all over his big dick. He buried his face in my shoulder, groaned deeply as his own orgasm ripped through his body.

Hayden collapsed down beside me, his breathing was still labored. "I'm sorry, I couldn't help myself."

"Don't be sorry. I needed that just as badly as you did."

He raised himself up on his elbow and stared down at me for a moment with a small smile on his face. "I love you so much." He whispered softly before leaning over and kissing me lightly on the forehead. He rested his head against mine while his breathing returned to normal.

Neither of us said anything. There was nothing to say. We were madly in love, deeply in love, passionately in love, truly in love, and yet, forbidden. It wasn't fair.

***

Hayden's breathing had turned into a steady rhythm of sleep beside me. His head lie on my shoulder, one leg draped comfortably over mine.

I aimlessly ran my fingers through his hair. My heart ached. My thoughts filled with hope, desire, and sorrow.

At least I know there's an expiration date on our affair, the same as I did with the one with Mason. It seemed so unfair. Just because I know about the date and put up walls to protect myself from the heartache doesn't necessarily mean I felt completely immune to it.

It still hurt. I didn't want to lose him even though I knew it was coming. I knew he would return to Chicago and I would remain here.

He subconsciously tightened his hold on me in his sleep. Almost as if he knew what I was thinking. I sighed deeply still running my fingers through his hair. Our time together was growing short. I closed my eyes and did my best to push the thoughts out of my head.

But they weren't going anywhere.

CHAPTER 26

TUESDAY EVENING, CHRISTMAS EVE, the boys and I were snuggled up together on the couch watching Ron Howard's, *How the Grinch Stole Christmas*. We had turned all the lights out except for the soft glow from the twinkling white lights on the Christmas tree and the embers in the hearth. The stockings with each of our names sewn across the brim hung from the mantle waiting to be filled.

I sat between my sons with a bowl on popcorn and M & M's in my lap. Billy was curled up on the floor in front of us snoring softly. The sounds of the boy's laughter was like music to my ears.

Halfway through the movie my cell phone rang. I glanced down at it lying on the coffee table and noticed it was Danny. I paused the movie and answered the phone.

"Merry Christmas," I answered cheerfully, not for him but for the joy I felt with my boys.

"Well, Merry Christmas to you too. You're in a particularly good mood." He noted. "Are you guys at home?"

"Yes, we're watching a movie." Henry sat up a little straighter and looked over at me with big anxious yes waiting to talk to his dad. Max, on the other side of me, huffed at the interruption to his movie, tossed the blanket off his lap and went into the kitchen.

"Sounds fun. Are the boys with you?"

"It's Christmas Eve, Danny. What do you think?" I tried not to roll my eyes in front of Henry, my good mood disappearing fast.

"Just checking because I've got a surprise for them for Christmas. Can you put me on speaker?"

"Okay," I clicked the button and held the phone out between Henry and me. "You're on speaker."   "Hi Daddy, Merry Christmas!" Henry said a little too loudly.

"Merry Christmas, little man. Are you having fun?" Danny asked.

"Yes, we've been pigging out tonight and watching Christmas movies." Henry climbed up on his knees sideways on the couch.

"Is your brother in the room?" Danny inquired.

"Nope," Henry immediately responded.

"Yes, I am." Max reentered the family room and plopped down on the couch beside me.

"Merry Christmas, buddy." Danny said cheerfully.

"Merry Christmas, Dad." Max grumbled back.

"Well, now that I have the three of you together I wanted to tell you my big Christmas gift." Danny continued. "Are you ready for this?"

"Yes," Henry bounced.

"Sure," Max mumbled.

I remained silent almost holding my breath.

"I got you both tickets to Arizona leaving the day after Christmas and returning on the seventh." Danny sang out.

"What?" I felt the bottom drop out of the room. "Danny, you never mentioned anything about this to me."

He never made travel plans for the boys without discussing it with me first. "The boys and I have plans for winter break."

"Well, plans change, darling." Danny could have cared less, and I knew it.

I clicked the speaker button off and walked back into my room closing the door behind me. "Danny, this isn't funny. You didn't even ask me. Why did you buy tickets without talking to me first?"

"Alex, I missed Christmas with them last year. I'm missing it with them this year. Let me have New Years with them." He sighed heavily. "Can't you do this for me? I already paid for the tickets."

"Danny," I sat down on the bed, tears burning my eyes. "How can you take my boys for the holidays?"

"They are my boys too, Alex." Like I needed to be reminded.

"I realize that, Danny. But since you have missed so many holidays, we already made plans."

"I'm trying to make it up to them," he exhaled loudly. "Jesus, Alex. I figured if I let you keep them for Christmas you'd be happy to let me have them for New Years. Now you get to spend it with your little boy toy." He mocked.

"Seriously," this was not the time for him to mock Mason. "Danny don't be an ass."

"Look, if anything it will give you a break from the boys. Relax. Enjoy yourself. Go out for New Years for a change."

"Whatever," I muttered trying not to scream, cry or both.

"I will email you their itinerary."

"Okay," I conceded without being given a choice.

"Can I talk to the boys now, please?" His voice took on a sugary sweet tone.

"Yeah, hold on a sec," I got up and walked back out into the family room and handed the phone to Henry who took it eagerly.

I went into the kitchen and fixed myself another root beer. I wanted a glass of wine but resisted. Max followed me, and it was clear from his body language that he was none too happy about his Dad's surprise.

"Do I seriously have to go?" He leaned against the counter with his arms folded.

"What do you want me to do Max?" I was ready for a full-blown explosion that was surly going to ruin the rest of the evening and most likely tomorrow as well.

"Tell him no! I don't want to go. Aaron and I have plans," he huffed. "I'm old enough. I don't have to go if I don't want to." His voice went up an octave.

"Why are you yelling at me? I didn't do this. Do you really think I want you jetting off to Arizona just because he says so?"

"Then tell him NO!"

"Lower your voice, young man." I warned him. "Your dad has visitation rights and I cannot stop him from exercising them. And look at it this way, while I'm freezing my butt off up here, you actually get to enjoy some warmer weather." I tried to make him see the brighter side.

"Do you really think I care?" He lowered his voice but was now glaring at me.

"No, but..." I shrugged my shoulders. "What do you expect me to do, Max?"

"Don't make me go?"

"I don't want you to go, but my hands are tied, Max. I'm sorry." I truly was.

"This sucks..." Max muttered loud enough for me to hear before storming out of the room, shortly followed by the sound of his bedroom door slamming shut.

"Great!" I said to the empty room and walked back into the family room where Henry was still chattering nonstop with his Dad.

I flopped down on the couch beside Henry and closed my eyes. I let him finish his conversation and then he handed me the phone back. "I'm gonna go pack!" Henry announced excitedly and bounced back to his bedroom.

"Yeah," I held the phone up to my ear trying to calm down.

"Oh, come on, Alex. Is it really that terrible? You get to enjoy New Year's without the boys under your feet. You should be happy." Danny's voice grated on my nerves.

"Thanks," I muttered.

"I'm trying here, doll. Can you at least cut me a little break?" The enthusiasm and cockiness left his voice. He just sounded defeated.

"Fine," I took a deep breath. "Just email their itinerary. I'll make sure they're at the airport on time."

"Thanks, Alex. I appreciate it." He said softly.

"No problem."

"Tell the boys I'll call them tomorrow. And Merry Christmas, doll."

"Merry Christmas, Danny."

I set my phone back on the coffee table and went to see about the boys. Henry had half-hazzardly packed his suitcase. I took everything back out and set it aside. "Come on, you." I patted his bed and he hopped up. "I'll take care of your suitcase tomorrow. It's time for you to get some sleep."

"But I'm not tired," he complained while trying to stifle a yawn.

"If you don't go to sleep, Santa isn't going to bring you lots of presents." I tucked him in and kissed his forehead.

"You don't really think I still believe in Santa, do you Momma?" He looked up at me with his big brown eyes that had somehow lost some of their innocence. "You know I haven't believed in him for a couple years now. I just let you think that I do." My heart died a little hearing his confession.

"You know, Henry. When I asked my mom about Santa when I was six after a neighbor girl Janie told me he wasn't real, do you know what she told me?" My little boy shook his head. "She said that as long as I believe in my Dad, then Santa would always be real." It was one of the few rare memories from my childhood that I cherished.

"But what if I don't believe in my Dad?" It was like a knife cut through my chest.

"Why don't you?" I couldn't stop myself from asking.

"Because he chose to leave us. I know he loves us in his own way, but he left all of us and moved across the country." His voice sounded so young.

"Ah, sweetheart," I wrapped my arms around him and held him tight. "I'm so sorry."

"But I believe in you, Momma. I know you'd never leave us." Henry turned his head and kissed me on the cheek.

"Never in a million years." I choked back some tears.

"When I grow up, I'm never going to live more than five miles from you. That way we can still see each other every day." He smiled and rested back against the pile of pillows at the head of his bed.

"I'd love that." I leaned down and kissed him again. "Goodnight, little man. Try to get some sleep." I got up and turned his light out.

"Goodnight, Momma. Sweet dreams," he replied before I shut his door.

"Sweet dreams."

I found Max sitting on his bed playing on his laptop. I wasn't surprised he hadn't begun packing anything. "Hey sweetheart, how are you?"

"Pissed," he muttered.

"Language," I went over and sat down beside him.

"Ticked off," he glanced over at me. "I suppose I have to go, don't I?"

"I'm afraid so," I reached over and patted his leg.

"Fabulous," he shut his laptop and put it beside him on the bed.

"I know you're upset and I'm sorry. I wish you didn't have to go either." I told him.

"Then tell him no," Max glared at me.

"He has rights, Max. You know that."

"What about my rights? When do I get to have a say in whether or not I want to see him?"

"Perhaps you should be having this conversation with your Dad once you get there?" I passed the buck to Danny.

"Yeah, right. Like I can talk to him." Max folded his arms and leaned back against his pillows.

"You can try," I suggested.

"Have you met him?" I knew he had a point. Danny never listened to me the entire time we were together.

"Yes, I know what you mean." I didn't know what else to say to him. "Try to get some sleep." I leaned up and kissed him. "We'll talk more about it tomorrow. I love you."

"Love you too," he muttered picking up his laptop again.

I closed his door softly and returned to the family room, exhausted from the turn of events Danny had sprung on us. I sat down on the couch and flipped mindlessly through the channels. I settled on *Miracle on 34th Street*, the original black and white version and curled back under the blanket.

Billy jumped up beside me wiggling her way under the blanket with me. I stroked her black fur and closed my eyes for a moment.

I couldn't believe my boys were leaving again. I knew when Danny moved across the country I'd have to deal with this, but until now, I hadn't had to worry about it much. Danny had been more concerned with his own life more so than his role of being a father.

This was the first time he had ever exercised his right to see them over the holidays even though he had been promising it to the boys ever since he moved. And I, like them, no longer gave much thought to his empty promises and always made our plans without ever considering the possibly of them leaving.

I finally got up and went to my room in search of all the little things I'd gotten to put in the stockings. I grabbed the bag out of the back corner of my closet on the top shelf and took it to the family room. During our marriage Danny had always overseen the stocking stuffers.

It was something silly and trivial that he enjoyed, buying small gifts and candy to surprise me and the boys with. It was also something I'd never given a second thought to until that first Christmas after our divorce when I had to take care of it myself.

I placed Max's new Fossil watch in his snowman stocking. It was the one he had wanted so desperately at the beginning of the school year and I had told him it was too expensive.

It was, but I finally caved since he was getting more difficult to buy for. I included the video game, Skyrim that he wanted and then an assortment of chocolates and candy. For Henry, I got him his own copy of Skyrim, an Avengers watch and then the same various goodies I'd given to his brother. I tossed in a bottle of body wash and lotion from Bath and Body Works in my own stockings and included some candy for good measure.

I spent the following half hour crawling around in the attic pulling out the boys' gifts. I picked a few things up here and there throughout the year, but with school now consuming my life I put most of my shopping off until the last minute.

So far, at least as far as I knew, Max hadn't found my hiding spot yet. But that hadn't stopped him from relentless searching. And I was sure that Henry had joined him on the quest a couple years ago. Probably, about the time he had stopped believing in Santa.

Once everything was finally done I crawled into bed with Billy. It had been a long night and I had the feeling that tomorrow was going to be even longer. I was just about to drift off when my phone rang on the nightstand. I reached over blindly trying to grab it in the dark, just to make the noise stop.

"Hello," I fumbled with the phone.

"Merry Christmas Eve, darling. How are you?" Hayden's voice was as soothing and warm as a cup of hot chocolate.

"I'm good, just crawled into bed. How are you tonight? Is everything going well?" I knew Mason was staying at his place for Christmas.

"Good, I suppose. Mason's still upset about the recommendation letter so he's being pretty stand-offish to me."

"I'm sorry. I know he can be stubborn when he wants to be."

"It's okay. I'm used to it. I'm glad Kennedy is overwhelmed with the Christmas spirit. But she's been hounding me about this special lady I've been seeing.

She doesn't understand why you're not here right now." Hayden chuckled. "I explained that you live out of state and that you're spending the holiday with your children and your family."

"I hate to think of what she'd say if she knew the truth."

"It's hard to say with her. Kennedy is more like me in a lot of ways, whereas Mason has more of his mother's personality traits. I'm not sure if that's good or bad." He confessed.

"You'll never believe what surprise Danny got the boys for Christmas." I said.

"What did he do now?" Hayden asked sarcastically.

"He bought the boys tickets to Arizona. They leave on the twenty-sixth and return the day before they go back to school."

"Wow! I didn't expect that."

"Me neither. Henry is thrilled or at least I thought he was until I tucked him in and Max is so pissed that his dad is ruining his Christmas breaks and all the plans he'd made with his friends." I explained.

"I'm sorry. I know you were looking forward to spending some time with your boys," he sighed. "What are you going to do?"

"Cry," I laughed half-heartedly. "I have no idea. I had all this stuff planned to do with the boys and that all went up in smoke."

"What if I came down and spent the next ten days with you?" Hayden asked.

"Are you serious? What about work? What about Mason?"

"The office is closed until the Monday after New Years and I believe Mason would be thrilled if I left. He's not exactly been here much anyway." He said what I already expected.

"I kind of figured. But that's a good thing. He's moving on with his life." I was torn between being thrilled and hurt...and a tiny bit jealous.

"She's over here," he confessed. "She joined us for dinner. I think he invited her just to piss me off over the recommendation letter. It worked. It's been an uncomfortable evening to say the least."

"I'm sorry. I wish he wouldn't have done that. I know he has a vindictive streak." Memories of Cancun ran through my mind.

"Yes, he gets that from his mother," he laughed. "She's mastered it."

"Ex's have the tendency to do that." I admitted.

"What time do the boys leave?"

"We have to be at the airport at ten in the morning. Their plane leaves at 11:30." I informed him.

"Okay. I'll leave here around nine and meet you back at your house around lunch. How does that sound to you? Would you mind being held up in your house for days on end with me?"

"I would love that," I couldn't stop grinning. It was the first time I'd smiled since Danny called.

We finalized the details of his trip and as much as I hated the boys leaving me over the holidays I was thrilled at the possibility of spending the time alone with Hayden.

I missed him so much and it felt like forever since I'd seen him. I hated this constant back and forth, the hidden truths, the outright lies, the deceit. As much as I cared for Mason, my heart belonged to Hayden and I knew in my soul my future was with him and there was nothing Mason could do or say to change that.

CHAPTER 27

THE BOYS WERE UP BRIGHT AND EARLY
Christmas morning, just as they were every year. By the
time I had dragged myself out of bed and started a fresh pot
of coffee Max had already crawled under the tree and
started making piles out of the gifts for him and Henry.
Henry, instead, had opted to dig through his stocking first. I
found him sitting on the corner of the ottoman chewing on
his chocolate Santa and looking over the various candy and
games.

"Can I play Santa?" Max poked his head out from under
the tree.

"Didn't you play Santa last year?" I couldn't remember.

"No, Henry did." I glanced my youngest son who
surprisingly nodded in agreement.

"All right then, just let me get some coffee first." I got up
and went to the kitchen to fix myself a cup of morning
strength and glory.

Once I had it in hand I settled back on the sofa with my
comfy blanket tossed over my legs Max handed a small gift
to his brother and started ripping the paper off one for
himself. The boys opened numerous articles of clothing,
video games, sports equipment and silly little trinkets.

They seemed genuinely happy with what they had, but
of course I made them wait until the end to open what
Hayden had brought them.

Both boxes were the same size but wrapped differently with their names on them and a card saying they were from Santa.

Henry carried his over to the couch and sat down beside me. Max remained seated in the middle of the floor as they both started tearing into them. My surprise was every bit as real as theirs when they uncovered new Xbox Ones complete with Connects.

I couldn't believe Hayden had been so generous with my sons. But it was also his nature to do it.

"Oh, my gawd, Mom! I can't believe you did this!" Henry jumped up and threw his arms tightly around my neck. "You are so awesome!"

"Merry Christmas," I stuttered. "I'm glad you like it."

"Are you serious? I love it! I've been dying for one of these!" He bounced back over to the game system and started opening it.

Max was so stunned he sat there silent just running his fingers lightly over the box. "Hey Max, what do you think? Do you like it?" I grinned.

"Yes, I love it." He said in a small voice.

"What's wrong?" I reached over and put my arm around his shoulder.

"Nothing," his voice perked up and he shook his head as if erasing some far-off thought.

"Can you help me hook it up?" Henry picked up the box.

"Of course." I followed my son down the hall with Max close behind me heading to his room to hook up his new system.

The poor pre-teen was literally bouncing with excitement. I was so happy and still in disbelief that Hayden had done something so amazing for my boys.

My boys spend the rest of the morning playing with their new Xbox Ones leaving me time to clean up the mounds of discarded paper and bows and start preparations for our Christmas dinner. I was so happy that we were keeping it low key this year.

I had spoken with my sister, Samantha who called the other day and asked if she and Oliver could come by. I hadn't mentioned it to the boys hoping to surprise them.

She was their favorite relative and they always enjoyed her stories about all her travels around the globe. Sam was famous for her crazy antics although I curious as to whether her recent engagement to Oliver had curved her behavior any. I doubted it, but I was hopeful.

I put the ham in the oven, made the green bean casserole, and prepared everything else for our mid-afternoon Christmas dinner. I could hear the boys in their rooms trying out their new games and hollering at their televisions.

I cleaned up my mess and fixed myself another mug of coffee before returning to my spot on the couch. I turned on the television and found Tim Allen's The Santa Clause movie and settled back to relax for a moment.

Two commercials later Max came down the hall carrying a little box wrapped in silver paper with petite gold ribbon. He handed it to me along with a folded note.

"I found this in my bedroom behind my tv a couple weeks ago when a game fell behind it on accident. I don't think I was supposed to find it until this morning when I hooked up the new system. It's in the same handwriting as the tag on the gift. It must be from Mason." He explained.

I glanced down at the folded note that simply said; 'Max, please give this to your mom for me on Christmas morning. Thanks'. I couldn't find the words to respond with.

"Did Mason buy us the Xboxes?" He sat down beside me and asked. "It doesn't look like his handwriting."

I took a deep breath and sighed. "Ah Max, it's complicated."

"Does this have anything to do with that Megan girl he's always talking to on facebook and texting? I know things aren't the same between you two." The kid was too observant for his own good.

"Mason met her last summer while he was working in Chicago. He spent Thanksgiving with her and he's with her now." I told him.

"Doesn't that make you mad? Why would he be there with her and still live with us?"

"Like I said, it's complicated, Max." I ran my fingers through my hair trying to find the right words. "Mason is young, and Megan is his age. They have more in common with each other than Mason and I do.

And he should be with someone younger than me. Someone he can build a future with. Someone whom he can someday marry and have children of his own with.

That's what I want for him and I can't give him that. I'm done having children. I'm very happy with you two." I smiled at my son. "

And I believe that Mason is still here not because of me but because of you and Henry. He's grown very attached to you boys and he loves you. He doesn't want to hurt you guys."

"But he's graduating in May and moving back to Chicago, right?"

"Yes."

"So, he's sticking around here just to be around us?"

"I believe so, yes."

"Are you seeing someone else too?" Max asked.

"Honestly? Yes, Max I am."

"But I don't understand why? I thought you were happy with Mason. I thought you loved him."

"I do love him, sweetheart. But I'm not in love with him. There is a big difference." I reached over and took my son's hand. "I have been seeing someone closer to my age as well who makes me very happy, someone whom I am in love with, but I didn't know how to explain it to you and Henry." I confessed. "I never wanted you two to get hurt. I know you both love Mason and I know it's going to be hard on you guys when he does leave."

"Shouldn't Mason move back to where he was living before he moved in here?"

"Yes, he should, but like I said, I didn't want you and Henry to get hurt."

"I'd rather see you happy, momma. If you love this other guy and Mason is with Megan, you guys shouldn't be living together." He reasoned.

"You're right, we shouldn't." I agreed.

"Did you go on your trip with this other man while we were in Arizona last summer?" Max tilted his head to the side and narrowed his eyes as me a bit as if he was just now figuring it all out.

"Yes, dear."

"And Mason knows about him too?"

"Yes, we talked about it. He wasn't happy about it, just as I wasn't thrilled learning about Megan, but I believe we both knew it was going to happen sooner or later." Max nodded in agreement as if he was miles wiser than his years.

"And this new guy is the one who got us the new Xboxes for Christmas?"

"Yes," I grinned at my eldest son.

"And are you going to open up the gift he got you?" He grinned back at me with a slight smirk.

I had completely forgotten the small box in my hand. "Of course," I laughed a little.

"I'll bet it's jewelry. Men always buy ladies jewelry for Christmas."

"Really?" I raised my eyebrows at him as I ripped the corner of the paper and slide out a white velvet box.

"Yeah, don't you ever watch commercials?" Max asked as if I was stupid.

I opened the box and gasped. Inside was a gorgeous delicate white gold chain with my name spelled out on the charm. It was simple, elegant, and perfect for a first Christmas gift. I absolutely loved it. "Look,"

I passed the box over to Max. He glanced down at it for a minute and smiled.

"Sweet, I like it." He handed it back to me. "I think you should wear it today."

"Me too," I took it out of the box and put it on. "How does it look?"

"Like he really likes you too."

"I think he does." I couldn't help but grin at the thought of Hayden.

"So, do I get to meet him or not?" Max asked in a cocky voice.

"Well baby, that's where this whole thing gets extremely complicated and I'm not sure I'm ready for you and Henry to…" I didn't want to say 'know the truth' so I kept stopped short of finishing my response.

"To what?" I knew Max wasn't going to let me off the hook so easily.

"You realize that in life, sometimes, you have no control over who you fall in love with, right? You don't always plan to fall for the right person or who someone else thinks is the right person. Sometimes you find out you have chemistry with and feelings for someone you probably shouldn't and there's nothing you can do about it. Do you understand?" I rambled.

"You're babbling, momma." Max stated flatly.

"I can't tell you because I don't know how to tell you. I'm still trying to figure that one out." I said as honestly as I could.

"Why don't we just leave it at that for now?" I almost pleaded with him to drop the subject.

"Seriously, momma? After all that you're going to leave me hanging?" Sometimes his quick wit aggravated me so much. "How bad can it be?"

"Pretty bad," I admitted with hesitation.

"Really?" Max tilted his head in disbelief. "Momma, you've never done anything bad in your life." He giggled a bit at me.

"I might surprise you this time, my love. I even surprised myself because I've been seeing someone whom I really shouldn't be involved with at all."

"Who?" I could tell he was dying to know. I took a deep breath and sighed heavily.

"Do you remember last spring when Mason got into trouble for using his Dad's credit card without permission and his Dad drove down here from Chicago to talk with Mason about it?" I tried to jog his memory.

"Yeah, I answered the door when he came over and then you sent me to my room." Max narrowed his eyes a bit as he did whenever he felt I was treating him like a child.

"Well, anyway regardless of all the details, Hayden and I started talking because of some things that Mason was doing and then, well…" I didn't want to finish the sentence, but I knew my son understood.

"Got it. Wow!" Max whistled a long low blow. "And Mason doesn't know that this other man in your life is actually his dad?" I shook my head. "So, he doesn't realize that you spent your vacation this summer with him."

"Nope."

"But I thought Mason was in Chicago working with his Dad over the summer?" His forehead crinkled a bit.

"He was, but his dad took a three-week vacation with me to Europe." I felt suddenly guilty.

"Who did he tell Mason he was going with?"

"He didn't. Mason and his sister know he's seeing someone, but they have no idea who." I admitted shamefully.

"I can see where it could be a problem." He pinched his lips together to keep from laughing.

"It's not funny." I rolled my eyes at him and shook my head slightly trying not to laugh myself.

"Well, most people trade in for the newer model, but not you, you trade for the older." He couldn't stop himself from giggling.

"Okay, mister. Let's keep this little conversation between us. All right?"

"I promise," Max stood up and kissed me on the cheek. "But I would love to be a fly on the wall when Mason finds out." He kept giggling as he walked down the hall.

I leaned back on the couch and stared down at the necklace Hayden got me. I really hoped I hadn't made a horrible mistake in being honest with Max. I really didn't think he'd betray my trust, but I also hated the way it made me appear in his eyes despite the way he played it off with humor.

I knew that I had fallen in love with a forbidden man, at least forbidden to me. And it was both a guilt ridden and phenomenal thing. I didn't want to lose Hayden and I wanted to let Mason go. If Hayden was any other man in the world this wouldn't even be an issue.

Oh, why does he have to be Mason's Dad? Life is so unfair.

I ran my fingers through my uncombed hair with frustration and sighed heavily. I drug my exhausted butt off the couch and decided that a hot shower was exactly what I needed. The boys were still consumed with their new gaming systems and I knew they'd be in there until I called them out to eat.

Samantha and Oliver stopped by late afternoon just as we were finishing our Christmas dinner. Since we weren't expecting anyone the boys were surprised when the doorbell rang. Max, always my curious child, jumped up first and ran to the door.

"Aunt Samantha!" I heard him exclaim from the great room.

"Hey Buddy, Merry Christmas!" My sister's voice rang through the house. "I'm so happy to see you."

Henry leapt up from the table and sprinted to the great room. "Aunt Sammy!" His voice echoed off the walls.

"Merry Christmas little man!" I heard Samantha say as I followed the sound of their voices into living area.

"Merry Christmas, Oliver." I hugged my sister's fiancé. "How are you doing?"

"I'm doing well, thanks. How are you doing?" Oliver embraced me back.

"Good. Busy, as always, but good." I reached over for my sister who finally released Henry. "Merry Christmas, stranger. It's great to see you!" I hugged her tightly.

"You too. Merry Christmas little sis."

"You look fabulous." I stood back and looked her over. She looked stunning with her dark hair pinned back and wearing her stylish Christmas attire.

"Thanks," she mock twirled for the boys and laughed. "I have to keep up appearances." She winked over at Max. "So, are you going to spill the beans on who you went to Europe with?"

"What?" It was the last thing I expected to pop out of her mouth.

"Mom said something about you cavorting all over Europe with a man you won't introduce her too." She explained.

"And with good reason." Max added with a smirk.

"Long story," I shot Max a look that told him to shut it. His smirk turned into a low grin and I knew exactly what the little monster was thinking. Problem was he was right.

Samantha and Oliver made themselves at home. The five of us made ourselves comfortable by the Christmas tree after dinner. Oliver had gotten a fire roaring in the hearth and I had turned on some Christmas carols.

Samantha had brought an expensive bottle of wine from France that was simply to die for. She, Oliver, and I were gathered around enjoying a glass while the boys returned to their new gaming systems.

"So, explain little sister." Samantha eyes me suspiciously.

"Explain what?" I asked even though I knew precisely what she was referring too.

"Mr. Mysterious European guy." She raised her eyebrows at me. "What's the story there? I thought you were still living with the college boy?"

"I am sort of, I suppose. I mean he's still staying here, but mainly because of the boys. He met someone his age during his internship in Chicago last summer and he's spent the holidays with her." I explained.

"And you're not pissed all to hell about that?" Samantha questioned.

"No. He needs to be with someone his own age. Someone he can build a future with and that's never going to be me." I told her.

"You're nicer than I am. I'd beat his little ass." She told me.

"Why? It's true."

"But he's living in *your* house!" She declared.

"Only because of the boys, not me." I stated again.

"Still, that's disrespectful to you. I wouldn't stand for it." She took another drink of her wine.

"Well, it's complicated to say the least. And it's difficult to say anything to him considering what I've been doing behind his back. He knows I've been seeing someone else also. He knows I went on a trip with someone, but he doesn't know where I went or with whom."

"Explain." Sam shifted herself drawing her legs up beneath her getting more comfortable. Oliver topped off his glass and then added a bit more to each of ours.

"It doesn't make me look good." I told her.

"Yeah, little Miss 'I've never done anything wrong'." She laughed. "I'm sorry, but…me yes, you – yeah right."

"I'm serious…" I continued with my story explaining everything that had occurred between my initial introduction to Hayden to my conversation with Max earlier today.

The look on my sister's face was priceless. I knew Samantha could never imagine me doing anything remotely close to what I'd done. She sat there stunned and speechless for several moments.

She finished off the wine in her glass and immediately reached for the bottle refilling her glass a little fuller than before and absorbing everything she's just heard.

"Wow." Oliver whistled in a low voice. His eyes were wide, and I could tell I'd caught him clearly off guard.

"So, let me get this straight." My sister finally managed to recompose herself. "For the last eight months you've been sleeping with both the father and the son. The father knows about the son, but the son doesn't have an inkling that this other man you've spent the summer cavorting around Europe with was his own dad?"

She shook her head in astonishment "Oh my God Alex! You slut!" She unexpectedly busted out laughing. "I've never been so proud of you!" Oliver shot her the strangest look. "No. No. You don't understand. I say that with admirable affection.

Alex was always the good kid who always made the right decisions, blah, blah, blah. And I was the wild child who never did anything right.

Now, I'm the one with a successful career and engaged to a wonderful man and she's the one who's in school, a single mom, living with a kid and having an affair with his father!" Samantha gloated still giggling.

I sunk down in my corner of the couch and felt horrible. She was right, I was now the fuck up and she was, for the first time ever, the daughter with her shit together. I gulped down the remainder of wine in my glass before refiling it once again.

"Sam," Oliver said in a low voice and nodded to her in my direction with a stern look of disapproval on his face.

"Sorry, Alex, but it's funny from where I'm seated. Our parents would flip. Well, at least Mom would. She's given you the 'holier than thou' lecture and you'd never hear the end of it. And Charlotte, oh good Lord, could you imagine what that tight-ass would have to say?"

She laughed whole-heartedly. "She'd freak! I still can't figure out what Colin see's in that prude. I miss the days when our brother used to be normal. Can you even imagine how sad his sex life must be if he even has one?" And that mere thought made me laugh out loud.

"I don't think they have one and if they do, you know there's no foreplay and missionary style only." I couldn't help from saying.

"She wouldn't know how to give a blow job if we told her!" Sam roared.

"Ew…that's gross. Only nasty girls would put a penis in their mouth." I mimicked Charlotte's voice making even Oliver laugh.

"She needs to be rode hard and left wet." Samantha concluded.

"Damn, you two are so sweet." Oliver smiled broadly.

"Truth hurts," I shrugged with a smirk.

The three of us ended up finishing off a second bottle of wine and having a marvelous evening laughing, teasing, and joking around. Neither of them was in any condition to drive anywhere so I insisted that they spend the night here.

I pulled out the sofa bed and put the air mattress on top of it in hopes of making it more comfortable for them. However, as intoxicated as the three of us were I don't believe they would have cared if they slept on the floor next to the Christmas tree beside the hearth.

CHAPTER 28

GETTING MY SISTER MOTIVATED in the morning proved to be more challenging then attempting to keep my sons on schedule. I ended up trying and left her and Oliver at my house when I took the boys to the airport. As stubborn as Samantha was, I knew the reason she was fighting me about getting ready was solely because she wanted to stick around until Hayden arrived. She was dying to meet the man who she claimed was responsible for knocking me off my moral high horse.

So, I left them there sleeping peacefully and loaded the boys with their bags in my car. The air was bone chilling cold and tore through our many layers as the wind whipped around us while we made our way through the airport parking garage.

Henry huddled close to me, but Max took off at an almost sprint towards the sliding doors. I hollered after him, but he simply waved in acknowledgment of having heard me to wait for us inside the doors. His puberty was beginning to take a toll on us all.

I kissed and hugged them both goodbye, hating this moment as always. It never got any easier no matter how many times I was forced into this. Max was not in the best of moods. He was never really a morning person anyway and the fact that he didn't want to take this trip just thrilled him to no end.

Henry, on the other hand, was literally bouncing. I almost felt sorry for the flight attendant that came to escort my boys to the plane. He wrapped his arms around me one last time, giving me a big kiss and telling me how much he loves me. I squeezed him tightly and told him the same.

***

Samantha was all dolled up and sitting at my kitchen table drinking coffee when I arrived back home. Oliver was rummaging through my refrigerator looking for something to eat when I entered and put my purse down on the table.

"Find anything interesting in there?" I asked with a chuckle.

"Yes, my favorite. Leftovers!" He excitedly started piling tubs of Tupperware on the counter.

"Is the coffee fresh?" I rolled my eyes at my sister about her fiancé 's behavior.

"Of course. I just made it." Samantha dumped another heaping spoonful of sugar into her freshly poured mug.

"Fabulous," I helped myself to some hot liquid heaven. I sat down beside her, took several sips of coffee, then rested my head on the table. "I hate it when they leave. Danny is such an ass for this." I complained like a child.

"He is their dad. As shitty of a dad as that may be, at least he's making somewhat of an effect." Samantha reached over and patted my shoulder. "So, Romeo should be here shortly, right?"

"Yes, and don't think I don't know that's why you've stuck around. I know you're dying to meet him."

I looked over at Oliver who was heaping mountains of leftovers on a plate and then stuck it in the microwave. I was grateful they weren't going to waste this year like they usually did.

"Guilty." Samantha laughed "And what's so wrong with that? You never let me meet the kid."

"And you never will." I shook my head at her from behind my mug. "There is no way I would subject him to being grilled by you." I teased her. "You'd shred him."

"You have a first aid kit in the house." My loving sister pointed out.

"The kid is what twenty-two years old?" Oliver got his plate and joined us at the table. "I love you dear, but he is not ready for the likes of you." He lovingly touched her hand.

"I'm sure my little sister has made of man out of him by now." Samantha batted her eyes in my direction.

"Good Lord, Sam. You are so ornery." Somehow, she never ceased to amaze or humor me. Interrupted by the doorbell, I let out a sigh of relief, but the knot in my stomach grew to the size of a watermelon. "Stay." I warned my sister.

I slowly got out of my chair and made my way to the front door. Hayden looked stunning in his Kakis' and navy-blue sweater. There were scattered snowflakes in his hair and across the shoulders of his full length smoky soft tweed overcoat that gave him an even dreamer look than normal if that was even possible. I leaned up and kissed him sweetly before pulling him into a full embrace.

"Hello darling, I missed you." He held me tightly.

"Me too. By the way my sister and her fiancé, Oliver is here. And she knows who you are so fair warming." I whispered in his ear.

"Okay," Hayden chuckled and took off his overcoat and soft black cashmere scarf.

I hung them up in the hall closet and took Hayden's hand, squeezing it gently. "Are you ready for this?" I smiled gazing into his gorgeous green eyes. Boy, how I'd missed them.

"No worries." He smiled reassuringly.

The two of us entered the kitchen where Samantha and Oliver were still seated at the table. Oliver had almost consumed the contents on his plate and hurriedly swallowed, choked, and took a long gulp of coffee to help wash it down.

"Sorry about that. Please excuse me." Oliver cleared his throat one more time, stood, and shook Hayden's hand. "I'm Oliver Ashton, Samantha's fiancé. Pleased to meet you."

"Hayden Brooks. Nice to meet you too."

"So, you're my baby sister's dirty little secret. My..." my sister rose from her chair and gave Hayden an obvious once over. "I can understand her reluctance to give you up, darling. You are positively delicious." She laughed coming around the table and gave Hayden a friendly embrace.

"My loving sister, Samantha." I smiled over at Hayden gesturing with exaggeration towards Samantha showing him I was not in the least bit shocked by her words.

"Easy now, I was warned about you." Hayden, thankfully, dished it right back at her.

"Oh, I am sure you were darling." Samantha patted his arm before returning to her seat.

"Would you like some coffee?" I offered him the empty chair in the nook.

"Love some, thank you sweetheart. It's really coming down out there." Hayden said sitting down between my sister and me.

The four of us enjoyed a lively conversation about careers and family. Hayden was completely intrigued by Samantha's career and talked to her at length about it. I sat there feeling ridiculous that I had nothing to contribute to the conversation.

It seemed that all the adults in my life were busy living adult lives and I was the one walking a decade behind them. I hated it. I felt so ridiculous that all I had as a *job* was my teaching assistant position.

I ran my finger lightly over the brim of my mug thinking about how I couldn't wait for school to be done so I could have a career I could be proud of. I sighed lightly and recalled the words my father had once spoken to me in anger when I told him I was pregnant with Henry.

"I really thought you'd be somebody in this world, Alex. I thought you'd be so much more than just a mom." I knew he was only expressing his disappointment in my having another child instead of going after my degree, but those words had cut deeply, and the scar had never fully healed.

By late afternoon the four of us had decided to go downtown for dinner. It seemed the outside world had transformed into a winter wonderland with several inches of freshly fallen snow. If it continued at its current pace, we could have a good foot of snow by morning.

The roads weren't too bad yet as we headed out in Oliver's rented Silverado. Christmas decorations hung off the streetlights in the early twilight sky. I knew it would be completely dark by five o'clock. Such is so typical of a winter evening in the Midwest.

We parked in the garage adjacent to the Circle Center Mall and took the skywalk into the mall. We fought our way against the hoards of unsatisfied gift receivers and bargain shoppers trying to seek out the best post Christmas deals.

We crossed through the impatient crowd as quickly as we could and cut through Macy's department store to the bitter cold fresh air once again.

The sidewalks were covered in a slushy layer of trampled snow, salt, and dirt. In a fruitless attempt to ward off the bone chilling wind, we crossed the busy city street, and huddled closely to each other walking as quickly as our half-frozen bodies would allow.

Finally, we made it to Fogo de Chao restaurant. They had some of the best food in the city and I was starving. I clutched Hayden's arm and tried to keep the wind from biting into my face as I hid behind a woolen scarf. I was glad I had put on my thick fuzzy socks and leather snow boots.

It was almost nine o'clock before we returned home. We had engorged ourselves on the most delicious dishes and mouth-watering tender meats in the city. We shared a bottle of white wine and enjoyed a splendid conversation.

I wished that Samantha lived closer and we could spend many more evenings together with her and Oliver. They were the closet thing I think I'd ever seen to a couple who were truly meant to be together.

They complimented each other so well and played harmoniously off each other attributes. I couldn't have been happier for my sister for finding the right man for her.

Hayden and I snuggled up together under a thick cashmere blanket on the couch in our pajamas after a long hot shower. It had done wonders to rid my bones of the freezing temperatures and biting wind. I felt almost hypothermic by the time we'd reached the truck after going along with Samantha's brilliant idea of walking around the circle in downtown Indianapolis to see the world's largest Christmas tree.

She had insisted because Oliver had never seen it. So, against my better judgment, Hayden and I were dragged along. Thankfully, we did stop at this small little chocolate shop of the circle and treat ourselves to a large steamy cup of hot chocolate and some freshly dipped chocolate covered peanuts.

My sister and Oliver were camped out on the loveseat almost completely hidden beneath the fleece blanket that was usually draped over the back of the couch.

Hayden had started a roaring fire in the hearth while they were in the shower and it was finally starting to take a little bit of the chill out of the air. I had let my sister pick out a movie and she had selected *The World According to Garp* because she was a huge fan of Robin Williams and Glenn Close.

Not to mention John Lithgow's brilliant performance as a new lady was priceless. When Samantha had learned that Hayden had never seen it she insisted on putting it in. I couldn't argue it was one of my personal favorites as well.

Shortly after the movie was over and we had all called it a day, Hayden and I finally retired to the privacy of my bedroom. I remembered I still hadn't given Hayden his Christmas gift, so I waited until he was brushing his teeth and pulled the two elegantly wrapped boxes out from beneath my bed.

I set them down on his pillow and slipped out of my pajamas. I crawled beneath the covers, naked and trying not to shiver. The bed felt so cold after fire from the family room, my flannel pajamas, and the heavy blanket.

Hayden walked out of the bathroom looking breathtaking in his birthday suit. His chest was ripped and accented with just a small amount of hair that I loved to run my fingers through.

Everything was nice and trimmed, toned, and well defined. I loved the way he looked. He smiled a devilish little grin and crawled up the bed making little growling noises.

I giggled and reached for him as he crept up my body. I wrapped my arms around him, his strong powerful lips found me, his tongue searching, probing.

Breathing heavily, I reluctantly pulled myself back. "Aren't you curious what I got you for Christmas?"

"Edible panties?" A cocky grin slid across his shapely lips.

"Not quite," I lightly traced my finger down his jawline to his lips. They were so full and luscious.

His eyes drifted over to the two beautifully wrapped boxes resting on the pillow beside us. "You really shouldn't have."

"Neither should've you." I grinned seductively and played casually with the delicate gold chain. "But I love it." I kissed him once more. "I'm afraid mine aren't quite as extravagant as your gift, but I wanted to do something special."

Hayden maneuvered himself around with his legs crossed and picked up the bigger of the two boxes first. Like a little child he tore the paper off the front of the box, stared at it for a moment, wrinkled his brow, and looked at me utterly baffled. "Lucky Charms? You wrapped up a box of Lucky Charms?" His eyebrows went up a tad.

"Open it," I told him.

"Okay," He tossed the remaining wrapping paper onto the floor and opened the box. His eyes drifted back to me still looking confused. He opened the bag and burst out laughing. "Marshmallows! You made me a box of just marshmallows!"

He leaned forward and kissed me excitedly. "You know how much I love them and don't like the oat crunchy things."

"I know, you always pick them out." I grinned and shook my head at him.

"They are the best part." He reasoned. "How many boxes did it take to make one box?"

"Eight." I laughed. "My boys will be eating the crunchy oats until Easter."

"Well, thank you. I love it!" Hayden set the box on the nightstand and picked up the smaller box. He shook it just a tad. Nothing rattled. He opened the side that was simply a little black box with no identifiable markings. "Did you get me a tie clip or cufflinks?"

"Nope," I beamed with anticipation. "Better."

"I don't know," he teased. "I don't think anything can be as sweet and thoughtful as my box of Lucky Charms marshmallows."

"Will you stop being a pain the ass and just open it?" I reached around for a pillow and then playfully smacked him with it.

"Don't rush me. I'm working on it." He turned the box over and started slowing peeling open the corner just to tease me.

I rolled my eyes at him with a heavy sigh. He adored his little torments. Finally, he tossed the paper off the bed where it landed next to the other. "What's this?" He turned the box over and studied the writing on the side. "You got me a vibrating cock ring?" He chuckled with disbelief.

"I couldn't help it after I read the reviews." I confessed.

"Really?" He sounded intrigued and studied the box a little closer. "Rechargeable, waterproof, vibrating cock ring by Lelo." He looked up at me with a smirk. "It's purple?"

"It only came in black, green, or purple." I stated. "I thought purple was more us."

"It's made out of silicone, stretches and has six different patterns and speeds." Hayden continued reading the box. "It has to charge for a couple hours before we can use it. So, we'll have to try it out tomorrow." He carefully opened the box and examined his new toy. "It's soft." He played with it with his fingers and picked up the charger out of the box.

"It's charged." I admitted.

"What?"

"I couldn't help it. I didn't want to wait for it to charge so I opened it and charged it before I wrapped it up."

Hayden pushed gently down on the one button and the little toy sprang to life. "It's got a good little kick for something so small." He noted. "This is going to be fun." He winked at me. "Come here, you!"

Hayden wrapped his arms around me and pulled me beneath him. I loved the feel of the weight of his body beneath mine.

It was the feel of it, but not the actual pressure of it. My hands traced over the muscles in his back, the smooth silkiness of his skin, the heat radiating off it. The smell of his cologne was enticing.

My fingers caressed his firm muscles across his back and slipped down to his shapely ass. I pulled his body closer to mine. I wanted him desperately. It felt like forever since I'd been lost in his arms.

Hayden's hand cupped my breasts, squeezing it, teasing my hard nipples between his fingers. I moaned softly at the jolt that shot through my body and burned between my thighs. He brought his mouth down to my breast to tease me some more. I leaned into him arching my back towards him, my legs wrapped around his waist. I wanted him.

He traced his tongue across the small of my stomach making me squirm beneath him. He moved his body slowly down mine. I closed my eyes and danced my fingers through his curls. His hands gently nudged my thighs further apart.

Hayden's fingertips trailed lightly over the sensitive areas of my inner thighs. I squirmed in delight and the mere pleasure of the torture and anticipation. He kissed the top of my pubic lips ever so softly.

Then the absolute pleasure of the soft moist probing of his tongue. I moaned in ecstasy arching my hips into his face. Hayden wrapped his arms beneath me and around my hips and thighs holding me into place, so I could not escape his. He loved to torture me like this because he knew how much I dearly loved it.

Hayden had a way about him. A way of pleasing a woman in ways that only entered into the far recesses of their mind. It was those dark desires that they would never admit aloud to anyone, even their self's.

He had an innate ability to read a woman's body language down to her smallest whisper, slightest moan, and knew exactly how to use that pleasure against her in ways that she never dreamt imaginable. He was every woman's dream lover as well as her worst night terror matrixed into the most desirable man possible.

Hayden tongue explored me thoroughly. He lapped up my juices and probed deep inside me. His fingers tightened on my thighs. My head was swooning. I was lost in the world of exquisite delight he had engulfed me in. His tongue playfully teased my clitoris as he slid his fingers inside me.

I moaned loudly and tightened my grip on his hair unintentionally. He quickly found his and my favorite spot and gave it its due attention until I was trying to thrust my hips to him or away from him or both. I did not know which and I did not care. My brain had stopped working and all I could feel of intense sensational pressure rippling through my body.

"Just let go baby," Hayden whispered.

"Oh my God!" I screamed out and relaxed into his movements, the rhythm of his fingers massaging me tirelessly and ejected cum all over his face. But Hayden wasn't satisfied with that, he kept going, kept pushing me for more.

But I was exhausted. I screamed out in unimaginable lust, love, desire, hate, passion, intensity. My body was spent.

With every strength I had left in my body I tugged and pulled to break free of his grip. I could barely breathe. I was severely dehydrated.

I collapsed back on the pillows trying to catch my breath. Hayden sat up between my legs with a proud grin under his messy face. "That's my girl." He patted my thigh, hopped up and disappeared back into the bathroom to clean up.

I closed my eyes and tried to clear my head. I didn't know if I should hate him or marry him immediately. No man had ever brought me to such heights before. And there was nothing like it. My entire body was numb. I wasn't sure if I was going to be able to walk again.

Moments later Hayden crawled into bed beside me, his face freshly washed, his hair hanging in short loose curls. He looked incredible. "Did you miss me?" He propped himself up on his elbow and stared down at me.

"Very much so."

"Are you sure?" He leaned down and kissed me lightly on the forehead. "Cause I couldn't tell." The biggest cockiest grin spread across his shapely lips.

"You're such an ass." I rolled my eyes playfully at him. "I don't know why I tolerate you."

"Because no other man can do that to you." His voice was full of confidence.

"Maybe not but who says I can't take care of it myself?" I countered. I couldn't but he didn't need to know that.

"Seriously? That's impressive." His grin took on a smirk twist.

Well played Hayden, well played.

"What am I going to do with you?" I held his tender gaze.

"Just love me." He shook his head slightly. "That's all I'll ever want from you. Just love me."

"That's all?" I wasn't fully buying it.

"That's all." He leaned over and kissed me hungrily. "So, do I get to try out my new toy?" a sly grin spread across his face.

"You bet your sweet ass you do," I reached up and pulled him on top of me.

The new toy slid on with ease. I was amazed by how sturdy it was but still had so much give to it. And it was so soft. It turned his penis into my own little real vibrating dildo.

It was fabulous! His new toy immediately became my favorite new toy. I was in love. It didn't matter which position we tried...and we tried four before neither of us could take anymore, but whichever way we were, it hit perfectly on my clitoris and I couldn't get enough of him.

When all was said and done and we both lay in two sweaty heaps on the bed, dehydrated and exhausted, we agreed it was the best Christmas gift either of us had ever gotten.

CHAPTER 29

MY SISTER AND OLIVER spent the next couple of days with us because the weather had taken a nasty turn for the worse. They slept in Max's room and complained nonstop about his full-size bed. I told my sister more than once to be happy she wasn't on Henry's twin captain bed. But all in all, we had such a great time. The men got along like two old friends who hadn't seen each other in years and Samantha and I spent our evenings cooking lavish dinners for our men. Each evening we would all retire to the living room around the blazing hearth and bask in a glass of red wine, a mug of hot apple cider with cinnamon or a steamy mug of hot coco.

I truly loved every minute of it. The time spent with my sister, with Oliver, and mainly with Hayden, was just like being in Europe again…only this time with another couple tagging along for good measure. But it felt so perfect, so peaceful, and I was head over heels in love. I curled up beside him every night with my head resting on his chest, listening to the strong rhythm of his heartbeat, playing lightly with the hair on his chest. I knew in every fiber of my being that this was where I was supposed to be.

The day before they left, the day before New Year's Eve, my sister and I decided we wanted to make a snowman. It was silly, and childish, and absolutely freezing outside but was also necessary.

We hadn't done it in years and for whatever strange reason we both were in the mood to go outside in a foot of snow and act five years old again.

We bundled up in layers and I lent her a pair of Max's snow boats, luckily, he has big feet, and she borrowed various other items she found in my hall closet of the boys' winter gear stash.

I hate to admit how comical we truly looked in our mix-matched apparel. The men looked up from the game they were battling on the X-box long enough to laugh at the two of us.

Samantha and I pranced around in front of them acting like models, being goofy and enjoying the silliness of it before we headed outside. It was a perfect winter day. It was light outside and not bright, which was wonderful since it can be blinding when the sun reflects off the snow.

There were a few scattered clouds drifting lazily across the bluish grey sky, but nothing much in the way of a breeze. The snow was wet and thick. Great packing snow. It held together easily and could be molded into shapes without much effort.

But that also meant it was heavy and wet heavy snow was good at clinging to your clothes. Once that happened it didn't take long before it soaked in and chilled the wearer to the bone.

We began forming two softball size balls with our hands, packed them firm and began rolling them across the yard.

We watched each other out of the corner of our eyes and quickly found ourselves racing to see who could make the bigger ball the fastest. It was something she and I had done for as long as I could remember. We were always in silent or open competition with one another regardless of the task. Soon we were laughing and tossing snow back and forth.

Finally, we rounded the house and realized that we had two huge bottoms for the snowmen that we could barely move rather than one taking the bottom and the other building the body and the head.

"We'll simply make two." Samantha reasoned catching her breath. "Man, I am not used to this anymore. I can't even remember the last time I'd played in the snow." She leaned back against the giant snowball.

"It helps if you have kids." I grinned over at her.

"Yeah, throw that one in my face. Mom is never going to leave me alone until I give her a grandchild." She complained.

"I didn't think you wanted children?" I rested against the large ball I'd created.

"I never really thought about it. You know I adore your boys more than anything, but I always liked the fact that I could give them back and go home. From what I understand you can't exactly do that when they're yours." Samantha chuckled.

"No, you're kind of stuck with them 24/7." I told her.

"But with Oliver…" she shrugged. "I don't know. Things seem different now and I'm thinking I might not mind having a little Ollie running around."

"I think it'd be great."

"What about you? Are you done?" She perched up her lips and narrowed her eyes as she looked at me.

"Are you kidding?" I snorted.

"No, you're still young."

"I'm not talking about my age. But hell, Sam. My personal life is a mess. I can't even fathom having another child. Besides, Max is hitting his teen years. Henry isn't a baby anymore. I've got another three semesters of college just to complete my bachelors. I don't have time for a baby." I explained.

"What about Hayden? Does he want more kids?"

"His daughter, Kennedy is 24 and Max is 22. I don't really think he wants to start all over at this point in his life." I reasoned.

"Oh, I don't know." The sound of his voice made me jump. I had no idea Oliver and Hayden had been eavesdropping on our conversation. "I wouldn't mind having a baby with you." Hayden walked over and wrapped his arms around me. "We'd have a really cute kid."

"Oh, have you thought about it?" I teased just to play off my surprised reaction.

"Of course, and I think we should have at least two, maybe three. Cause we don't want it to grow up an only child. They'd have no one to fight with and that's no fun." Hayden squeezed me and kissed my hooded forehead.

"Okay, it was funny for a second but now you're starting to scare me." I took a couple steps back and Samantha and Oliver laughed at me.

"Careful Hayden, I think she might bale on you." Oliver teased.

"You hush," I pointed my authoritative gloved finger at Oliver. "My sister just admitted she wants four kids, so you've got our own problems."

"What?" Oliver's face visibly paled as he stared over at Samantha.

"She's kidding, darling." My sister put her hand on her fiancé's chest. "But good to know where you're at." She looked over at me and rolled her eyes.

"Well, I mean, um…" Oliver stammered. "We talked about two, but,"

"If we have two. Most likely, it will only be one. I'm not as young as my sister." Samantha pointed out.

"So, you guys are making progress on the snowmen, I see." Thankfully, Hayden changed the subject.

"Yeah, we kind of got stuck. We can't seem to get them around to the middle of the front yard over there." I pointed over between the two big maple trees.

"Women," Oliver muttered under his breath in a teasing manner loud enough for Samantha to smack him on his shoulder. But both men pushed, shoved, grunted, and moaned but got the snow boulders over to the area I had indicated.

For the next two hours the four of us built four snowmen, two forts on either end of the yard, and proceeded to have the best snowball fight I'd ever had in my life. We were half frozen and soaked by the time we made it back into the house.

We had played couples and I quickly learned that it was a great asset to have two former pitchers on one team verses an outfielder, Oliver, and one that couldn't throw much more than a wild tantrum…Samantha. We bombarded them relentlessly for almost a half an hour straight until they both came out with their hands up.

Thankfully, it was all in good spirits and no one got upset about snowballs in the face…and there were a few, or the occasional one snuck up behind you while we were building snowmen. It was one of those afternoons that I'd hoped would never end. I wanted to cherish each moment with the three of them.

It seemed for a short while all the world was perfect, and the fates were smiling down on Hayden and me. This was our time, our first holiday season together. And while we may not have been able to wake up on Christmas morning together, we were going to start off the New Year in each other's arms and seal it with a kiss at midnight.

CHAPTER 30

NEW YEAR'S EVE…Samantha and Oliver had flown back to the East coast leaving Hayden and me to attend Debbie and Mark's party with Lisa and Erik. Hayden put on a pair of black slacks and a cranberry dress shirt. Most men couldn't pull off such a color, but on him, it was breathtaking. He even put on a pair of festive holiday suspenders he'd specifically purchased the other night downtown for this evening. They matched perfectly, and I loved that he had such a playful easygoing way about him.

I spun around in front of the full-length mirror in my bedroom trying to decide if I should change or not. I felt overdressed considering I was only going to a house party across the street. I had slipped into a black strapless little dress that came down mid-thigh. It was fitting in all the right places without being tight. Beneath it I hid a black corset, guarders and black stockings. My three-inch heels were perfect for the dress, but I was going to freeze from wet frozen feet or slip and break a hip if I tried to cross the street in them.

I wonder if I could get Hayden to carry me?

"You look amazing!" Hayden came up behind me and wrapped his arms around my waist. "Are you sure we have to go? I'd rather stay home and celebrate alone with you." He leaned down and kissed the back of my neck lightly.

I melted.

"We need to at least make an appearance. I promised Lisa and Debbie we would." I confessed but now I wanted to rescind the agreement.

"Okay, fine. But we're home by 12:30." He traced his lips softly across the skin on the back of my neck, caressing my shoulders with his strong hands. Butterflies fluttered about wildly in the depths of my soul. My knees began to feel weak as if they could no longer hold my body upright.

"Maybe we can tell them we caught the flu." I spun around in his arms and kissed him fiercely.

"We can do that," he exaggerated a fake cough making me giggle. "See, I'm congested." His adoring dimples deepened with his broadening mischievous smile.

"Very convincing." I firmly grasped a hold of his muscular backside and pressed his body against mine.

"I thought so," he said in a throaty whisper before devouring my mouth with his.

"Okay," I said breathlessly retreating from the fire of his clutches. "If we don't stop now we'll never make it."

"I'm good with that." Hayden's devilish grin touched my soul as he reached out for me trying to embrace me again.

"I'm serious," I tried to step back and collided with the mirror almost knocking it and myself over. I quickly grabbed it and steadied myself.

"So am I." I had to side step quickly to escape him. Hayden shook his head at me. "Fine. Be that way." He pretended to pout. "You're no fun." He exited my bedroom with his head bent low in a defeated manner.

Before I could even spin back around in the mirror Hayden came rushing back into the room with a big smile upon his face. "I'm not going to give up that easily." He picked me up and easily tossed me over his shoulder. I squealed and shouted to be put down, which he did oblige by throwing me onto my bed. He slowly, seductively, crawled up beside me with a little devilish grin growing all the wider the closer he got to me.

"You can wipe that shit-eatin' grin right off your face, Mr. Brooks. We don't have time for hide and seek." I propped myself up on my elbows and watched him.

"What about a quick pickle tickle? Do we have time for that?" The twinkle in his eyes made my heart race.

"Definitely not," I shook my head slowly but held his intense gaze.

"Damn it." Hayden leaned down over me and pressed his mouth against mine.

We slowly sunk back onto the bed. His tongue playfully teasing mine.

An hour later we finally arrived at Debbie's. There were about fifty people scattered throughout her living room, family room, dining room, and kitchen. The large majority of who were co-workers, old friends, or relatives of our hosts. I held onto Hayden's hand wandering about looking for my friends or at least a familiar face.

We finally found Erik in the kitchen helping himself to a plateful of goodies Debbie had put out for her guests to enjoy at their leisure. She loved to cook, especially to bake so there was a large variety to select something from.

She often told me it was always better to have too much than to have an empty table midway through a party.

Over in the corner of the kitchen I noticed a large washtub filled with ice holding numerous bottles of bubbly to be opened at midnight. Surrounding it were tiers of elegant frosted wine glasses. This was also a staple at all of Debbie's New Year's Eve parties since I'd met her over a decade ago.

"Happy New Year!" I touched Erik's shoulder to get his attention.

"Hey, happy new year," he leaned over and kissed my cheek and then shook Hayden's hand. "Lisa has been looking for you." He told me.

"Where is she?" My eyes scanned about the room but didn't find her.

"In the living room talking to Debbie." Erik returned his attention to filling up his plate.

Noticing Hayden eyeing the food hungrily, I left him with Erik to engorge himself and wound my way through the crowd in search of the only females I knew here. I found the two of them already enjoying their second round of cocktails hovering by the hearth gossiping about their favorite topic…me and my father/son duo.

"Aren't you two bored with this topic by now?" I asked as I approached after overhearing our names.

"Nope," Lisa lifted her glass to me before taking a drink.

"Not really," Debbie laughed. "Which piece of eye candy did you bring with you tonight?"

"Hayden is here." I rolled my eyes in a teasing manner at the two of them.

"Where's beanie boy?" Lisa asked.

"Chicago for the holiday break." I told her.

"So how exactly does that work? Mason stays down here and is your lover during the semester. On breaks he goes back home to Chicago where Daddy jumps in his car and rushes down to fill the vacancy in your bed?" Debbie inquired causing Lisa to choke on her drink.

"Lovely ladies, very lovely." I shook my head at the two of them. I knew they were only having fun with me, but I was also aware of how my situation truly looked. "How long have you been waiting to say that one?"

"We just came up with it." Debbie confessed.

"Nice to see you're both making good use of your time." They were a disaster team to put together. What one of them didn't think up, the other one did.

"You love us and wouldn't want us to change." Lisa put her arm around me and kissed me on the cheek.

"We keep your life interesting." Debbie added but then turned towards Lisa. "Actually, she does a pretty good job of that on her own."

"True, very true." Lisa agreed.

Hayden and Erik wandered over with loaded down plates in one hand and holding a drink in the other. The three of us ladies were still giggling when they approached. They looked at us like we were insane.

"What'd we miss?" Hayden asked.

"Nothing," we three answered in unison and then began laughing all over again.

The evening was perfect. I had danced with Hayden, Erik, and Mark on the make-shift dance floor in the family room, meaning all the room's furnishings had been cleared out and placed in the garage for the evening. A blast of 80s music was flooding the room thanks to Mark's amazing surround sound system.

It was eleven-thirty. I had consumed three long island ice teas and was just starting on my fourth. Hayden was still two up on me. We were dancing slowly to U2's *With or Without You.*

I tightened my arms around his neck pulling him closer to him. The smell of his cologne was making my head swirl. I leaned up on my toes and kissed him firmly on his soft luscious lips. His mouth opened slightly, his tongue reaching out slowly searching for mine.

They touched. I held my breath, eyes closed, my fingers running through is short blond waves. Electricity pulsated through my body flowing rapidly into his.

I kissed him more forcefully, longing to stay in his arms forever, to feed the fire that burned between us. I couldn't wait to get him home. Only thirty more minutes and we can toast the new year, slam a glass of bubbly, kiss, cheer and five minutes later he'd be all mine.

Hayden's hands slid lightly over my bare shoulders. The touch of his warm fingers only heightened my desire and lust for him.

He moved his lips across my cheek and down my neck. I leaned my head back with my eyes closed enjoying the soft caress of his lips.

"What the hell!" an all too familiar voice threw a bucket of ice water over us. My head whipped around, eyes wide and alert, buzz completely demolished, a knot the size of Texas formed instantly in my stomach. "How could you do this to me?" I felt Hayden's body immediately tense in my arms as we both realized my college boyfriend…his son…was standing beside us.

AUTHOR BIO

A. L. Waddington, writing as Addison Winters, graduated with her master's in military psychology. She is an avid reader, researcher, and when she is not lost in a world of her own creation, she can be found exploring the southwest region of the country with her husband and their girls. She and her husband, Eric live in Arizona with their girls, four dogs, and a bearded dragon.

And don't miss out on the exciting conclusion of the With Honors series coming December 2018!

Transferring Credits

the With Honors series

Book 3

CHAPTER 1

MASON STOOD THERE RED FACED AND FUMING. I could see the glistening in his eyes as he fought hard to keep the tears welling up in his eyes from spilling out into a world he couldn't imagine ever being in. The music was still engulfing us, drinks were being consumed, all around us people were laughing and preparing for the countdown to the new year, but for the three of us the world had stopped.

"Mason?" Hayden took a small step in his son's direction, but Mason took a step back. He shook his head slightly, turned and walked as quickly as he could to the front door.

"Oh, my God," I whispered in astonishment as Hayden and I both followed closely behind Mason.

Hayden caught him by his arm in the front yard of my house. Mason spun around and faced his father.

"How could you? Of all the women in this world, you go after mine?" Mason shouted.

"Have some respect." He pulled Mason along with a firm grip on his son's arm. "Inside."

I followed the two men into my great room where a low fire was still burning and the Christmas tree lights continuing giving their festive glow. However, nothing felt festive. I closed the door behind me and watched the two men before me having a silent face off as they stood inches apart in front of each other.

"You say she is yours, then how come when I was here last spring you let me believe she was the mother of your girlfriend, not your girlfriend?" Hayden inquired.

Mason held his ground but didn't have a rebuttal for his dad. His hands went up on his hips and his shapely lips were perched together as if he was struggling to keep silent.

"And what of Megan? You spent your entire summer with her, Thanksgiving break with her, and when I left a few days ago you were still with her." Hayden questioned.

"You don't understand," was all Mason could come back with.

"Please explain." Hayden gave him space.

"I can't cause you just won't get it." Rushed out of Mason's mouth reminding me strongly of a retort that Max would say to me when cornered and questioned on his behavior.

"Oh, I'm fairly quick. Try me." Hayden glanced over at me and then back at his son.

"What do you care anyway?"

"What? You want your cake and eat it too, is that it? You believe it's okay to live with Alex and see Megan on the side?" Hayden asked.

"Like I said, you wouldn't understand." Mason slowly shook his head in frustration.

"Does Megan even know you're not living in your dorm any longer?" Hayden raised an eyebrow at his son.

"This isn't about Megan. This is about you sleeping with my girlfriend. The woman I live with. The woman I love." Mason spat at his father.

"But you told me she was Alex's mother. Are you now admitting to me you lied?"

"The point is..." Mason turned on his heels facing me. "I knew you were involved with someone else, but you never said it was my Dad! Is this who you went on vacation with?" Pieces fell together in his mind as he turned back towards his dad. "Seriously? She was the one? All this time?"

"Yes." Hayden said. "And wasn't it you who told me that things between you and Alex were over when you first arrived last summer?" I watched Mason's eyes drop to the floor and yet he said nothing.

"That doesn't matter. Even if things were over between us, it's still not okay for you to sleep with her. It wouldn't matter if you ran into her five years from now, it's never okay." Hurt and anger flashed in Mason's eyes.

"Do you think we planned this? We did everything we could to deny our feelings for each other. I tried to stay away from her. I couldn't. I'm sorry, but I couldn't." Hayden told him.

Mason let out an audible sigh, shook his head and rolled his eyes in disbelief. "Really? I'm so sorry for your struggles. But you fucked my girlfriend! And it's never okay to fuck your son's girlfriend, Dad!" Hayden gestured wildly as he raised his voice at his father.

"I'm sorry, son. But I love her." Hayden's voice remained calm despite Mason's constant fidgeting and fuming only feet in front of his nose.

Mason's jaw tensed, he continued shaking his head in disbelief, and then took a step back with his right foot. I knew in my gut what was coming as my face winced up bracing for the impact, but I couldn't manage to unseal my lips. Mason's right hand balled up in a fist and before I could do anything, he took a swing at his father's jaw. Hayden took a step back but held firm. His green eyes flashed for a second and then calmed just as quickly. His hand rubbed the side of his jaw.

"Is that your best shot?" Hayden taunted his son. "I'll give you one more, so you'd better make it worth it. Any more than that and I'll beat your ass."

"Fuck you," Hayden glared at his dad. He doubled up both his fists, took a jab at Hayden's jaw with his left just before he tried to hook him with his right. But Hayden blocked the blow. And the next thing I knew the two men were exchanging blows, cursing wildly and behaving worse than I had ever seen my son's act.

I stood beside my front door witnessing the exchange in utter disbelief. Never in my life had I witness such outrageous and ridiculous behavior.

I tried to sneak behind the two of them and escape into the kitchen but had to dodge them a couple of times just, so I wouldn't get slammed into or hit.

I shook my head at them, incredibly angry that they would do this in my house. Finally, I made it past them and into the kitchen. Their voices rang throughout the house as if I were still in the same room with them. I leaned back against the counter with my arms folded across my chest. Out of the corner of my eye I noticed the clock on the stove. It read; 12:01.

Happy Freaking New Year!

A loud crash startled me, and I ran back into the family room. In the middle of the floor were the splintered remains of my coffee table, several broken picture frames, a couple broken knik-knacks, and my remote in three different pieces. I was livid.

"Damn it! Stop this right now!" I suddenly felt like I was talking to my own sons. "You're grown men. Stop acting like children!"

They were wrestling in the middle of my living room floor screaming and trying to hit each other. Their heads turned towards me at the sound of my voice as if only then remembering I was still there. "I can't believe you're acting this way. This is my house!" Hayden scooted away from Mason and climbed to his feet.

"I'm so sorry, baby. I will replace your things." Hayden reached for me, but I took a step back. I was too furious with the two of them.

"Don't," I stepped back again. "Clean yourselves up. And then clean up this mess!" I turned on the balls of my feet and almost stomped down the hallway. I was so upset with them and was struggling to maintain any type of composure. I slammed my bedroom door behind me just for emphasis.

I stood in the middle of my room practically fuming. Not so much at them, but at myself. I was the one responsible for creating this mess. It would be easy to blame Hayden because he had persistently pursued me.

Or Mason for behaving his true age more often than not. But when it came down to the truth of it, I alone was responsible. There was no one to blame for actions I had taken myself. I was the one who gave in to Hayden. I was the one who went to Europe with him.

I was the one who spent the fall sneaking around every opportunity I got to spend time with him. The fault rested solely upon my shoulders and I honestly didn't know if they were broad enough to handle the repercussions for my deceitfulness.

This is not exactly how I envisioned starting off a new year. If this is any indication of how this year is going to go I might as well stay in bed until a new calendar is required.

I slipped out of my dress no longer caring about how I'd put on something special for Hayden for after the party. None of that no longer mattered at all. I walked into my bathroom and started up the shower letting the bathroom fill up with steam and heat while I brushed my teeth.

I pulled my hair out of the beautiful elegant French roll and let my hair fall across my shoulders. I made a face at myself in the mirror and spit the toothpaste in the sink.

You're so stupid.

The hot water did little to ease the tension built up in my muscles. I closed my eyes and let the hot water rain down upon me. I could only be grateful that my boys were not here to witness this horrific event. I slid down the back wall of the shower, hugged my legs closely to me and rested my head down on my knees.

The anger had finally given way to tears and they were flowing freely. I sobbed until all the hot water had long disappeared and my body was covered in goose bumps, shaking and shivering. And I still didn't feel any better.

I couldn't hear any noise or the men moving about my house. Instead it was eerily quiet. I was half tempted to investigate what they were up to, but after a moments consideration, I figured I'd rather stay right where I was.

Call it cowardice, call it selfish, call it whatever you like, but I couldn't bring myself to face either of the men in my life.

I put on a pair of flannel pajama bottoms and a long sleeved thermal hooded shirt, brushed out my long locks and crawled into bed. This was the worst New Year's of my entire life and the sooner I could put it behind me the better I would feel.

Hayden, however, felt differently.

I barely heard the soft knocking on my bedroom door.

"Alex?" His voice was a smooth and thick as luscious dark chocolate. I heard the door creak open an inch or two. "Alex, honey. Are you awake?" I remained still.

"Sweetheart?" The door creaked a little more and I heard his footsteps approaching the bed and finally his weight as he sat down beside me. "Alex?" His hand gently rubbed my shoulder, moved lightly up my neck and gently tucked some scattered strands of my hair behind my ear. "I'm so sorry, darling." He leaned over and kissed me softly on the forehead. I felt five.

"I'm sorry too," I opened my eyes and looked sleepily up at his bruised but gorgeous face. I couldn't make out the extent of his injuries but could clearly see some shaded areas. "Oh, my goodness. Are you all right?" I reached up to touch his face and pulled myself into a seated position. Hayden stopped my hand just before my fingers touched his skin.

"I'm fine. Just a little battered and bruised." He half smiled. "That was the first time he and I ever went to blows."

"I'm so sorry." I whispered. "I never meant for..."

"I know, sweetheart. I know." He stroked my hair softly and just gazed at me for a few minutes. "But at least everything is now out in the open. No more hiding or sneaking around." A phony chuckle half escaped from his chest but instead he managed to choke on the other half of it. "Don't worry, Mason and I had a good long talk while we were cleaning up the mess we made. I promise I will replace everything that was broken."

"I'm more worried about you and your relationship with your son. Despite everything, I do care dearly for him. I love him." I reached over and took his hand in mine. "But I'm in love with you."

"I know. I believe you. And don't worry about Mason and me. We will be fine. This has bruised his ego a bit, but he will recover. We talked, and he finally confessed that the only reason he came back tonight in hopes of spending New Year's with you was because he and Megan got into an argument this afternoon and she decided she wanted to go out to the clubs with her girlfriends tonight. So, he jumped in his car and drove down there trying to salvage his New Year's Eve." Hayden rolled his eyes. "I believe that backfired on him."

"Slightly," I snorted. "Where is he now?"

"He just disappeared into Max's room. I told him to get some sleep and drive back in the morning. I could tell he was tired." He told me.

"Of course," this whole situation was weird and uncomfortable.

"Are we good?" Even in the darkness I could see the sadness and concern in his eyes.

"Yes, we're good." I swung my legs over the side of the bed and wrapped my arms around his neck. I squeezed him tightly and felt the warmth of his love flow through my body. I closed my eyes and sighed deeply. "I need to go talk with Mason." I kissed him softly on the lips before I let him go.

"I understand," Hayden remained seated on the bed.

I got up and walked over to open my door. "I'll be back shortly." I glanced back at him and felt horrible about everything all over again.

I closed my door behind me and leaned up against the wall in the hallway for a moment trying to gather my thoughts. I had no clue what I was going to say to him, where to even begin.

I couldn't fathom what must be running through his mind. I looked up at my eldest son's door and felt my stomach churn. I really didn't want to do this but didn't see a way out of it either.

Coward

I reached out and turned the doorknob swallowing hard.

What I wouldn't give for a hot cup of coffee right now…

"Mason? Are you awake?" I could see the outline of his figure stirring on Max's bed.

"Yeah," he muttered pulling himself into a seated position. "I thought you went to sleep?"

"I couldn't sleep," I sat down on the edge of the bed beside him. "Mason," I reached over and put my hand on his leg. "I don't know what to say except for I'm sorry."

"I'm sorry too, Alex. I wasn't honest with you either. I didn't tell you the truth about my relationship with Megan. I didn't want to give you up and when I found out you'd met someone else who was closer to your age and that you were happy with him, I got really jealous." Mason confessed.

"I understand. I've grown rather attached to you as well. And I do love you, Mason. You need to know that." I tried to explain.

"I do understand. You love me, but you're in love with him. You and I are at very different points in our lives."

"Yes, we are." I agreed.

"I know. I just had no idea who the other man in your life was. I admit I was shocked when I saw you two together."

"I am sorry about that. I know I should have told you, but I honestly didn't know how. I've been wrestling with this for months because it seems so twisted." I shook my head slightly.

"True. It is a little twisted." Mason finally grinned.

"I never wanted to hurt you or for you to find out this way. I feel terrible."

"I know things changed over the summer. They weren't right when I came back last fall and I knew you were trying to keep us together until I graduated so the boys wouldn't be hurt." He reached out and took my hand in his. "I never wanted to hurt any of you."

"I know, and I love you for it." I smiled at him weakly. It was clear to all us that even though this was all wrong. It was obvious that Mason and I could never have kept up this charade for my sons. Our hearts lie elsewhere. "Your Dad and I..." I couldn't find the right words.

"He told me." His eyes dropped to the bed and his voice became softer. "I'm not mad at you or him for that matter. I just wish one of you would have told me."

"I am sorry, Mason. I should have, but I didn't know how." It was as honest an answer as I could give him.

"Yeah," he slightly smirked. "How do you tell your boyfriend you're sleeping with his dad too?" He looked up at me with big tears in his eyes. My heart broke.

"I don't know, that's why I didn't tell you." I gently brushed a tear off his cheek.

"So, where do we stand?"

"What do you mean?" Certainly, he wasn't talking about us.

"Well, I guess I'm with Megan and you're with my Dad, right?" I nodded. "But are we friends?"

"Of course, we're friends." I leaned over and wrapped my arms around him. "I love you, Mason."

"I love you too," I could feel the quivering in his chest as he fought breaking down in front of me.

"Well, I'll let you get some sleep." I kissed him on the cheek and rose off the bed. "Sweet dreams, Mason." I whispered as I closed the door behind me.

I paused for a moment in the hallway and looked between the two doors. One held my past, the other my future. I felt totally drained. I took a deep breath and sighed audibly before I opened the door.